THE FAT GIRLS CLUB PARIS BOUND

by

Lila Johnson

ISBN: 9780692056929

Cover Art: Maria Lis Cabriza – Find Maria on Etsy.com
Cover Design: Acclaim Graphics

Acknowledgements

"Your talent is God's gift to you. What you do with it is your gift back to God."

- Leo Buscaglia

First and foremost, I must give thanks to God for blessing me with the talent to string words together to make a sentence, a paragraph, and a page that turns into a story.

To my sister, Loretta. Thank you for digging through the raw and crazy words of my manuscript to help me bring it to the light.

Hugs and love to Maria Lis Cabriza. Your work as an artist always delights my senses when you bring my characters to life for my book covers. There would be no Sissy, Angela, or Nicki without you.

To my Acclaim Graphics family. You are gems! Without you, no one would know about me or *THE FAT GIRLS CLUB*. You are the kindest and best people I know. You bless me always because of what you do.

To my father, Leonard Johnson. Thanks, Daddy, for allowing me to hover in a corner of the kitchen and peck away on my keyboard. For this and all you do, I love you.

To my newest team member, Joyce Mochrie. Your expertise as a certified copy editor and proofreader took my manuscript to a new level. You mastered my pages with the swift hand of a Ninja warrior and brought the best to light. I look forward to traveling down the editing road with you again in the near future.

Finally, with a grateful heart, I want to thank my family, friends, and fans. Without your love, belief, and support, I would not be where I am today—books two and three in my series. I look forward to making you laugh, cry, and smile with more books in the future.

"*A woman in love can't be reasonable - or she probably wouldn't be in love.*"

-*Mae West*

Dedications

To my aunt Angela Allen

January 7, 1957-August 29, 2015

You believed I could, and I did. Thank
you.

To my cousin Edrenia Johnson

April 17, 1981-April 5, 2016

May your soul be at peace as you stand
with God and your mother beside you.

LILA JOHNSON

CONTENTS

1 | DREAMS AND DRAMA

"You may want to serve Robert something hot. He doesn't do frozen anything."

Sissy bolted upright in her seat and looked around the partially lit airplane cabin. Her subconscious had played a horrible trick on her. Why was Candace's snooty voice running through her head? She closed her eyes and opened them to regain her bearings. "What the—" She pushed the window shade up and noticed several clouds and a fading sun that left in its trail a pale-pink sky.

"You'd think that after having dropped 18 pounds, I'd earned the right to a little nap without being interrupted by Robert's 'I'm too sexy' ex. After all, *I am* wearing a size 12 now." Sissy sighed as she slid her hands along the sides of her skinny jeans. "Wasn't that the purpose of this little trip to London and Paris with my childhood friends? A celebration! My personal Declaration of Independence! Independence from fat and self-doubt, from Candace and Robert . . . whoa! Where'd that come from? I love

Robert, right?"

She avoided having to answer her own question by turning her head to stare at Nicki, seated next to her, and chuckled. She was the perfect image of a crash test dummy. Her coifed head fell forward as her chin rested atop her size 36 triple D breasts. Briefly, the cranium rose in an attempt to right itself but failed miserably and plunged forward to its original position.

She looked past Nicki and noticed Angela across the aisle. Her head had fallen backwards on the chair rest while a leopard-print mask covered her eyes. Her weave, full of highlighted curls, was in disarray as her mouth gaped open. Heaven forbid, but is that a trickle of drool seeping from the beauty queen's rum-colored lips? Sissy yanked out her tote bag from the seat in front of her. After nearly digging to China, she pulled out her Nikon pocket camera and snapped a few close-up photos. *"This is* a true Kodak moment. If she ever gets out of line on this trip, these shots will prove useful."

The overhead intercom crackled to life. "This is the captain. We are flying into partly cloudy skies as we prepare for landing in fifteen minutes." Sissy could hear the wail of the mechanical gears below as the vibration beneath her feet indicated that the equipment was shifting into place.

The first part of their journey came to an end as the wheels screeched when they made contact with the tarmac. After the "all clear" was given by the captain, the lead stewardess stepped into the aisle, the cord trailing behind her as she held the microphone in her hand.

"Ladies and gentlemen, welcome to Washington, DC with its sixty-one-degree weather. On behalf of the crew, we hope you enjoy your stay if this is your final destination. For those of you with connecting flights. . .."

Sissy's heart fluttered. After releasing a deep breath to steady herself, she tuned out the rest of the information. Peering out the window again, the buildings grew larger as they approached the airport. The hour-and-forty-eight-minute trip placed her just that much closer to London and her brother. Turning from the window, she was surprised to find Nicki awake and stifling a deep yawn. Her other hand tugged at the items underneath the seat in front of her. Angela, to no surprise, had not moved.

"Baby girl, you better wake up your sister

before the stewardess does. You know how evil she can be, and I don't need all that craziness right now."

"Excuse you," a drowsy voice interrupted.

"Oh no! It's alive! It's alive!" Nicki said mockingly in the voice of Dr. Frankenstein.

"Come on, ladies, they're disembarking," Sissy said while standing. "First class is empty, and by the looks of things, the front of coach is almost gone."

Nicki shifted into the aisle and reached for her case in the overhead bin.

"What's the hurry?" Angela asked after a deep stretch. "Just because everyone else is jumping up like Pop Tarts out of a hot toaster doesn't mean we have to. The plane is only half-empty. They better not come around here trying to start some mess about. . .."

Before Angela could say another word, an older, hefty, dark-blonde stewardess in a double-breasted, navy trench coat paused at their row. The three women turned to look at her.

"I'm sorry to rush you, but we have to turn this plane around in ten minutes and depart for our next flight. So, if you wouldn't mind—"

"Yes, we do mind! Don't you see we're

trying to—"

"Ah, we understand," Sissy practically shouted over Angela. Nicki had already made her way through first class and out the door of the airplane as Sissy gathered Angela's belongings that were strewn on the seat.

"Come on before we miss our next flight," Sissy called over her shoulder as she scooted her rolling suitcase down the aisle while juggling their purses that slid down her arms. Just as they stepped onto the jetway, Angela took her things and continued to grumble.

"Did you hear that hussy? If you don't mind—"

"Angela, they have a job to do."

"She won't have a *job* if she talks to me or someone else like that again."

"Don't let that woman spoil your trip. Let's find our connecting flight and get something to eat," Sissy said over her shoulder before stepping into the crowded waiting area.

They found the tram and boarded the car that would take them to the other side of the Washington-Dulles Airport. They exited through the doors, then stepped onto the escalator, searching for the signs that directed them to Gate D7. Once they found their area, they backtracked to one of the limited eateries in the terminal and purchased veggie burritos. Twenty minutes later, they returned to their boarding area, finding a row of seats away from the crowd as they ate and completed their own final check of their items.

"Do you have your boarding passes, passports, and credit cards?" Sissy called out. "And make sure those pink poly binders I gave you are within reach.

"Check," Nicki answered after swallowing her food. "Hey, do you have your driver's license and cash?"

"Got it," Angela called out. "And be sure you have the most important items on the list: camera equipment, clean underwear, and a toothbrush."

Both women looked at her and shook their heads, trying to hold back the laughter that threatened to burst out.

"Laugh if you want to, but that's a must! Those French dudes will not give you the time of day if you're funky and have yucky teeth."

"Only you would think of that," Sissy said.

"Ladies and gentlemen," a female voice blared through the seating area. "Boarding will begin for United Airlines Flight 4613, Washington-Dulles to Heathrow in ten minutes. We will begin with passengers who have disabilities and families with small children."

The area buzzed with movement and noise as people stood, collected their items, and made their way toward the designated lanes for first class and economy. The digital display above the boarding gate read four thirty-five p.m.

"We're on our way!" Nicki shrilled, causing a few heads to turn in her direction. "I can't believe it. London and Paris, wow!"

"Calm down, baby girl. I'm off duty and refuse to give CPR to anyone while I'm on vacation."

"Yikes. So much for compassion," Angela joked.

When boarding group number three was announced, the women made their way to the line. After the agent checked each woman's passport, scanned their ticket, then checked for the appropriate number of carry-on pieces, she allowed them to walk down another jetway for the second time that day for boarding. A flight attendant greeted them as they stepped into the cabin.

Just as they twisted through the aisles, Nicki whispered to Angela, "Check out the seating in first class! They are so spoiled. Hey, are they serving cocktails?"

"Don't look; it'll only make you sick. Keep moving. You know we're in steerage," she sneered, then made a 'mooing' sound for effect.

"One day, I'm going to fly first class," Sissy sighed. "Until then, I have to use coach—the poor man's way to travel."

"Well, when you do, don't forget me," Angela said as she scooted into her seat. Neither one noticed that Nicki had paused to speak to the steward. It wasn't until they were settled and Sissy turned to search for her friend, who was to take the middle seat, that she found her one row back and to the left of them.

Sissy gave her a curious look, and Nicki mouthed "I'll tell you later" while fastening her seat belt with the attached extender.

2 | THE LONG FLIGHT OUT

Passengers were crowding the aisles, seeking empty overhead bins to store their personal belongings; others forced tote bags, purses, and packages under the seating space in front of them. Stewardesses swiftly moved down the aisles to complete their final boarding checks while reminding passengers to fasten their seat belts.

"Where's Nicki? Why didn't she sit here?" Angela asked while pointing to the vacant seat in row twenty-four.

"She said she would explain later. I have a feeling that she didn't want us to be uncomfortable; even though we have lost some weight, we're still three hefty women. After all, this *is* a sixteen-hour flight."

"I guess." Angela shrugged her shoulders, not fully convinced of the explanation given. "I feel like I'm dreaming," she said, changing the subject. "I can't believe the three of us are on our way to London."

"You see that screen on the back of the seat," Sissy pointed out. "You can follow the flight route when we start, as well as listen to music or watch a movie." She showed Angela how to work the controls to find the different features, and afterward leaned back as the plane pulled away from the terminal.

"I can't wait to see William. It's been months since we laid eyes on one another," she sighed.

"Come on, sister girl, don't get weepy on me now." Angela gave her friend's forearm a squeeze.

"I'm all right. My emotions are getting the best of me." They dropped their conversation once the safety video began.

An hour into the trip, after people were settled, Sissy pulled out her journal and began to jot down her thoughts as the flight crew served dinner and drinks.

Wednesday, November 5th. I've said a silent prayer regarding our trip. We're flying over Boston in the direction of Halifax and Nova Scotia, according to the flight plan on our personal television screens. Earlier, we hit deep pockets of turbulence that caused quite a stir, but it finally calmed down. The stewardesses were passing out newspapers to anyone who wanted them. I guess they noticed that the natives were restless and decided that we needed the distraction. We've covered 1,073 miles with an outside temp of 77F and a full moon that is shining oh so brightly. We have thirteen hours and five minutes before reaching our destination. At this rate, I could have flown to Sydney, Australia! When I booked this trip, it said we had one stop. Where are we going to land? In the ocean for a fuel top off?

This time zone thing always throws me off course. I think I brought my Benadryl because I need some deep sleep, like Snow White. Well, maybe not that deep!

I still haven't figured out why Nicki moved to the back, away from us. It's been busy, and there is no way to get to her as of yet. Dinner is being served with our choice of pasta, chicken, or a vegetarian dish. Not the best selections compared to what the folks in first class are eating, but it's something. Later!

***

Once the activity on the plane died down, Sissy made her way to the row where Nicki sat. She took a seat across the aisle from her and wasted no time in questioning her friend.

"So what's the deal?"

"The deal?"

"Why are you sitting back here instead of hanging out with us?"

"Ah, yes. Well, after speaking to the steward and finding out that this wasn't a full flight, I asked to move."

"Nicki, we could have switched places if you wanted to move out of the middle."

"Nope, this is fine. Now I won't cause a disturbance when I need to go to the bathroom with my size 20 butt, and everyone can at least stretch out and be comfortable."

"Stop saying that! You've lost twenty pounds and will lose more, trust me. I just wanted to make sure we didn't give you the impression that we—"

"Girl, stop. We're solid."

Sissy nodded her understanding, then returned to her seat.

Nicki picked up the journal that she stowed under a blanket when she saw her friend approaching. Removing the satin bookmark, she began her note.

7 p.m. We're on our way. In fact, we've covered 1,606 miles with too many hours and a bunch of minutes from our destination. I have to admit, if only to myself, that I'm nervous about this trip.

Just the thought of meeting Sissy's handsome brother makes me so ashamed that I didn't lose more weight. It's not so much about him as what he'll think. I can see him whispering to her and asking why she couldn't find some slender friends to hang out with. He may not want to drive us around the city for fear that we'll flatten the tires on his car!

OK, maybe I'm exaggerating a bit, but it is something to consider. My biggest fear is that I may not be able to keep up with all the walking we'll do. I don't want to spoil Sissy's visit, but I also don't want to be the 'fat girl' who ruined the party.

You know, it's an eerie feeling knowing that the ocean is below you as you hover above in the clouds, but since I can't jump out of the plane, I'll just have to deal with whatever comes my way.

She closed the journal, moved the headset into place, and tried to concentrate on the music.

3 | WILLIAM

Sissy was startled by the rattle of food carts being pushed down the aisle of the plane. She felt slightly disoriented after being jolted out of her sleep, when bam! The overhead lights went on without forewarning.

"Dang, can't they give a sister a chance to come to life before they throw the spotlight on her?" Angela protested as she shielded her eyes. "I feel like I'm being interrogated for a crime I didn't commit!"

Before Sissy could answer Angela, a stewardess stood in front of her and practically threw a plastic-wrapped tray at her as if she were at a feeding trough. The woman might as well have said, "Here piggy, piggy. Sooie!"

Without making eye contact, she mechanically rattled off a list of drink choices.

"I'd like an orange juice, plea. . .." Sissy watched the stewardess' broad behind hustle down the aisle as her last word hung in the air.

"Hold on, girl. I'm going to send her a telepathic message to get your orange juice." Angela placed her first two fingers on her temples, closed her eyes, and in a mysterious, muffled voice said, "Or-ange-juice, or-ange-juice."

"Your face looks a little crusty, Sis. I'm glad I packed these disposable facecloths," Angela huffed while pulling a couple of the moist wipes from the package and handing one to Sissy. "These heifers won't even give you a towel or a Brillo pad to wipe your hands or clean your eyes."

The two women settled down and ate the continental breakfast, consisting of a cellophane-packaged blueberry muffin, a hunk of cheese, juice, and coffee or tea.

Midway through their meal, the captain announced that they were thirty minutes from Heathrow Airport. Sissy turned and looked back to make sure Nicki was awake. They waved at each other, then returned to their meals.

By the time the plane pulled up to the jet bridge, the cabin swarmed like a disturbed hornets' nest as people jumped up, ready to escape the long, confining flight. It was nine thirty-five in the morning.

***

The women followed the crowd from their flight to customs, only to be welcomed by several long, slow-moving lines. As they waited their turn, Nicki rummaged through her London guidebook, while Angela pulled out her compact and checked her makeup.

Sissy pulled the little gnome from its box. Robert's going-away gift was a hint of his sense of humor, one of the things she enjoyed about him. The brief but intense kiss that they shared at the airport—along with a lover's promise that he breathed in her ear—sent a tinge of excitement through her.

A customs agent waved Sissy up to the next window. She presented her passport and that of the gnome. The agent looked at her, then turned to the guard who stood behind him.

"Would you mind stamping his passport for me?" she asked when he faced her again. With a timid smile, she placed the character on the counter in plain view.

The guard explained to the bewildered agent that it was the travel gnome from the television commercials and chuckled afterward. The agent shrugged his shoulders, stamped both passports, and handed them back to her. She politely thanked him, grabbed the stowaway, and joined her friends.

"I know he *did not* stamp that little book," Angela said with her left hand on her hip.

"Yes, he did, after the guard explained it to him."

"You nut," Nicki said while shaking her head. "You know you'd have cried if they had confiscated that little creature."

"I would have found a way to bail him out," she said while stuffing the gnome back into his box. "Let's find our luggage and then my brother," she added while turning on her cell phone. "I'm glad I arranged for this special overseas phone. It's a godsend."

Once everyone's luggage was accounted for, they moved to the 'Passenger Pick-up Area' while Sissy dialed William. His phone rang twice before she heard his voice on the line.

"Darling girl! Where are you? I'm downstairs trying to find you, but there's such a crowd."

"We're leaving the United Airlines baggage area." Her eyes darted back and forth as she spoke.

"Are you in Passenger Pick-up?" he asked.

"I'm wearing a black wool Peacoat and a black-and-red knit cap," he explained.

"Well, you can't miss us: three hefty, sexy-looking soul sisters with a bunch of junk." She laughed.

Before she could say another word, she saw him! He passed the information counter, unknowingly walking toward her. Sissy took off in a run, leaving her baggage behind with the cell phone clutched in her hand. She dodged in and out of the crowds and almost collided with a few people.

Nicki and Angela stopped in the middle of the terminal, trying to figure out what was going on. Nicki's eyes followed after her friend. "I think she found William," she shouted back to Angela. "We better move this luggage out of the way before someone trips over it." Angela yanked on Nicki's jacket sleeve and pointed just as the reunion was taking place.

"William!" Sissy shouted. In one fell swoop, William gathered his sister tightly in his arms, rocking her back and forth. He held her at arm's length and stared at her, then threw his arms around her once more, kissing her on the forehead.

Once they got their emotions in check,

they made their way back to Angela and Nicki. The girls noticed the siblings dabbing away tears.

"Ladies," Sissy beamed, "this is my brother, William."

"Welcome to London, ladies."

"Hello and thank you. I don't know if you remember me, but I'm Nicki." She couldn't stop staring at his luminous, velvet-brown eyes as she shook his hand.

"None of that," he said. He gave her a big hug, then stood back and smiled.

"And I'm Angela." Stepping between the two, she opened her arms wide.

"Ah, yes!" he laughed. "How could I forget you?" He almost crushed her in his bear hug. "Ladies, I'm so glad to reacquaint myself with the famous characters in my sister's life."

"And we're happy to finally see Sissy's fine-looking brother again after all these years," Angela said while giving his six-foot, robust frame a seductive look.

"Flattery will get you everything," he teased, then turned to his sister. "Let me help move your things to the curb, then I'll go after the car to pick you up so we won't waste time."

Once he had them settled, he jogged across the street to the parking garage.

"Ooh, I ought to beat you, Sissy," Angela started. "Why didn't you tell me William had blossomed into such a hunk? The last time I saw him, he was this lanky kid starting junior high school. Now look; the military has worked wonders for him."

"Yeah," Nicki interjected. "Honey, did you see his eyes? *Those* are bedroom eyes."

"And that five o'clock shadow is so sexy," Angela added.

"Sissy, is your brother pumping iron or running marathons?" Nicki asked.

"Probably, why?"

"Because I think his body is calling my name," she said and let out a deep sigh while pressing her hands to her chest.

"Oh, you got it wrong, my sista'. That was *my* name you heard him calling with that melodic voice."

"Ladies! That's my brother you're drooling over and playing sinful mind games with."

"Oh, we don't mean any disrespect," Nicki said, "but girl, he is rocking that body!" She and Angela did a high five and broke out in laughter.

Sissy couldn't help but join in the frivolity after admitting that they were right. She hadn't seen him in such a long time and was as surprised by his looks as her friends were. Just as Angela was about to make another salacious remark, a horn blew, followed by, "Come on, ladies, time's a wasting."

William stowed the luggage away in the cargo section of the Ford Focus. *The four-door sedan should make the ride more comfortable for Sis and her friends,* he thought.

Sissy settled into the passenger seat, placing her tote on the floor between her feet and her purse in her lap. When she turned to share her excitement of the upcoming adventures, she was met with body parts instead.

Nicki's backside wiggled, then pushed through the door. She toppled backwards, landing on her back as she came eyeball to eyeball with Sissy.

"What in the world?"

Nicki sat upright and pulled the rest of her body in. "Don't say one word," she huffed. "So much for a graceful entrance."

Suddenly, from the back-left side of the car, a black Coach, drawstring leather purse landed on the back floor of the car. A bright-orange tote bag flew through the door, landing on Nicki's thigh with a thud.

"What the—"

"Hey, watch your mouth," Sissy warned.

Through the open passenger door, a thick calf, followed by a thigh, a hip, and finally the rest of Angela's body, tumbled in. "Now I know how those circus clowns feel getting into those tiny cars," she said.

"Shush," Sissy whispered, "William is coming."

"Okay, is everyone buckled up?" he asked. Once they answered, William cautiously moved into traffic.

"I can't believe that you're driving a Ford Focus," Sissy commented as she looked at the interior.

"Why?"

"Well, I mean it's so, *American*."

He chuckled at her statement. "I guess you thought I would pull up in a BMW or Renault?"

"Well, yes. After all, they are European-made cars."

"Ah, but that's the rub. Believe it or not, this vehicle is one of the bestselling cars in the country. And with gas prices constantly climbing, you choose economy over style or class."

"And it's in my favorite color, black," Angela chimed in.

"Excuse me, but when did black become your favorite color?" Nicki whispered.

"When I saw him behind the wheel," she snorted.

***

As he dodged in and out of traffic, William spoke of his plans for the trio. "Well, since it's early, I thought I'd take you to the hostel first so you can check in and freshen up. You're staying at St. Christopher's Inn in Greenwich. Do you think an hour would be enough time?"

"I'm sure it will be. What will you do while you wait on us?" Sissy asked.

"I'll run by my crib, check my computer to make sure my boss hasn't sent any important notices. Although he's given me two days to spend with you and your friends, I still have to monitor any messages that are sent. Remember, I do work for the government. Anyway, I think the best way for you to see London is first with a drive to the most popular sites, and then we'll park, walk, and I'll treat you to lunch. This town is widespread with numerous suburbs."

"William," Nicki called out from the back seat. "Could our first stop be Buckingham Palace?"

"And Big Ben?" Angela added.

"Whatever you'd like to do, *love*. I'm at your beck and call." Both women looked at each other and pretended to swoon at the sound of his hypnotic voice.

"*Love*? William, what's with this British speech?" Sissy questioned.

"Sorry, but I don't notice it much. After all, I have been living over here for a year. I work with a lot of British personnel and I live in the burbs, so it's bound to rub off."

"It's kind of cute," she said.

While the girls pointed and squealed at the sights, William tapped his sister's forearm, then lowered his voice to speak.

"You look great, Sis. I can tell by your face that you've lost weight. It's such a change from the old photos that you sent. I'm so proud of you."

"Thanks. It means a lot to hear you say that. I still have a way to go—"

"But," he interrupted, "you've done a fine job so far. Remember, 'Slow and steady wins the race.'"

She nodded in agreement, then turned to look out the window in awe. As Big Ben came into view, she felt a ping of excitement. They really *were* in London.

4 | LET'S TAKE A SPIN

William assisted the girls with their luggage, leaving them at the counter as the trio made their way into the building. "Don't forget to pack a *brolly* . . . um . . . I mean an umbrella. There's a chance of some light rain late this afternoon," he warned before hugging his sister and reminding her that he would return by eleven.

After completing the preliminaries of registration, with keys in hand, they rolled their luggage down the hallway. Sissy opened the door and peeked in before stepping aside. When the other two women entered the small room, they paused and turned to face their friend.

"You forgot to mention we were going back in time," Angela sneered.

"What do you mean?" she asked after shutting the door.

"Dorm rooms! Bunk beds! Are you serious?" she squealed.

"Well, all I know is," Nicki started as she

headed to the first stack of beds, "I'm taking the bottom bunk. My fat butt refuses to climb up there," she said, pointing upward and shaking her head.

"Look, Angela, I know you like things your way, but for once, could you please just work with us? If you insist on having your own room, go for it, but it will cost you a hundred and ten dollars as opposed to twenty-seven and some change."

"You've got to be kidding!"

"No, little mama, I'm not. Oh, and by the way, there are no bathrooms in here. You have to go down the hallway to relieve yourself." Sissy walked over to another bed and inspected the mattress. Like Nicki, she, too, refused to sleep on the top bunk.

"All right," Angela pouted. She grabbed the handle of her suitcase and took the last bunk with a lower mattress. After tearing away the sheets and checking the seams, she looked up and noticed Sissy and Nicki staring at her. "What are you two hoot owls looking at?"

"What are you *doing*?"

"I'm checking for bedbugs. You know there's been an infestation lately, and I'm not having that." She dropped her tote and purse in the nearby chair, then plopped the suitcase on the bed, opened it, and began to rummage through the items inside.

"Just think of this as an adventure," Sissy said as she changed into her walking shoes. She picked up her comb and tugged at the snarls in her hair that refused to be removed. "Did you know that hostels—or at least the very first youth hostel—was established inside a castle in 1912 in Altena, Germany?"

"Oh no, the walking encyclopedia has begun," Nicki teased.

"I know you're not trying to crack a joke," Sissy said. "I thought you would run into a pole while you were reading that guidebook." She climbed into the bed and released a sigh. "Not bad, but I'd better get out of this bed before I fall asleep. Ooh, I need to find the bathroom." She stood up and walked out the door and down the hallway.

Sissy stood outside the bathroom, debating the phone call she should make but didn't want to. "I told him I would," she reasoned, "and then I won't have to speak to him the rest of the trip." She pulled the phone from her pocket and dialed Robert's number. He picked up on the third ring.

"Hi, sweetie. I've been waiting for your

call. Is everything all right?"

"Things are great. We had a wonderful trip for the most part and we're all safe. The girls are giddy with excitement."

"How's your brother?"

"I didn't recognize him at first. He's so handsome and fit. I can't wait to hang out with him. In fact, I'd better get going. We checked into our room, and he's coming back to show us around."

"Well, just know that I miss you. Enjoy yourself; stay safe. Tell the girls 'hi' for me."

"I will. Bye."

"Bye."

Wow, if I didn't know any better, I'd think she was trying to get rid of me, he thought. Robert leaned back in his chair and stared at the phone on his desk.

***

William returned promptly as promised to find all three women standing outside, clutching paper cups, blowing on the contents inside. It was thirty-nine degrees outside, and they had the good sense to dress warmly, wearing jackets and trench coats. He jumped out of the car and ran around the front and to the side to open the passenger doors. Angela and Nicki stared at his muscular frame, dressed in black loafers, jeans, and an indigo, tweed, zip-front sweater that stopped at the top of his hips. A red, plaid, button-front shirt peeked out from the top of the sweater, and on his head, he sported a dark-blue newsboy cap.

"Oh, my goodness," Angela said while grabbing Nicki's arm. "It's a crying shame for anyone to look that good."

"Hey, you're squeezing the life out of my arm, girl," Nicki cried out as she broke free from Angela's death grip.

"Ladies, it's cold out here. Are you coming or what?" he asked as he held the car door open while moving back and forth to generate heat. Sissy had already taken her place up front while shaking her head at the mesmerized women. They finally gathered their senses, ran to the car, and scooted inside.

William slid behind the wheel, snapped his seat belt in place, and said, "Let me shut off my mobile, and I'm all yours."

"What, no calls? We have your undivided attention, brother dear?" Sissy teased.

"Considering I only have you and the ladies for two days, everything else can wait."

As they dealt with the burgeoning traffic, William seemed to enjoy his role as a tour guide. "OK, here's a brief history of London. From what archeologists have found, the first settlements were concentrated near the banks of the River Thames —the longest river entirely in England. The origins of modern London can be traced to 43AD when the Romans invaded Britain. The name of the city, they believe, is derived from the Celtic word *Londinios*, which means 'the place of the bold one.' In the 500s, monks arrived from Rome and began the task of converting the population to Christianity. A series of foreign invasions dominated London's history until 1042, when English rule was restored under Edward the Confessor. He made London the capital of England and established the foundation for Westminster Abbey. After Edward died in 1066, without a clear heir to the throne, the Battle of Hastings was fought between the French-Norman William of Normandy and Anglo-Saxon King Harold. William's victory at Hastings marks the start of the famous Norman conquest of England, which would have a profound impact on the country, affecting everything from governance, to society, to language."

"Wow!" Nicki exclaimed. "So, when's the exam, prof?"

"So I'm a geek!" William laughed. "I'll save part two of my lecture for later!"

Refusing to take a back seat to anyone, Angela abruptly cut in, "That must be the River Thames over there," she said, pointing at the dark body of water.

"That's right," William replied. "It separates north and south London. We can take a river cruise if you want. Plus, there are lots of museums—some of them free—fantastic buildings, and other wonderful historical sites around here." He rounded a corner and jumped in front of another car that blew its horn at him.

"Sorry about that," he shouted to no one in particular and continued down the street. "Today, we'll just concentrate on the small section of London that most tourists frequent: the British Museum, Westminster Abbey, the Tower of London, and so forth. Tomorrow, we'll take the Tube, or the Underground as most people call it, to get around the city. Never say 'subway' here because that refers to a pedestrian underpass." He snagged a spot in a car park near Victoria Station just as another car pulled away. "That was sheer luck," he insisted.

Everyone piled out of the car and waited as William put on his black, double-breasted Peacoat and deftly buttoned it while a paper bag dangled between his teeth. Removing the bag from his pearly whites, he joined the group, exclaiming, "It's chilly out here! The high will only be fifty-three. By the way, I have some orange scones for you to munch on until we have lunch." He pulled one out and passed the bag around.

"We'd better get started. There are only three good hours of daylight for photos, and we have quite a bit of ground to cover."

He held out his arms and beckoned Angela and Nicki, who promptly ran up and took their places on either side of his muscular frame while he wrapped his arms around the pair and started across the street. "Hey, what about me; I'm your sister?" Sissy asked in mock anger.

"You'll have to get your own date," he called over his shoulder.

"William Bennett Bakersfield," she yelled out. "You'll be sorry!"

The trio took off running when they looked behind them and noticed Sissy hot on their trail. They paused at the River Thames Bridge, winded and laughing like kids. Once they were under control, he continued.

"With the waters that flow eastward, you'll find businesses like shipping, manufacturing, and things of that nature. On the west end, the affluent and leisured class built their homes."

"Sort of like the city and the suburbs back home," Angela added.

They walked to the corner and waited for the light to change.

"I love those little black taxi cabs," Angela said while pointing one out.

"In my book, it said that they replaced horse-drawn cabs." Nicki held up the tome she was referring to. "The new vehicles had to be able to turn like the old, two-wheeled hansom cabs in a circle of twenty-five feet. They still have to follow the same rules even today." Everyone stared at her. Sissy was the first to speak.

"What did you do, memorize the book?"

"With sixteen hours on an airplane and nowhere to go, I had to pass the time between movies, music, and reading. Reading gained the majority vote." Everyone broke out laughing and finally crossed the street to Buckingham Palace.

"Well, William," Angela started as soon as everyone was together, "I thought your sister was the history buff?"

"She is to a degree, but I beat her out in that category. I loved reading so much as a child and well into my teens that in my nerdy days, I even read the Encyclopedia Britannica."

"That's why he works with the top-ranking officers in a high-level security position," Sissy said with pride while giving him a fist bump."

"Well, at least being a *boffin* paid off in more ways than one."

"A *boffin*?"

"A nerd," he corrected himself.

"So, dear brother, are you dating yet?"

"No, Ms. Nosey," he teased. "I date casually but nothing serious. Now that your friends are here, I can make all the men in London jealous as I strut down the street with two fine sisters, one on each arm."

"I know that's right," Angela yelled out, tossing a lock of hair over her shoulder.

"Oh brother," Nicki laughed. "Please *do not* get that girl started!"

5 | LESSONS LEARNED

After a short walk along Buckingham Palace Road, they paused outside the gates of the famous six-hundred-room, forty-acre official London residence of the reigning monarch of the United Kingdom. Buckingham Palace was majestic beyond all they had imagined. They darted in and out of the crowd gathered before the long, black-and-gold iron gate, trying their best to get a good view of the famous white stone façade. While they snapped away on their cell phones and cameras, William explained, "It's too bad you didn't come two months ago. You could have viewed the staterooms that are now closed to the public. Oh, hey, Nicki. The queen asked that I give you her regards," he teased. "She isn't home at this time."

"Really? How do you know?" She moved left and right, peering through bars of the gate as if she could catch a glimpse through one of the glazed windows.

"The Royal Standard—the red, gold, and blue flag—is raised whenever she's in residence. So, you probably won't be able to keep that tea date, but you never know. Maybe you should check with that guard over there." He gave her a wink and waited until they were finished with their pictures before moving on.

"Let's go across the street to the Victoria Memorial," he said. "You'll get a better vantage point for your pictures." The group dodged cars in the traffic circle opposite the palace and made their way to the enormous, eighty-two-foot marble monument located on its own private island.

"Impressive!" Sissy gasped. "So, what's the history behind this, William?"

"Well, plans for the construction of the monument began in 1901, just a little less than a month after the death of Queen Victoria. It was her eldest son, King Edward VII, who suggested that a memorial be constructed in honor of his mother, the longest reigning monarch of the United Kingdom at that time. Queen Elizabeth II now holds that record, having reigned for sixty-four years as opposed to Victoria's sixty-three years."

Nicki smiled and opened her ever-present guidebook. "Now it's *my* turn to play tour guide, William." He made a courtly bow in her direction and moved aside, giving her center stage.

"Of course, the centerpiece of the memorial is this eighteen-foot marble statue of Queen Victoria dressed in her royal robes and holding the emblems of her authority, the orb and the sceptre. The queen is oriented so that she faces the city over which she ruled for so many years. Around her are smaller marble statues representing 'Motherhood,' 'Truth,' and 'Justice'—all virtues that the queen was said to possess."

"And the bling at the top? What's that?" Angela butted in.

"I assume you're referring to the gilded bronze statues at the very top of the monument, ma'am. That is a representation of 'Winged Victory' flanked by smaller statues of 'Constancy' and 'Courage'—all of which are personifications of the British Empire."

William laughed as he leaned against the monument's balustrade while the girls raced around, snapping photos.

They had just made their way back onto the sidewalk near the palace when William took off in a sprint and yelled, "Hurry, so we can catch the bus!"

He reached the stand before the red double-decker arrived. The trio ran and made it just as the bus came to a stop. As William paid, the girls, breathless, climbed the stairs to the upper deck.

"Wow!" Nicki exclaimed after settling into her seat.

"Just like in the movies," Angela added as she sat next to her.

"William, thanks for everything you're doing for us," his sister whispered as she snuggled in the seat next to him.

"How often do I get the chance to take out three beautiful women and spoil them?" he asked.

Before she could answer, he continued, "I'm having fun, Sis. This is the happiest I've been in a long time, so sit back and enjoy yourself."

***

The group tumbled off the bus with a large crowd of fellow tourists and looked around, trying to orient themselves.

"Welcome to Trafalgar Square, one of the most popular landmarks in Central London."

"Oh yeah, the Battle of Trafalgar, right? I remember this from history class," Sissy chirped, pleased with her pristine memory.

"That's right," William said, politely applauding his sister. "It commemorates Admiral Nelson's naval victory over the combined French and Spanish fleet off the coast of Spain near Cape Trafalgar. But it was a costly triumph, since Lord Nelson died from wounds suffered during the battle. Nowadays, the square is used as a meeting place for political rallies, demonstrations, and cultural events. There are also lots of museums and historical buildings surrounding the square. At one time, over thirty-five thousand pigeons flocked here, drawn by residents and tourists that used to feed them as a popular pastime. In 2003, laws were passed to ban feeding the birds because of the mess and disease that could result from all the droppings.

"You see that tall pillar down there?" William pointed straight ahead. "That's Nelson's Column. I read an article last year that said it cost over $199,000.00 just to clean all the pigeon droppings off the column! And on that appetizing note, it's about time I *fed* you," William said, glancing at his watch.

"Really, little Bro?" Sissy asked. "I think that story could have waited until after lunch."

William ignored the comment as he guided his flock to an elegant little restaurant nearby. The sedate, but comfy, interior featured dark wood paneling and a set of large picture windows that looked out on the square. At William's insistence, the hostess seated them next to a window that offered a delightful view of the fountains and buildings surrounding Nelson's Column.

"Excuse me, ladies." William politely tapped on the table as the three women turned away from the window to stare at him. "Could you focus on the menu for just a few minutes? My stomach's growling."

"Sorry," they laughed as a waiter arrived to take their order.

Soon afterward, the women were sipping black tea from elegant porcelain cups decorated with delicate pictures of ferns, lilacs, and gilded butterflies. A matching teapot covered with a dark-blue cozy sat in the center of the table. William leaned back and took another taste of the crisp Riesling that sparkled in his wine glass, and then he began answering the questions that the girls were peppering him with.

"OK, so that domed building across the

square with the grand staircase," he pointed, "is the National Gallery. It contains one of the greatest collections of paintings in the world, with over 2,300 of them spanning the mid-13th century to the early 20th century."

"Have you been there?" Sissy asked.

"Oh yeah. They have everything from Botticelli's *Venus and Mars* to Van Gogh's *Sunflowers*." He smiled at his sister, remembering her fondness for the brightly-colored masterpiece. "And all of it is free to the public. I belong to a program called the 'Picture of the Month Club.' One Tuesday each month, during the noon hour, a curator describes one of the paintings in depth while members eat a sack lunch and ask questions. Seven years from now, I'll know everything about the entire collection," he laughed.

A waiter arrived with a tray filled with bowls of warm pumpkin soup, wheat bread, and wedge salads.

"So Nicki, since you've been doing so much reading, do you know what that building is across the way with the Gothic spire?" William asked in-between spoonfuls of the velvety soup.

"No, but give me a minute," she said as she reached into her tote bag to retrieve her guidebook. Just as he swallowed the last of his wine, she asked, "Is it the Church of St. Martin-in-the-Fields?" while her hand rested on the open pages.

"Very good," he said.

She continued reading. "The church was named for St. Martin of Tours, a French saint who died in 397 AD. St. Martin is best known for an incident that occurred when he was a solider in the Roman army. One winter day, he came across a beggar, dressed in rags and freezing. St. Martin took his sword and cut his military cloak into two pieces. He kept one for himself and gave the other to the beggar. His fellow soldiers called him a fool and laughed at him. That night as he slept, Martin had a dream in which he saw Jesus Christ wrapped in the cloak that he had given to the beggar, declaring to the angels, 'Martin wrapped Me in this robe.' "

"Correct," William added. "In fact, St. Martin is the patron saint of beggars, and since at least the early 20th century, this church has sponsored programs to care for the area's homeless population. Nowadays, it also houses an award-winning restaurant in the church crypt, as well as a world-renowned music ensemble, 'The Academy of

St. Martin-in-the-Fields.'"

"What does 'in the fields' refer to?" Sissy asked.

"Precisely *that*," Nicki laughed. "According to the guidebook, the current location was literally a field, and the church was constructed 'in the fields' between the cities of Westminster and London."

They took a break from their history lesson as William asked Angela and Nicki about their jobs and hobbies. In turn, he and Sissy regaled them with childhood stories about the mischief that got them into trouble with their parents and older siblings. The table erupted in laughter when William recounted the time he actually caught 'Mommy kissing Santa Claus' and in a fit of anger went after his baseball bat to show the bearded guy that 'we don't play that mess in our house.' Sissy's description of six-year-old William coming to his mother's defense, wildly swinging his little *Louisville Slugger* bat, was priceless.

"Afterward," he said between chuckles, "I was going to have a long talk with Mom and give her a piece of my mind, but by the time I returned, Santa was gone and Mom was playing dumb!"

The waiter and his assistant soon appeared with large serving trays. Platters of trout, sautéed shrimp, and strips of sliced rib eye steaks were placed in the center of the table, along with steaming bowls of broccoli, boiled potatoes, and asparagus, which teased the nose. They bowed their heads as William said grace.

"Father, thank you for delivering my sister and her friends to me. I'm so grateful for this day to laugh, dine, and share memories. In Your Son's name, Jesus Christ, Amen."

Before you could blink, forks stabbed at the platters of food being passed around. Spoons dipped into the bowls of the side dishes that moved in the opposite direction.

"I think I'm going to hurt myself," Angela insisted. "This steak and shrimp is so tender and well-seasoned."

"Try the trout," Sissy said between bites. "I feel like swimming upstream after eating so much."

"Well, don't leave without me," William laughed.

"The veggies must have been steamed," Nicki commented. "They taste so good, and the colors are so bright. Angela, pass the boiled potatoes before William takes another one."

"Ah, Nicki, I thought we were friends," he joked while his fork hung in midair, missing a chance at the butter-and-parsley-flavored delights.

The comradery was palpable and the meal filling as the hour and a half passed. When the plates were cleared away, three desserts replaced the platters in the center of the table: a slice of cheesecake with whipped cream, strawberries and juice over a thick biscuit, and a slice of chocolate mousse cake. All of the dessert plates were filled with a small sampling of each delight without an utterance of guilt. After their last cup of tea was drained and the bill had been paid, the recharged group took off on their next undertaking.

6 | THE TOUR CONTINUES

"I wanted to bring you here first to avoid the crowds, but it's slowed down a bit and we should be all right."

"William, what are you talking about?" Sissy asked.

"We're going to the Tower of London," he said as they left the Tower Hill Tube Station and began the six-minute walk toward their destination.

"Ooh, we get to see the Crown Jewels?" Nicki asked in wonder.

"Yes ma'am, that—and more."

***

The Tower of London has served a number of different roles throughout its history: a royal residence, military base and barracks, prison, royal mint, and home to the famous jewels—but most famous of all, a place of execution for those convicted of treason. Less well known is that during 1235, the medieval fortress was first a menagerie, accommodating three leopards.

The White Tower is the oldest and most

famous part of the tower complex. It was built around 1078 by order of William the Conqueror. In addition to serving as a fortified residence for the king, it also served as a prison, an armory, and an astronomical observatory. On the second floor of the tower is the Chapel of St. John the Evangelist, one of the earliest examples of Norman period church architecture in England; services are still conducted there periodically. On a more macabre note, there's an interesting little piece of real estate within the complex called the Tower Green—a peaceful, open patch of land where VIPs of bygone ages were allowed to be executed without having to endure the leering eyes of thousands of spectators. A privilege of rank, you might call it!

***

"Ah, here we are!" William smiled, "Waterloo Barracks."

His charges turned their heads to stare at the long, fortress-like, stone structure rising before them. They approached the impressive entryway, flanked on each side by a massive, crenellated tower. Above the door, on a sign with large gold letters emblazoned against a ruby-red background, were the words "The

Crown Jewels." Angela stared at the sign and let out a low whistle. "Now that's what I'm talking about," she said as she lined up behind a middle-aged couple.

"I thought the queues would be longer," William stated. "Now I'm glad we came late in the day."

Thirty minutes later, they found themselves standing inside the Jewel House, the large vault that holds the 141 ceremonial objects that make up the Crown Jewels. The dazzling array of items included orbs, scepters, crowns, robes, and priceless jewels. "I'll take the Sovereign's Scepter with Cross," Sissy said, as though she were checking off a grocery list. "Look at that rock," she said.

"That *rock*," Nicki laughed, "is a 530.2 carat Cullinan I diamond," she read from her tour book. "They say it stands as the largest colorless cut diamond in the world."

"I'm not greedy," Angela chimed in. "I'll take the Imperial State Crown. With 2,868 diamonds, 273 pearls, 17 sapphires, 11 emeralds, and 5 rubies, I could be happy until the day I die."

After exiting Waterloo Barracks, they continued their tour as the Yeoman Warders paraded the grounds. "Hey, what are those guys dressed up for?" Angela asked.

"Those are the famous Beefeaters," Sissy answered. "They're known as the guardians of the tower. I believe the highest ranking Yeoman lives here at the castle."

"And to be a Yeoman, they have to have served in the armed forces for at least twenty-two years with an honorable record," William added.

William pointed at an area on the grounds and signaled for the girls to hurry. "It's the Raven Master," he called out. They joined the small crowd as a pink-cheeked, thick-framed gentleman spoke.

"We have six ravens in residence, as by tradition, and then a spare, giving us seven all together. Legend says, 'If the ravens leave the tower, the kingdom will fall. . ..'" The Raven Master walked over to one of the birds and threw some bread at it. "Although we clip one wing to keep them at the castle, we've had to sack a couple of birds for bad behavior." There was laughter from the crowd.

A little girl, who looked no more than eight years old, raised her hand and asked, "What did they do to get in trouble?"

"Well, Raven Grog," the man bellowed, "was seen at a nearby pub. Raven George was dismissed for eating television aerials." The girl clasped her hands over her mouth as the adults let out a laugh.

"We ask that you not approach or feed the ravens. We have built a sort of trust with them. They eat 170 grams of raw meat per day and what we call bird biscuits soaked in blood. Once a week, they get a special treat—an egg."

"That's so nasty, blood biscuits," Angela whispered to Sissy.

Before their exit, they took last-minute photos of the Yeomen, ravens, and the tower. Sissy covered her mouth and yawned deeply.

"I guess that's a sign that you ladies need to go home," William said. "After three hours of gathering jewels, scolding the ravens, and eyeballing the Yeomen, I guess you're a little worn out."

"Not before we have something to eat," Angela said while holding on to her stomach. "Can't you hear it growling, 'feed me, feed me.'"

William draped an arm over her shoulder. "Never fear, William's here." The girls let out an audible groan while he laughed aloud.

***

The bedroom door flew open at ten p.m., and three exhausted bodies stumbled through like zombies from the grave.

"My feet and legs are killing me," Nicki whined as she fell across her bed. "I need to find my Icy Hot and do a rubdown; otherwise, I won't be able to move in the morning."

Nicki stood and changed into her pajamas as the vapors from the cream filled the air. She stretched, then climbed back into bed and onto her left side.

"Why do I feel like I'm in a nursing home?" Angela sniffed.

"Good night, Grandma Thomas," Nicki called over her shoulder. "I'm going to dream of life in Buckingham Palace."

"Not me. I'm dreaming of Sissy's hunk of a brother."

Dressed in a nightshirt, Angela wiggled under the bed sheets and blanket. "I can see his lips close to mine," she yawned. "Come to me, William."

Sissy listened to the rhythmic beat of music from a nearby club as it drifted up from the street. Slowly, she pulled herself from her chair and wobbled over to her suitcase. The light snores from the girls entertained her as she changed into her pajamas. Before climbing into bed, Sissy walked over to the window and glanced at the light foot traffic below. What an emotional and exhausting day it had been. Absentmindedly, she looked at a couple in a lip-lock underneath a neon sign. For a brief moment, she thought of Robert and smiled. Sissy slowly closed the blinds and moved to the bed. Five minutes after her head hit the pillow, she was sound asleep.

7 | PAUL

Paul threw the charcoal pencil on the desk, not caring when it fell on the floor with a light 'thud.' His eyes burned from weariness as he squeezed them tight then reopened them. Deadlines drained him, pulling every life force from his body, and yet, he was like a junkie in the midst of them.

The Carrington apartment and shopping district plans were complete—finally—and one week before the deadline. The countless hours of late-night work would not only pay off financially, but mentally as well. He looked forward to a few days of relaxation before meeting with his client next Thursday.

Paul placed the drawings in the black, leather portfolio, then cleaned off his drafting table. Just as he was about to pull the chain to the old brass desk lamp, he paused, staring at the tarnished hood that covered the bulb. He remembered how proud the senior Michaelides appeared as Paul, still dressed in his cap and gown, joined the family on the grounds of Cornell University after the graduation ceremonies.

Now, twenty-five years later, he was one of the top five architects at Bradshaw and Hampton Architect and Design. He knew his papa would be so proud of him if he were still alive. Paul smiled to himself and tugged on the chain, throwing the room into darkness.

He walked down the softly lit hallway until he reached the bedroom in the ranch-style home. After changing into a pair of gray-and-blue plaid drawstring pants, Paul crawled into the unmade bed. "One of the joys of being a bachelor," he chuckled while pulling the sheet and blanket to his chest, "is that you don't have someone nagging you on the days you don't feel like doing anything—and that includes not making the bed."

He lay on his back after settling under the rumpled sheets. Paul closed his eyes, awaiting the hands of slumber to carry him away when, of all people, Angela came to mind. What was it that the secretaries referred to her as? Ah, yes, "a hot mess." He shook his head at the analogy. Smiling, he remembered the day six months ago when she strutted through the lobby of Bradshaw and Hampton in her tight pinstripe suit and stilettos for her interview as his team's new interior designer. He knew at that moment that she was a force to be reckoned with.

Paul liked Angela. She was clever, always one step ahead of the team, and oh, was she sassy! The day he caught her pretending to choke their new client, Marie, the spoiled, eccentric celebrity chef, was a prime example. He couldn't blame her. From time to time, he had wanted to do the same thing, but no matter what the situation, one had to have a certain amount of decorum. Besides, the company was counting on this lucrative contract. Any misstep could have resulted in the end of both of their careers. Still . . . Ms. Angela Thomas just may be worth checking out.

8 | SHOPPING AND SECRETS

Four hours had passed when the group stepped from the doors of Harrods onto the sidewalk.

"Well, that was something else," Sissy said after taking another peek at her purchases inside the trademark green-and-gold-lettering tote bag. "After dealing with three hundred departments and seven floors, I'm ready for a break."

"Tell me about it," Nicki agreed. "And thanks to William for arranging a wonderful afternoon tea. I believe we walked that food off after tapping a few of the departments on each floor, but what an experience!"

"I couldn't believe that guy in the green jacket. He told that lady who was standing behind us wearing a pair of Daisy Dukes that she wasn't allowed to enter," Angela said.

"Oh, yeah," William began. "You have to remember that Harrods is a premier department store. They work hard to keep that reputation, and that's why the 'Green Men' patrol the doors and turn people away whom they consider improperly dressed. If it's revealing, it's a no-go at Harrods."

"Well, Angela, it's a good thing you didn't wear your muffin top shirt," Nicki joked.

"Whatever," and then she made a hissing noise while curling her fingers, pretending to be a cat with her claws showing. "Hey William, can we get a bite to eat? My stomach's growling."

"Sure, let's find a *chippie* stand, then we can take the Tube to Piccadilly Circus," William said.

"Chippie?" Nicki asked.

"Oh, sorry, I mean fish and chips. Afterward, Angela, I'll take you to Bond Street; that's where you can find Donna Karen, Gucci, and Versace."

"You know I have to get my designer shopping on," she said while tossing the green Harrods bag over her shoulder.

"While she's doing that, I want to go to Waterstones," Nicki said, combing through her tour book.

"Always the bookworm," Sissy laughed. "Hey William, while they're shopping, how about you and I take a break and chat?"

"Not a problem," he replied. William leaned closer to Sissy and whispered, "Let's you and I hold off on the fish and chips. I have a little surprise for you."

They had walked one block when Nicki called out, "Hey, isn't that a fish and chips stand over there?" They dodged the traffic as they crossed the street.

"Great, the queue's not too long," William said as he guided the girls to the end of the line.

"William, what's that stuff?" Nicki asked with alarm as she watched a woman dip a thick French fry in a white bowl of green slop.

"Mushy peas," he laughed. "A 'must-have' side to any authentic order of fish and chips."

"Well, it looks like monkey vomit," Angela sneered.

"Really, Angela?" Sissy chided.

"OK, OK," Angela apologized. "Let's just say that my Gerber baby food days are over. William, I'll take my fish and chips straight, please."

"Aye, aye, ma'am!" William said with a tip of the cap.

Five minutes later, Nicki and Angela huddled together, holding cones of wax paper filled to the brim with golden fish filets and piping hot fries.

"This is good!" Nicki muttered between bites of fish.

"Yeah, grease on top of grease. What are you trying to do, William, give me a coronary?" Angela joked.

"Oh, come on, it's not that bad. Anyway, you only live once, as they say," William responded.

Two more fish filets later, William led his charges down the stairs of the Knightsbridge Station, arriving at the platform just in time to push their way onto a crowded train.

Nicki descended two stops later at the Piccadilly Station and headed to Waterstones. After backtracking, the remaining three arrived at the Bond Street Station where they got off.

"Angela, this is your stop. All you have to do is. . .."

Without waiting for William to finish his instructions, she hurried away like a Tasmanian Devil, ready to inflict maximum damage on designer row.

"Angela has an internal GPS when it comes to finding designer shops, you know," Sissy laughed.

"So, Will, where are *we* going?" Sissy

asked excitedly.

"Good things come to those who wait," he answered mysteriously.

"Well, that depends on how long one has to wait, Brother dear."

"Not long—just a ten-minute walk from here." He caught hold of her hand as they weaved their way along the busy sidewalk. Sissy turned this way and that, taking in the fashionable storefronts and elegant façades lining the streets.

"So what's this area called?" Sissy asked as she glanced at a smartly dressed woman entering a chic restaurant.

"This, my dear, is the famous Mayfair District. Lots of major corporations have offices here; you'll also find tons of foreign embassies, upscale eateries, markets, hotels, and auction houses. Speaking of which. . .." William stopped abruptly in front of a gracious whitewashed Georgian building.

Sissy looked at him, and then glanced up at the large, black awning covering the entrance and read the single word inscribed in bold, white letters— "S-o-t-h-e-b-y's," she said, smiling. "Oh, William!"

"I know what an antique nut you are," he laughed.

"Well, *these* antiques are definitely out of my price range. Maybe I can come back when Publishers Clearing House surprises me at the door with a check," she joked.

He opened the door and ushered her in.

"OK, we'll hold off on placing any bids today, but you *will* permit me to buy you a bite to eat, won't you? Sotheby's is one of the best-kept secrets in London."

"So that's why you insisted that I not purchase anything at the chippie place," she said.

"That's right, little sister," he smiled.

***

Voices engulfed them as they entered the hallway of the auction house. She passed a smartly dressed woman in white leather pants, a bold turquoise silk blouse, and . . . were those Jimmy Choo's? The man she conversed with was casually dressed and sported a pair of red Chucks. Sissy tried to guess at the unmentioned rich and the common man. Everyone caught her interest. She observed exceptionally beautiful men and women mingling with the less favorably endowed who swept through the building. Who were the pretenders and who were the real millionaires?

As William guided her through one of the display rooms, a breath escaped her as she viewed the museum-quality work. Sissy had read of the famous Sotheby's white glove and evening auctions. Collectors from around the world—bidding in person or by phone— were now to go toe-to-toe in order to own a particular piece of artwork. In 2015, she read that the portrait of Gertrud Loew fetched an astounding 2.2 million pounds in a twelve-minute bidding war.

They weaved between pillars displaying landscapes, passed by exceptional period furniture, and noticed displays of decorative art in bronze and silver. These priceless collections represent some of the finest examples of French, Italian, and British workmanship.

"Darling girl," William whispered, "we need to go. Remember lunch?"

It took a moment before Sissy's eyes finally pulled away from a dark-framed, richly painted portrait of a mother and child.

"Lunch?"

"Yes," he chuckled, and raised his left wrist up to her face, pointing at his watch. "We must eat and then pick up your friends. Come along." He gathered her hand in his and practically snatched her away from the bronze sculpture she leaned in to view.

She left the intensely rich world of the auction house. They walked down a pale-beige hallway, pausing in front of a bank of steel elevator doors. The doors opened, and the spell was broken. They exited and moved through a hallway of light colors, glass, and photographs. A hostess seated them in the contemporary restaurant at a small, white-linen clothed table with high back Lath chairs. The noise level was that of a whisper as they looked over their menus. When the waitress arrived, William ordered for them.

"We'll have the Beef Sirloin with Beer Onions and Hazelnuts. I would like to add an order of Fine Green Beans."

"Yes, sir. Would you care to add a glass of wine?" the petite waitress asked, her eyes fixed on William's.

With a sly grin, he said, "Let's add the 2014 Soave Classico, a glass each."

"Thank you, sir." She gathered the menus and smiled broadly at William before walking away.

"Another mesmerized fan," Sissy teased.

Just as they settled into a light conversation, their food arrived. "I'm starved," Sissy said before bowing her head, mumbling some part of a prayer, then stuffing a hunk of sirloin in her mouth.

"Yikes," William teased. "I didn't know we invited *Jaws* to lunch."

"Sorry," she muttered while holding a napkin in front of her mouth. She slowed her chewing before filling William in on all the news from home.

"Did you know that Ms. High and Mighty Karen Jean on Daddy's side of the family is pregnant—and no, she isn't married?"

"You mean that chick who was always telling Mom that I was kissing some girl, and how I would have some chick knocked up with a baby?"

"That's the one. And Aunt Kathy's husband . . . what's his name . . . James, passed away two months ago?"

"Oh wow."

"Honey, she didn't grieve long because he set her up tight."

"Don't tell me he left her with some major cash flow?"

"Please. That woman is spending a month on a tour in Italy."

"Mom and Dad are heading to Mobile, Alabama for the family reunion. Being here with you is much better than hanging out with a bunch of people I don't remember. And if you repeat what I said, I will deny everything and disown you."

"Scouts honor," he vowed, and held his fingers up in the traditional pledge symbol. "Tell me what's going on in *your* love life."

"Oh, well, it's OK."

"Just OK? That's not the impression I got when I spoke to you six months ago."

"Things have changed." She picked up her water glass and took a sip, trying to avoid her brother's gaze.

"On whose part?" He stared in her direction and dared her to lie.

"You know I don't like to rush into anything. My work as a travel nurse keeps me busy, plus my next contract may place me in the Pacific Northwest or California."

"Excuses, my darling girl. Just say you're afraid of getting involved in a relationship. I'd believe that a lot better than the bull you're trying to feed me."

"William!"

"Sissy!" he mocked. "I love you, but I also know you. You've lost some weight, and I must admit, you look great. But knowing you as I do, you'll lose a few more pounds and really start to shape up. Then boom! The men will come at you from everywhere."

"So, what if they do? What's wrong with a little chase? You know all carnivores want fresh meat to eat."

William nearly choked on his wine. "Oh, it's like that, Mary J. Blige, or is it Halle Berry the second?"

"Neither," she said in a huff as her fork dangled in the air.

"All I'm saying is don't get too greedy. You may lose a good man and be very sorry in the end."

"How can you talk, player?"

"Hold on now," he said while pointing at Sissy. Her barb stung, and he had to set her straight. "*I* was the guy who got played."

"What? You? The smartest guy I know?"

"Yes, darling girl. Someone, Victoria Flower, taught me to hold back on love, at least for a while."

"I wish I could kick her behind. How dare she mess with you!"

William snorted. "Listen to yourself. Anyway, after we dated for a year and a half, she decided that I didn't make enough money for her tastes. She found one of those corporate types who believed in climbing the ladder at any expense. They've been married for at least three years, and he's beat her at least four times the last time I saw her. When his social drinking got out of control, she became the target of his frustrations."

"Wow, that's sad."

"Yeah. She called me a few times in the past when I was still stateside, crying, asking to see me. One day, her conversation was different from the last. She wanted some help and asked if I would come over. I said the only thing I could do was take her to a friend's house or an abuse shelter." He sipped his drink and placed the glass on the table, spinning it absentmindedly.

"William," Sissy gently called out. "Are you all right?"

He gave a half grin. "Yeah, I'm fine. It was after the fourth beating that I went to her home to pick her up, along with a couple of suitcases that she haphazardly packed. That sorry excuse for a man had left the house, but not until he gave her a bloody nose, a swollen, bruised eye, and bruises on her arms. All I can say is that God was watching over that punk because I would have kicked his a-- and would be serving time at the United States Penitentiary in Leavenworth."

"Wow," was all she could say.

"I took her to the emergency room. When I walked in with her, they wanted to arrest me until she finally convinced them that I wasn't the one who messed her up. Three hours later, after doing the whole photo array, police reports, and anything else attached to a situation like that, I drove her to her cousin's house. Ella Jean is an older, hefty, black woman who looked like she'd break a brother into pieces. Before I walked away, Victoria apologized for the way she treated me in the past. She said that I was a good guy and that she messed up by not staying with me. How do you respond after someone tells you that? I said that it was all in the past and that I'd pray that she would be safe. I walked back to my car and stepped in. She waved, turned, and walked back inside her cousin's house. I pulled off and never looked back."

They sat, staring out the window, lost in their own thoughts as the foot traffic passed by. He sighed, threw back the rest of his drink, and said, "We better gather your friends before they think we forgot about them. That Angela seems like the type who would have a few choice words to say."

Sissy let out a slight chuckle. "Oh, you've figured her out already?"

"I've dated a few Angela's in my life. Nicki, on the other hand, seems like a sweetheart. How is she coming along with her diet?"

"Baby girl has lost twenty pounds so far. She knows it's a long road ahead, but she keeps plugging away. She'll turn a few heads when it's all said and done. She's smart and very likeable."

He called the waitress over and settled the bill. They walked along New Bond Street, turned onto Piccadilly, and met Angela and Nicki at the designated spot in front of the Eros statue at Piccadilly Circus. The statue was always mistaken as the Greek god of love, but after some complaints about its sensuality, it was renamed the Angel of Christian Charity in order to placate offended sensibilities.

"Well, ladies," William began, "I know it's your last day in London, so let's wind it up with two more sites. Then I'll drop you off to rest and return around eight so we can have dinner and shake a leg at one of my favorite clubs for a bit. After that, it's back to the hostel so you can pack and sleep before flying out tomorrow."

"Are you sure you're up for all of that? I mean, don't you have to work in the morning?" Sissy asked.

"I'm doing a half day and won't have to be there until noon."

"Well, as long as I can get a couple of dances out of you, I'm all for it," Nicki said.

"Not before me," Angela insisted as she looped her arm through his.

"Ladies, ladies, you're talking to a powerhouse. I've got enough energy for everyone." They all laughed and headed toward the Tube for the next leg of their journey.

9 | GOODBYE

The Underground delivered the group to the area of 96 Euston Road, the first of their last destinations. The British Library's ranking equaled that of the National Library of Congress and the Bibliotheque Nationale de France. One of its known facts is that it holds every publication produced in the UK and Ireland. Over 150 million items in its collection are in most known languages. It is also a known fact that if a person viewed five items each day, it would take 80,000 years to see the whole collection.

***

"This is my treasure chest," William stated while taking pride in showing portions of the building to the girls. "Sometimes I come here to study, do some reading, or just sit and wonder," he said.

The massive interior triggered an audible gasp from Nicki. "I love it," she whispered as she drifted away from the group in awe of the surroundings.

"Reel her back in," Angela teased.

"The library basement, reportedly, is the

equivalent of over five stories. It holds five hundred miles of shelving with at least twelve million books in this section alone. The total collection is well over fifty million." William moved the trio into the dimly lit John Ritblat Gallery with its almost hallowed atmosphere. Principal pieces like the Lindisfarne Gospels and Bedford Hours brought out a sense of reverence from the girls.

"This place is incredible," Sissy said while shaking her head. "The architecture is fantastic."

"Come over here." Nicki practically pulled Sissy's arm out of its socket. "Look." She pointed at the glass cases that displayed the manuscripts of Jane Austin and Charlotte Bronte. Angela and William walked over to the middle showcases that exhibited the musical scores of Mozart and Handel. An hour later, to the girls' disappointment, William explained that it would take days to scour the library. "I only wanted to whet your appetites," he explained.

"Well, I'm ready to devour this place," Nicki said.

"Would you settle for the gift shop?" he offered.

"Let's go." She grabbed his hand as he led the way.

"Let's try to keep up, ladies," Nicki called over her shoulder. "We *are* on a time schedule."

"I didn't know the Queen Mum was hanging out with us," Angela retorted.

"Now, now peasant," Sissy teased as she dodged Angela's grasp.

***

Their final stop placed them back at the River Thames. They took several pictures of the 120-year-old Tower Bridge and then posed for each other. As the bell chimed in the clock tower, Angela shouted, "I read up on that."

"On what?" Nicki asked.

"The clock, Big Ben. It's the name of the clapper or bell inside the tower and not the clock itself," she said proudly.

"Check you out," William replied.

"Well, I wanted you to know that I'm smart and beautiful."

"I had no doubt," he said.

As they traveled along the walkway, Nicki called out, "Did you know they are required to raise the bridge to registered vessels with a superstructure or mast of thirty feet or more,

365 days a year?"

"And," Sissy started, "they have to do so any day or night free of charge as long as they have a twenty-four-hour notice."

"I'd be ticked off if I were the bridge master," Angela said.

"Why?" Sissy asked.

"Maybe the guy wanted to take a nap at one in the morning and here comes some stupid sailboat flowing down the river. Now you have to open the bridge to him, the only one on the water. I would take a blow horn and tell them the bridge is out of order. Turn your behind around and go back home." They all laughed and continued touring the structure.

They walked to the bridge's pier, paused, and looked into the murky water that contained hundreds of fish species and rumored sightings of seals. Each person was lost in their own musings. Sissy's heart was heavy as she leaned against her brother, his right arm wrapped around her shoulder.

"Hey, none of that," he whispered after noticing the tears on her cheeks.

"I hadn't realized until now how much I've missed you. It's been so much fun."

"Don't toss me to the side already. You're

not leaving London without giving me one turn on the dance floor."

She smiled and dried her eyes. "OK, Mr. Dancing Machine. This I'll have to see." With that, they finished their last photo and headed back to the London Underground.

***

Angela ran across the room when she heard a knock on their door. She pulled it open before asking who was on the other side.

"I could have been a mass murderer," William reprimanded her. "You've got to be more careful, Ms. Lovely One."

"If whoever's on the other side of that door can rumble, let them bring it on— murderer or not," she said.

"I'm scared of her," William said while pointing his thumb sideways in Angela's direction as he walked across the room. "Oh, my goodness, its Diana Ross and the Supremes," he joked while pretending to wipe his brow.

The girls were decked out in gorgeous, figure-flattering, cocktail-length dresses and high heels. They quickly lined up and sang the chorus to "Stop! In the Name of Love." When they took a bow, William clapped and shouted, "More, more."

"Maybe another time," Sissy said while catching her breath. "In the meantime, we better go."

"Yeah, so I can show you how a real man brings the house down."

***

An hour later, William pulled up to an old, colonial-designed building that sat near the end of a one-way street. The styling reminded Sissy of an old established banking firm—grand and of great importance in its day. People milled in and out of the front doors. Others hung along the side of the building and stairs, pulling drags off their cigarettes while talking. The music pulsated like a heartbeat as the vibrations drifted, finding its way inside of the car.

"Go ahead and wait for me in the lobby while I find a place to park." As they watched William pull off, Nicki fidgeted with the neckline of her dress.

"Leave it alone," Angela called out, pushing her friend's hand away. "It's fine, Nicki; you look great. I love the way the fabric pleats and flares over your frame. And you're rockin' those crystal-and-black earrings."

"I like those sling-back pumps. Where did you find them?" Sissy asked.

"In the back room at DSW; they're Calvin Klein's."

"Well, I think we all look good," Angela said. "I'm loving this wrap dress, and Sissy, your scoop neck cocktail dress is really showing off those new curves."

"Why, thank you, ma'am. We better head inside before my brother gets back." They ascended the short flight of stairs, showed the security guard their driver's licenses, then moved forward to pay the entrance fee.

"Welcome, mates, to Broadmoor." A round-faced, biracial man with thick, light-brown, shoulder-length wavy hair took the cash handed to him. He and Sissy held eye contact for a minute before he said, "Have a good time, ladies."

"Now that's what I'm talking about," she said when they stepped to the side. "Did you see his hazel eyes? And those lips can call my name all night long." Nicki and Angela glared at her.

"What?"

"Have you forgotten about Robert?" Nicki asked.

"Yeah, your *boyfriend*," Angela stressed.

"Look, I'm here, and he's there. Why are you guys trippin'?"

"OK, now you're starting to act like this one," Nicki said while pointing at Angela.

"Excuse you!"

"I said—"

"Before this goes any further," William said while stepping between the two women, "I think we better head in. Someone owes me a dance." He guided the women inside as the electronic beat enveloped them.

***

The group was just about to settle into their booth when the beginning strains of "Blurred Lines" by Robin Thicke ft. T. I. and Pharrell Williams caught Angela's attention. "That's my jam," she shouted and headed to the dance floor. By the time William arrived, her hips spun in motion in the black-and-white marble wrap dress. He gave Angela's stilettos a run for their money. She had to step up her game to keep pace with him.

"Check out your brother," Nicki squealed. "William is tearing it up."

Sissy giggled and nudged Nicki, motioning in the direction of the dance floor. They were getting into the frivolities of the evening when the song "Treasure" by Bruno

Mars kept the dancers in motion. The rift that had taken place earlier was nonexistent as the girls shouted and took turns dancing with William. They twirled, booty bumped, and two-stepped to various songs. A stranger leaped onto the dance floor and moved in Sissy's direction.

She broke away from the group and matched her new dance partner, step for step, when the soft and sexy song "Adorn" by Miguel triggered the lights to go low. Sissy's heart fluttered as she looked into the eyes of the slender, olive- skinned man. "Not bad," she murmured when he wrapped his arms around her. Thirty minutes later, he escorted her back to the booth and asked if he could dance with her again. She agreed, and he smiled before walking away. When the rest of the group returned to the booth, Nicki was fanning herself with a napkin. She downed a glass of water before speaking.

"William, you're an amazing dancer."

"You weren't bad yourself," he said while giving her a fist bump. He turned to Angela. "And you," he began while shaking his head, "I thought you were going to put me out of commission."

"Honey, you don't know who you're

messing with," she shot back while dabbing away the moisture on her face with her handkerchief.

Sissy held up her glass of Castello del Poggio Moscato and said, "A toast." The others picked up their drinks to join her.

"To my brother. You are too fine, too kind, and too smart for your own good. I love you from the core of my heart and want to thank you for such a wonderful time."

"Here, here!" the girls cheered as they clinked their glasses and drank.

The waitress returned and took orders for a second round of drinks and appetizers before they returned to the dance floor. When the music slowed down, William and Sissy returned to their seats. Nicki and Angela took advantage of the dance partners who approached them as "I Hope You Dance" by Lee Ann Womack played in the background. The siblings took time to catch their breath.

"I'm going to miss you so much," she began while fighting back her emotions.

"Same here. I've had a blast with you and your friends. Angela is a laugh and Nicki is a sweetie. I'm glad she let her guard down and allowed herself some fun."

"Yes. Each time she moves out a little

more, trusting herself to be better."

"Hey," William said, picking up his drink, "a toast to us." Sissy lifted her glass; a small amount of wine rocked back and forth in the bowl.

"I love you, my darling girl. You have filled my heart with such joy. May love and happiness find its way back into your life."

"Right back at you," she said with a smile, then tipped her glass for a swallow. When disco mama and her sidekick returned, Sissy and William took off for another round of dancing.

***

The chimes from the clock tower rang at midnight as William cruised down the street, passing the London Bridge and the Houses of Parliament before returning his charges back to the nest. The dancing queens were sound asleep in the back seat. At one point, he caught a light snore from behind him and chuckled.

"That's probably Angela calling her sheep home," Sissy said jokingly. "I've never seen those two have so much fun."

"They were wild, but in a good way. Nicki kind of showed what she's made of on that dance floor. I take it she doesn't date much."

"It's been a few years since she's had a boyfriend. I guess she needed to release some pent-up tension. I can't imagine what she's going to be like when she loses the rest of her weight."

"Well, the men better watch out."

"I know. She can't see it yet because she's caught up in the mix, but one day."

"Hey Sis," William began. She could tell by his tone that something bothered him. "I hate to sound like a wuss, but man, I'm going to *miss you*. I didn't realize how lonely and homesick I've been until now." He let out a deep sigh and turned down another street.

"When will you return home?"

"In another year, but that's months from now and I don't like to think about it." They rode the rest of the way in silence. When he pulled up to the hostel, there were no parking spaces to be found. He drove to the next block and squeezed into the only available space he could find. Thank goodness for small cars.

Sissy had dozed off, and he gently nudged her shoulder. "Already?" she asked between a yawn. William turned in his seat and tapped Angela's arm.

"Mama, I didn't. . .." Angela called out

while bolting upright.

"Aw man, we almost got a true confession out of her," Sissy teased.

"What did I say?" Angela asked sheepishly.

"Don't worry, your secret is safe with us," William reassured her. He stepped from the car and walked the women back to the hostel. Before they entered the building, the girls gave him a hug.

"I'll see you all in the morning. In fact, I better call and make sure you're up by eight."

Sissy stifled a yawn before hugging her brother and saying good night. Once the door closed behind them, William shoved his hands into the pockets of his dark slacks. He let out a deep sigh as he slowly walked back to his car.

10 | BON VOYAGE

"So I guess this is the end," William said as the sadness crept into his voice. He stared absentmindedly at the foot traffic in the hallway outside the airport café.

"I really hate goodbyes," Angela said. She dabbed the corners of her eyes.

"So do I," Nicki added. "William, you were fantastic. My hips will never be the same."

"What?" Sissy asked with a questioning look.

"From all those gyrations on the dance floor, you nasty thing."

"Girl, I'm glad you cleared that up. I thought you'd been creepin' at night."

"And how do you know that we haven't?" William asked as a sly smile covered his face.

Angela and Sissy stared in disbelief while the two imagined lovebirds stood up with their empty trays and walked off to the refuse bin.

"That hussy," Angela said.

"I'd better hurry before they run off to find a preacher." Sissy laughed, then pushed through the café door to catch up.

***

The girls walked away from the ticket counter as William stood up from the hard, orange, plastic chair. "Everyone's good? Your tickets and luggage are all in order?"

Sissy stepped over to William and laid her head against his chest as his arms encircled her. Her body shuddered as she sobbed. William kissed her forehead. "Now, now," he whispered. "You're going to turn me into a sponge."

Through her tears, she started to giggle. She took in several deep breaths and let them out to compose herself.

"There you go; that's how I want to remember you." He turned to Angela and Nicki. "Thanks for brightening up my life. I haven't had this much fun in a while. It's no wonder my sister loves you so much."

The girls strutted over to William, each giving him a tight hug. He returned the gesture. They slowly walked to the security area and stood to the side. "Before you go," he said, "I want to say a quick prayer." They held hands before he began.

"Father, I hold my sister and her friends up to You. I ask for a hedge of protection to surround them during their journey to Paris. I ask this, in Your Son's name, Jesus Christ. Amen."

"Amen," they said in unison.

"OK, my darling girl, you'd better get a move on." They hugged once more while saying goodbye and I love you as Sissy stepped to the podium and showed her identification.

Angela and Nicki attacked him from both sides, wrapping their arms around him.

"Keep an eye on my sister, please."

"We will. Bye, William." He kissed their cheeks before they hurried off. Just as the girls headed down the hallway, they turned once more and waved. He blew a kiss and watched the trio disappear around a pillar. His smile waned when the reality of their leaving pulled him back to the moment.

William turned and shifted through the crowd until he reached the exit door. A lone tear coursed his cheek. He swiped it away just as he pushed the door open, stepping onto the busy sidewalk, all alone.

11 | BONJOUR PARIS

Paris, the capital of France, offers much in the way of history, art, and monuments. To the millions who travel the world over, it also suggests amour.

Its beginning was pieced together like a puzzle or, better yet, like a manuscript. The history of the Capetian dynasty pulled France together through the Middle Ages. As with any story, strife—like the Hundred Years' War and The Black Death—brought the country to its knees, but not for long. It struggled and reclaimed itself during the Renaissance and Louis the XIV's reign.

Many historic pages were written over time. For example, as France went through a period of the avant-garde, specifically Paris, it would introduce icons like Coco Chanel and Josephine Baker to the world. American musicians hung out in the local cafés. The French Riviera fascinated artists like Matisse and Picasso and writers such as Hemingway and F. Scott Fitzgerald. Art Deco, launched during The International Exhibition in Paris during 1925, gave way to geometrical shapes and utilitarian designs. *Par Avion* (airmail) showed the innovative skills of France in 1927.

Although the society changed after 1950, France put on a new face of modernism and offered contemporary ideas like Train à Grande Vitesse (TGV)—at that time, one of the fastest trains in the world. Other projects, like Centre Pompidou and La Defense, moved France into the international realm. Haute couture was no longer in high demand, but it did not diminish Paris as a major fashion center. As industries in technology increased, mass culture grew and the peasant farmer was pushed into the background and seen as old world.

It is the France of today that Sissy, Nicki, and Angela fly into. Historic buildings like the Musée d'Orsay, the Eiffel Tower, and Notre Dame will charm and fascinate the newcomers. The busy suburbs of Île-de-France will welcome and excite the world travelers throughout the commuter towns that are home to château's like the illustrious Versailles.

So we say, *Vive la France*!

LILA JOHNSON

12 | COULD THIS BE REAL?

A palpable energy filled the air as the girls moved their luggage through customs and looked for the nearest restroom. They snagged an abandoned luggage cart and loaded their things on it.

"You two go first while I stay and watch over the baggage," Sissy offered. "I know how difficult it is for you to hold your bladder," she teased.

"If I didn't have to go so badly, I would get you for that comment," Angela said while running into the open doorway.

Nicki didn't respond. She was busy doing her own type of leg cross, wiggle walk to the bathroom. Sissy sat on the nearby couch, pulled out her journal, and started a quick note.

I can't believe it. We're really here! Thank the Lord we made it safely and without a lot of drama. My small-bladder friends are handling their business in the ladies' room. I have to admit, my heart was a little heavy after leaving my brother in London, but I am grateful for the time we spent together. I have such wonderful memories and some great pictures to show Mom and Dad. They'll be so surprised to see how well their youngest turned out.

I have to put in a call to William and Robert to let them know we made it safely. I can't believe how my feelings for him have changed. I still like him and find him incredibly handsome, but there's something I can't quite put my finger on that has dampened my desire for him. I can still hear William's words of caution in my head. Oh well, I'm here and Robert is over there, and I plan to have my fun while I can. What he doesn't know won't kill him.

* * *

"Whew, that was a close call," Nicki said as she emerged from the restroom. "Your turn, Ms. Iron Bladder," she chuckled. Sissy tucked away her journal and made a beeline past Angela.

"Hey Nicki, are you going to stay here for a bit?" she asked.

"Yeah, why?"

"I want to brush my teeth and freshen up a bit. I'll hurry so you can do the same." Nicki waved her on as she rummaged through *her* tote and pulled out her journal and ink pen. She looked around, noticing the activity throughout the common area. Some tourists took time to change their shoes, use the restroom, make phone calls, or take inventory of their possessions. Three women had taken up space behind one of the couches and began pulling clothes from their suitcases. She turned her attention to the open page in the dark-blue, leather journal and began to write.

I think I'm dreaming! I'm in Paris, France! Twenty pounds ago, I would not have imagined this to be possible, but here I am, thanks to Sissy. If she hadn't brought up the crazy idea to do this thing, I would still be on my couch with my magazine, Now Playing, going through this week's lineup on Turner Classic Movies.

I'm wearing the necklace that Sammy, the company's receptionist, gave to me as a going-away gift. It's a silver medallion with the design of a sailboat on one side and the inscription from my favorite movie on the other. The quote, titled The Untold Want, is by Walt Whitman.

"The untold want, by life and land ne'er

granted, Now, Voyager, sail thou forth to seek and find."

"Nicki. Hey Nicki," Sissy called out.

"Huh? Oh sorry, I guess I was daydreaming."

"Do you want to freshen up? I'm finished, and your sister is putting on the last touches of her makeup. We may not be able to check in early, so whatever needs to be done, we better do it here."

Nicki stuffed the journal in her tote, gathered her cosmetic bag, and walked away. Sissy opened her suitcase and unloaded unneeded supplies from her backpack into it. She made sure her passport, money, and identification were secured to her body while placing her camera, tour book, journal, snacks, and the water bottle she just filled inside the pack.

When the other two women emerged from the ladies' room, they did the same before heading out. "Let's get some money at the ATM. William said we'd get a better rate than at the exchange office, plus we'll have money to pay the cabbie," Sissy informed them.

Angela was snapping away, taking pictures of the welcome sign painted on the airport wall, then turned and fired away at Sissy and Nicki as they waved. She shoved the Nikon camera into Sissy's hand and quickly withdrew some money before they exited the building.

"Does everyone have everything before we go?" Nicki asked while checking her own gear.

"I'm golden," Sissy called out.

"Me, too," Angela added.

"Paris, here we come," Nicki said with a big smile while leading the way.

As they followed the signs that directed them to the taxi stands, Angela spoke up. "Isn't there a cheaper way to do this?"

"We could take the subway, but with all of us pulling a medium and small suitcase, including our backpacks and purses, it will be hell on earth," Sissy explained.

"And girl, you know you would have a fit if the slightest bit of nail polish chipped off those darling digits," Nicki said, smirking.

"Come on, women. To the taxis," Angela pointed.

They walked through a glass hallway, then stepped outside into forty-six- degree winds and a pale-blue overhead sky. They waited their turn until a thin, dark-skinned,

Ethiopian male dressed in grayish-blue khakis and a matching work shirt waved them over to a white van. His broken English mixed in and out with his French dialect.

"Bonjour, Mesdemoiselles. To where are you going?"

"Best Western Hotel Left Bank Saint Germain," Sissy said while pointing to the printout with the address below."

"Oui." He stepped over to the driver and repeated the information in French. The driver nodded his head, turned, and motioned for them to bring their luggage cart over.

Once they were settled, the clerk explained that the drive would take an hour. As the van moved along the highway, they stared at the traffic and understood why. The morning rush-hour commute was in full swing. Nicki squealed a few times while clutching the door handle. The cars appeared to approach and almost slam into them as they changed lanes. The driver, who did not speak to them, dashed in and out of traffic like an Indy 500 racer. It worsened as they traveled down the Champs-Elysées and toward the Arc de Triomphe. This time, it was Angela who let out a yelp as cars and motorcycles seemed to create their own traffic lanes while darting in front of one another, horns blaring and vying for the right-of-way.

The driver continued to hum to the music on the radio, never speaking to the women. He pushed his way through rush-hour traffic without a care in the world. Occasionally, a reporter's voice dispatched the morning news, disrupting the cabbie's musical talent.

"It would be nice if he would give us a few details about the town," Angela whispered to Sissy.

"Maybe he doesn't speak English or he couldn't care less," she said.

They arrived at the hotel none the worse for wear and tear. Sissy paid the fifty-nine-euro fare with an additional eight euros as a tip and said, "*Merci.*" He unloaded the luggage from the back compartment and set the pieces inside the hotel lobby. This time, Angela and Nicki repeated the French compliment before he walked away.

"*Bonjour,*" Sissy said as she stepped up to the front desk.

"*Bonjour, mademoiselle,*" a brunette who looked about thirty spoke as she stood up from the chair that sat low enough to conceal her behind the desk.

"*Comment allez-vous?*"

"Trés bien."
"Parlez-vous anglais?"
"Oui."

"We have reservations," Sissy said while handing the clerk her information sheet and passport. She turned to ask the girls for their identification and caught them staring at her. "What are you looking at? Give me your passports." She took the passports and handed them to the clerk.

"It's early and the rooms are not ready," she said while completing the paperwork before handing the passports back to Sissy.

"That's fine; we have a tour to attend. If you could hold our luggage, it would help."

"Bien sur, mademoiselle; you can place them in the booth to my left. We will see you later. When you return, the night clerk will be here and will have the keys to your rooms."

They stowed their items once they secured the locks on the suitcases. The 'booth' was a defunct telephone room with only the wood plaques and some wiring left dangling from the wall.

"I would advise you to make use of les toilettes," Sissy warned the girls. "Public restrooms are hard to find, and some of them make you pay to use. Remember, we aren't in Kansas anymore."

Nicki looked at Sissy and shook her head. "I didn't realize you spoke French. I'm impressed."

"Don't be," she said. "I've been practicing the basics, and that's as far as it goes. I will still be doing the point and speak method while we're out."

Once their personal needs were complete, they read the itinerary one more time before stepping out the door. "The clerk said the subway is over there," Nicki pointed. The trio turned left, walked past a sidewalk café, and located the entrance to the Metro across the street.

13 | THE CITY TOUR OF PARIS

The girls descended the stairs and walked across the concrete platform. Nicki took out a small spiral notebook and scribbled Metro Cité. "Now we know which line brings us back home," she said.

"I'll go one better," Angela laughed. She pulled out her phone and took a picture of the sign.

The train pulled to a stop, and the girls gathered at the nearest door after they saw how crowded the cars were. Once they opened, a flood of people poured out. As soon as the opportunity presented itself, the trio pushed their way inside and huddled together to keep watch on each other's belongings. Sissy pointed to the diagram listing the subway route above the doorway as they looked for their stop, Rue des Pyramides.

***

They exited the Metro underground station like creatures from the night, pausing to the right of the stairwell to gather their bearings and their breath.

"Do they *not believe* in elevators or escalators?" Angela huffed.

"I guess not," Sissy answered while fanning herself. "Where's Nicki?"

"Here I come," she said after reaching the last stair and shaking her head. "I'm in big trouble."

"Why, what's wrong?" Angela moved to her side, placing a hand on her shoulder.

"I forgot my oxygen tank. I guess I'll just have to die right here."

"Look," Sissy started, "if you die, we all die. In the meantime, let's get going before we miss our tour."

***

The trio mustered all the strength they had and proceeded down the sidewalk to Vive la Ville Tours at 21 Rue des Pyramides. Nicki and Angela stayed outside and watched the other tourists while Sissy took care of the reservations. When she emerged from the building, she waved the girls over to the increasingly long line beside the tour bus.

"You need the paperwork I gave you earlier in those 8x10 poly-pink binders."

They rummaged through their backpacks and pulled out their vouchers.

"I have to admit, at first I thought you were some neat freak when you passed this stuff out to us, but now I'm grateful," Angela confessed.

"All of the tour information and entrance passes are in those binders. Without them, you won't be admitted. That's why I insisted on paying for a lot of these things in advance, as you can now see."

Assistants from the tour company called everyone to attention and gave a brief summary of the day's events. "Welcome to Vive la Ville tour number 455. If this number does not appear on your ticket, you're in the wrong line. Today, we'll commence with a city tour by bus. When we arrive at the Eiffel Tower, further instructions will be given to those who paid for the luncheon; the rest of you will proceed to the Seine River Tour."

"How about if you're doing both?" a man yelled out.

"They will explain more about that on the bus. Right now, let's get everyone seated so you can be on your way."

The trio moved to the middle section. Angela grabbed the window seat on the left-hand side of the bus, while Nicki snagged the one on the right-hand side.

"I have dibs on a window seat for the next tour," Sissy muttered.

The engine roared to life as the last few passengers excitedly stumbled into their seats. *"Bonjour, je m'appelle Élodie."* For those of you who do not speak French, that means my name is Élodie. Behind the wheel is Amadieu, our driver."

"Bonjour!" the busload of guests replied.

"The bus tour of Paris will take an hour and a half; the Seine River Cruise is an hour. For those of you who have paid for lunch at the Eiffel Tower, you will proceed to the river cruise after your meal. A guide will escort you to the restaurant and give you the tickets needed for the cruise."

***

"Let's start our grand introduction to the city by travelling along the Avenue des Champs-Élysées, Paris' most famous boulevard. We call this *'la plus belle avenue du monde'*—the most beautiful avenue in the world. Stretching over one mile, the Champs-Élysées connects the Place de la Concorde at one end with our crown jewel, the Arc de Triomphe, at the other end. Besides serving as the focal point for the annual Bastille Day parade, the avenue is also home to luxury stores, hotels, theaters, restaurants, and last—but not least—the finish line for the Tour de France.

The women snapped away on their cameras, Nicki at the buildings, street signs, and unique posters on glass doorways while Angela photographed the fashionably dressed people on the streets and famous landmarks. Sissy just continued to listen to the commentary, slightly steamed because she couldn't take any pictures from her aisle seat.

Élodie continued, "We are now rounding the Arc de Triomphe, one of the most well-known monuments in Paris. The arch stands 164 feet and is covered with bas-reliefs of armaments, equestrian sculptures, and military battles. Modeled after the Arch of Titus in Rome, the structure was started in 1806 but was not completed until 1836. Meant to be a show of Napoleon's military might—as well as to honor all who fought in the Revolutionary and Napoleonic Wars—the façades of the monument are covered with the names of important military victories and generals. In November of 1920, the body of the Unknown Soldier was laid to rest beneath the arch to commemorate the dead of World War I. If you dare to climb the

284 steps to the terrace, you will be welcomed by many unforgettable views of Baron Haussmann's splendid design of the twelve avenues that reach to the outside sections of the city."

The bus cruised down several avenues and throughout the busy streets. "Sissy, look!" was called out on more than one occasion.

Angela and Nicki "oohed and ah" at the different sites, reminding Sissy of her inability to view the wonders along the tour without having to duck and dodge, weave and bob between heads like a drunk boxer. On occasion, she would lean against Angela to snap a few pictures on her camera. Just as her friend's temper was about to pop, Sissy would press a finger against her lips to hush Ms. Thang and point to Élodie.

"And now, ladies and gentlemen, to your left is the Musée du Louvre."

Low whispers could be heard throughout the bus. "The Louvre is the world's largest museum, housing over 380,000 objects, including important collections in Egyptian, Greek, Etruscan, and Roman art, prints and drawings, paintings, and decorative arts, including the famous Regent diamond—still considered to be one of the most perfectly cut diamonds in the world. The museum also showcases other masterpieces, such as the Winged Victory, the Venus de Milo, Giotto's *St. Francis Receiving the Stigmata*, da Vinci's *Mona Lisa*, and Delacroix's *Liberty Leading the People*."

"In 1190, to protect the capital from Anglo-Norman threat, King Philippe-Auguste desired to reinforce its defenses with a fortress, which became known as the Louvre. Over four centuries, kings and emperors continually enlarged and improved the structure. The most recent addition—the famous Glass Pyramid—was not liked by all during its debut in 1989, but it remains as the entrance to the large reception hall beneath. Here you will find temporary exhibition areas, the history of the palace and museum, as well as public amenities."

"This chick is good," Angela whispered. Sissy nodded her head in agreement. The bus maneuvered deftly through both car and pedestrian traffic, arriving at the Place de l' Opéra.

"If any of you have a little time in your busy schedule, I would suggest you visit this beautiful giant, often referred to as the 'wedding cake,' the Opéra National de Paris

Garnier. This monumental Beaux-Arts-style masterpiece was constructed between 1861 and 1875. It served as the home for the Paris Opéra until 1989, when the Opéra Bastille opened. Today, it serves mainly as the site for ballets, musicals, and other cultural events. Inside this exquisite façade, you will find the magnificent Grand Escalier, constructed of white, green, and rose-colored Carrara marble, the 505-foot Grand Foyer, known as 'the drawing room for Paris society,' and the luxuriously appointed 1,900-seat auditorium, boasting the largest stage in Europe, a ceiling painted by Marc Chagall, and a seven-ton bronze-and-crystal chandelier. In 1896, a fatal accident occurred when the extravagant creation broke free of its counterweight and crashed to the floor, killing a member of the audience . . . and inspiring one of the most famous scenes in literature, immortalized in Gaston Leroux's, *The Phantom of the Opera*. There is so much more that I could tell you about this unique monument, but I strongly suggest that you take the tour and find out for yourself. You will not be disappointed. We will now proceed to the Cathedral of Notre Dame."

The road leading to 6 Parvis Notre-Dame-Place Jean-Paul II was inundated with foot and bumper-to-bumper car traffic on its narrow street. Horns blared as all movement came to a stop. Several tour buses with their swollen bellies interrupted the flow of traffic as they allowed tourists on and off, causing already impatient drivers to lean on their horns and wave their hands, swearing.

"Although you will not find any hunchbacks here," the group laughed, "you will find exquisite beauty, intense history, and historic finds such as the Holy Crown of Thorns, a fragment of the True Cross, and other precious relics. Oh, I should also mention that the Crypt, which can be entered from the outside, is often overlooked and contains additional archaeological treasures.

"Over the years, the cathedral experienced a demise caused by pollution and political and religious change. If you look out your windows, you will see the imposing West Façade of Notre Dame—probably the most famous view of the cathedral and the one that will give you a great overview of the painstaking detail typical of French Gothic architecture. The famous flying buttresses can only be seen from the east end of the cathedral. The use of flying buttresses was one of the revolutionary techniques of 13th century architecture. In earlier eras, thick walls were needed to support the heavy vaults of high-ceilinged structures. This new buttressing technique allowed for the construction of high ceilings and heavy vaults, but instead, with much thinner walls that could now serve as frames for the installation of delicate, stained-glass windows. Inside, you will find a quiet, almost revered spirit within the grayish walls. This effect is highlighted by the three magnificent rose windows, one of the glories of the cathedral, which fill the somber interior with jewel-colored splashes of light. The famous South Rose Window is forty-three feet high and depicts Christ reigning in Heaven. The North Rose Window is dedicated to the Virgin Mary. The West Rose Window contains depictions of the Virtues, Vices, and Zodiac.

"Once you've entered through the West Façade, you will find yourself in the main aisle, where you will be amazed by the high-vaulted central nave, choir, and high altar."

A little boy, who looked to be about ten and wearing wire-rimmed glasses, raised his hand.

"Yes, *monsieur*?"

"Are we allowed to get close and see the gargos on the outside?"

She smiled before answering. "Yes, you can see the gargoyles or *chiméres*, as we would say. Do you want to climb the tower's 422 steps?"

"Wow, that many?" he said with amazement.

"*Oui, monsieur*. There are no elevators."

"That's OK," he said with a slight resolve.

The guests roared with laughter. Soon the bus jerked forward, catching Élodie off guard as she grabbed the top of the seat to the left of her.

"*Excusez-moi*," Amadieu said into the speaker.

"All is well." Élodie said as she straightened. "Look to your left and right, everyone, and you will see the Seine, the longest river in France after the Loire. The Seine runs right through the heart of Paris, and a stroll along its banks would reward you with a history of the development of Paris itself." She continued to point out other minor buildings and answer questions of the guests. During the last ten minutes, the one monument that no one needed an introduction to came into view.

"*Mesdames, Mesdemoiselles, et messieurs,* you are facing la Tour Eiffel." The bus made its way down Ouai Branly, Champ de Mars as the group became restless.

"We will end here at this 1,063-foot marvel of engineering. Originally meant as a temporary design for the 1889 Exposition Universelle, it is reported that it took two years to build. It was meant to commemorate the centennial of the Revolution. Before the Empire State Building was completed in 1931, la Tour Eiffel was the tallest building. Met with opposition at its inception because of artistic objections *and* because the construction of such a tall structure was not considered feasible, Gustave Eiffel, the designer, was vindicated when it was found that the tower only sways 9cm, or 3.5 inches, in high winds. One thing to note: although the tower was the brainchild of Gustave, Stephen Sauvestre was responsible for the actual detailing of the structure, like the four arches linking the base of the tower at the second floor and the bulb shape at the summit."

The bus came to a gentle stop, and Élodie

held up her hand before people started to stand. "On behalf of my company, Vive la Ville, Amadieu and I want to thank you for touring with us and hope you enjoyed yourself."

A round of applause erupted. "Outside, you will find two guides who will help you with the rest of the tour. Enjoy your time in the City of Light and au revoir."

Élodie stepped to the side, allowing the passengers to disembark. A plum top hat, turned upside down, sat in an empty seat as some of the guests dropped coins and bills inside as a tip. Sissy contributed a few bills and stopped to tell the woman what a wonderful presentation she gave. Élodie smiled broadly and thanked her.

In the meantime, Angela was making eye contact with Amadieu. She gave him a sexy wink and he pursed his lips, tilting them slightly upward, and winked back. Nicki gave her a quick shove. "Leave that man alone, and let's get out of here."

"Don't be such a hater," she said and slowly went down the stairs after glancing back at him once more.

"Ms. Thang, you're going to break your neck if you don't watch yourself," Sissy teased.

"Whatever," Angela said and threw up her right hand. The girls paused outside the bus and searched for their guide.

14 | THE TEST BEGINS

"For those who are going to the luncheon, over here, please," said a slender woman dressed in stovepipe blue jeans and a blue-and-red, multi-colored cotton blouse with red hair cut into a pixie style, waving a card in the air. "Eiffel luncheon" was written on the laminated board.

They walked over and checked in with the guide. "Thank you," she said. "If you would wait over there, I will be taking everyone soon."

The girls walked to the left of her and mingled in the crowd. Sissy noticed several groups of schoolchildren gathered along the stairs, their backs against the Seine. Paper bags and lunch pails gave the indication that it was lunchtime. Sissy felt drawn to their curious, expressive faces. She listened as the children chattered away, their native language sounding so strange coming from their mouths. She picked up her Nikon camera and fired away, using her 55-200mm lens. Pleased with the results of the few pictures she photographed, she noticed the group moving up a flight of stairs toward the Eiffel Tower and ran to catch up.

"Glad you could join us," Nicki joked.

"The children are so adorable. You should hear them in their native tongue," she said. "It's so cute."

"Right now, we have to deal with this crowd," Angela interrupted. "Look at all these people. I thought it would be slow. It's November and the middle of the week. They should be at work." Nicki and Sissy chuckled as they walked with the group. It was true. A surprising number of people had flanked below the tower, causing the line to extend out about a mile.

"Have your vouchers ready to be scanned as you enter the elevator," the redhead called out.

"I can't believe that we are standing underneath the Eiffel Tower," Angela shrieked while grabbing Sissy's arm and shaking it several times.

"Yes, Cinderella," Sissy said while breaking her friend's grip. "We've arrived at the castle."

Nicki giggled while snapping away on her camera. Just as she angled it to take a shot looking upward inside the structure, from her peripheral, she noticed their group going through the gates to the elevator. "Hey, come on," she shouted and took off running. Angela and Sissy followed in haste and slid into the back of the line before the attendant placed a chain across the entry.

The brief ride up on the elevator placed them on the first floor, a short walk to 58 Tour Eiffel Tower, the restaurant. Their redheaded guide passed out the tickets to those who were taking the boat ride, then held up her smartphone.

"You can take a picture of the schedule. It will give you times for the Seine River Tour." Like a giant octopus, arms appeared from every direction with phone devices attached to the end of them. When the last hand retreated, she said, "Now to the restaurant."

***

They ordered from a short list that was included in the package deal and waited for the arrival of their meal. The view was surreal, as each woman was lost in her own thoughts as they scanned the panorama. A short while later, their first course was served. Sissy, who complained of hunger pains just minutes earlier, dove into the cup of creamy pumpkin soup, served in a white, ceramic goblet. The velvety-textured soup, with a complex, savory-sweet flavor, was garnished with a thin swirl of sour cream, causing her to shake her head in delight.

Nicki and Angela watched their friend relish the soup in ecstasy, then looked at their salads and sighed. There would be no such reaction as they stabbed into the variegated, mixed-greens appetizer with crumbled goat cheese sprinkled on top. The waiter whisked away the empty dishes before the second meal was served.

Sissy gently dabbed at the corners of her mouth, smiled, and turned toward Angela and Nicki as the plate of Comté cheese ravioli with ricotta and herb croutons was placed in front of her. "What in the world?" Her smirk fell flat once the cover over the meal was removed and stared back at her. "I could have gotten this mess at Olive Garden."

Angela and Nicki snickered as the waiter approached. A large casserole dish was placed between them.

"*Bon appetit!*" the waiter said as he stepped away with the lid that covered the dish. Large, off-white, tube-shaped macaroni, covered with a ham gravy garnished with grated Burgundy truffles, gave their eyes a visual feast. The women bent over the dish and inhaled the slightly musky, hazelnut-like aroma rising from the truffle sauce.

"Oh my dear, allow me to serve you," Angela cooed as she picked up Nicki's plate and deposited a generous serving on it.

With her hands outstretched, Nicki exclaimed, "Pierre outdid himself this time."

"Only the best for my guest," Angela said before placing the fork full of macaroni on the edge of her teeth.

"To die for," Nicki continued, "simply to die for." They paused long enough to look at Sissy, who was finding no pleasure in their antics.

Nicki continued. "You know that Burgundy truffles are best served slightly warmed so as to preserve their rich, earthy flavor."

"But of course," Angela agreed while waving her fork in the air. "And observe how a rich butter sauce brings out the full flavor of *any* truffle."

"All right, you two, knock it off," Sissy said as she gnawed on her pale, cardboard-like ravioli. After a few minutes, she gave up, pushing her plate to the side. She leaned forward, and with elbows on the table, Sissy rested her chin on her hands while staring at the women as they indulged in food and talk. She picked up her fork, scraping it against her plate, and said flatly, "Any time, ladies."

Angela jumped slightly in her chair and with startled pretense said, "Oh Sissy! How was your meal?"

"Lovely. Could we move on with dessert now?"

Nicki raised her hand and gave a slight wave, *"Garçon."* The waiter appeared straightaway at Nicki's side and bowed deeply. In a low voice, he said, *"Madame?"*

"Mousse au chocolat, s'il vous plaît." He smiled discreetly, gathered the dishes, and walked away.

Angela stared at her. "And when did you learn French, Missy?"

"Oh, here and there. I've picked it up as we've traveled."

Sissy shook her head and said, "Whatever." She closed her eyes and rubbed her forehead.

Angela reached across the table and patted her hand. "Never you mind that headache; the mousse is going to cheer you right up."

Sissy groaned slightly.

The waiter arrived with a tray of clear cups filled with a cloud of dark chocolate, topped with a swirl of whipped cream. After he served each woman, he said, *"Bon appetit."* They enjoyed the rich, creamy concoction as murmurs of delight escaped their lips.

As they rose to leave, Sissy said, "Now that was something we could *all* enjoy. Well, is anyone up for the challenge of climbing the stairs?" she asked, suddenly revived. "Or, like the tour guide said, we could pay the extra six euros and take the elevator to the second level of the tower."

"I'll climb the stairs if you two want," Nicki volunteered. They looked in Angela's direction.

"Well, I sure as heck am not paying another dime or euro. So, I guess it's to the stairs," she huffed.

"Atta girl," Sissy joked. She left the tip, and the trio exited the restaurant. First, they walked around the second level to photograph the skyline from different vantage points, then visited the gift shop. After their purchases, they approached the staircase. Secretly, Nicki wished they would forget the whole thing.

They made it up two flights when the reality of it all finally came to light. Nicki watched as a guy who appeared to be in his early twenties paused at the top of the staircase. He looked up nervously. "I have vertigo and can't do any more," he said aloud, excusing himself as he stepped around them to go down the next flight.

When they looked up and noticed there were five more flights to go, Angela shook her head. "Oh no, baby, my hips can't take all that. I have to go back down," she said while descending the staircase. The other two followed. When they found the elevator on the second level, a line of at least ten people waited in front of its doors.

"Well, there's no telling how long that's going to take," Sissy said. "Let's just do the stairs all the way to the bottom."

Nicki's heart raced as fear crept through her skin. This was not what she signed up for, but she dared not state so. She followed the girls and began the long descent down the black iron staircase. The embarrassment and pain that crept through her calves was too much. Just as she was about to call out to Sissy, she noticed several people impatiently waiting for her to continue. Nicki allowed them to pass and then began to take some of the stairs, one at a time, as her knees twitched with increasing pain.

Sissy paused on the fourth landing, searching the crowd for her friend. She yelled down to Angela to continue. Nicki appeared behind a middle-aged couple after they turned the corner on the landing.

"Girl, are you all right?" Her voice was full of concern.

"I won't lie; no, I'm not. My knees are killing me. I thought I would be okay descending the stairs, but the impact is worse. So much for all that exercising in the gym."

"Hey, before you start with that poor, pitiful me story, just stop. You wouldn't have made it as far as you have if you hadn't exercised. Just take your time and stay to the right. I'll follow behind you. When you need a break, just stand to the side on the landings and rest, then we'll continue. You know Ms. Thang is already downstairs, waiting."

"Of course," Nicki sighed before taking the next step.

When they finally reached ground level, Sissy gave her friend a fist bump with a few words of encouragement. "I know this was rough, but with every move we make, it makes us stronger—and I do mean all of us." She said the last line while staring in Angela's direction.

"What? Oh, you think it was easy for me to walk down that mess. Please. My hips haven't had this much of a workout since Cody left me."

"Too much information, Angela," Nicki said in a low voice.

"Girl, we are in Paris. You think these people don't know what I'm talkin' about? They invented the word sex."

Sissy couldn't hold back the laughter anymore and snorted out loud. "Whew, you are too much. I have to get away from you." And with that, she took off in the direction of the Seine River.

***

They were the first to arrive for the boat tour. Angela pointed out a guy who was walking on the upper level of the walkway. "He looks just like a French version of Usher."

"He is handsome," Sissy agreed.

"Who? Usher or this guy?" Angela was confused.

"Both!" Sissy said while staring at the man

until he disappeared from their view.

The temperature dropped slightly, and the girls retrieved their jackets from their backpacks. "I'm glad I didn't leave this behind at the hotel," Nicki said, and the others agreed with her.

After forty minutes, the crew approached the line and welcomed the visitors aboard. People of various races boarded and took a seat either inside or on top. Sissy was not surprised by the small crowd, considering that it was November. The captain spoke an impressive array of languages: French, English, Japanese, Chinese, and Spanish, explaining what channel to tune their headsets to for the tour description. The passengers clapped their approval of how well he handled each language.

The river was the heartbeat of the city. Both banks of the Seine were lined with numerous buildings that recounted the history of Paris.

"The word 'Seine' comes from the Celtic, meaning 'Sacred River,'" the guide began. "If you look to your left, you'll see a little island in the center of the river called 'Ile de la Cité'—literally, 'Island of the City.' Everything that you visit during your stay in

Paris started right here on this little tract of land because Paris itself started here. A small tribe of Celtic people called the 'Parisii' inhabited the island. Sometime around 52 BC, the Parisii were conquered by the Romans, who established a small settlement on the island and from there began to develop other settlements on the Left Bank. And the rest, as they say, is history!

"Let's move ahead several centuries and focus on the three important buildings that dominate the island. The first, the Cathedral of Notre Dame de Paris, is not only one of the most widely recognized monuments in France—and in all of Europe—but in many ways, it is also a mirror of the history of Paris and France. The building, located on the eastern end of the island and begun in 1163 on the site of a previous cathedral, has seen its fortunes rise and fall with those of France. From its original glory, it almost fell into complete disarray until the 1830s when Victor Hugo's famous novel, *The Hunchback of Notre Dame*, played a major role in the cathedral's restoration.

"If you direct your attention forward toward the western end of the island, we'll move ahead approximately seventy-five years to 1238 when construction of our next building, the Sainte-Chapelle, began. This diminutive, jewel-like structure was commissioned by King Louis the IX, Saint Louis, to house some of the most precious relics of Christianity—including the Crown of Thorns. The upper chapel is world-renowned for its exquisite, gem-colored, stained-glass windows. Unlike Notre Dame Cathedral, the Sainte-Chapelle is no longer used for religious services; however, it does host several classical music concerts throughout the year that are open to the public."

Sissy tapped Nicki on the knee and pointed to the building, then gave a thumbs-up, a signal she knew meant, "We are going there."

"Finally," the guide continued, "across from the Sainte-Chapelle, you might be able to catch a glimpse of the round towers of our last building, the Conciergerie, as we move away from the island. The structure, begun in the 10th century, was originally part of the Palais de la Cité complex, the residence of the kings of France until the 14th century, when it was abandoned for a new palace, the Louvre, which we'll pass shortly. The name

'Conciergerie' derives from the title given to the man who was in charge of the care and maintenance of the palace, the 'concierge.' The palace was eventually converted to a prison. In the 18th century, during the 'Reign of Terror,' one of the bloodiest periods during the French Revolution, over 2,000 prisoners were held here as they awaited execution at the guillotine, including the unfortunate Queen of France, Marie Antoinette.

"If you direct your attention to the right, you'll see the impressive Louvre coming into view. The Louvre Palace—one of the principal residences of the kings of France— appears to be a unified whole, but it is actually composed of a complex of structures that were constructed, renovated, and enlarged over a period of nearly 700 years. The Louvre decreased somewhat in importance when King Louis XIV moved the royal court to the recently enlarged Palace of Versailles, located about 20 km/12 mi from Paris, around 1678. During the French Revolution, the Louvre was converted to a museum with an initial collection numbering around 700 pieces. Today, of course, the museum has a stunning collection of over

380,000 items—only 35,000 of which are on display at any given time—making it the largest museum in the world."

"Not only is Paris a city of great monuments and art, but it's also a city of bridges. There are 37 bridges that cross the Seine, connecting the two banks of the city. If you take a quick look behind you, you'll get a final glimpse of the Pont-Neuf, or New Bridge, in English, which is rather ironic since it's actually Paris' oldest bridge, having begun construction in 1578. If you turn back to the front, we're now moving under Paris' most romantic bridge, the Pont des Arts. What makes it so romantic? Well, since 2008, lovers have been attaching padlocks with their names engraved on the front to the grates and railings of the bridge. What do they do with the key? They throw it in the river—a sign of their undying love. Unfortunately, there are now an estimated 700,000 locks on the bridge, which is putting extreme pressure on it and increasing the probability of collapse. The mayor's office has begun what they call the 'Love without Locks' campaign, encouraging lovers to take selfies rather than attach heavy locks to the bridge. Farther ahead, as we near the end of our cruise, you'll see what's considered to be the most beautiful bridge in Paris, the Pont Alexandre III. This bridge has served as the backdrop of a number of famous movies, including a recent music video. I'll tell you about that when we get there.

"If you look to the right, you'll see the Jardin des Tuileries, one of many former royal gardens in France that opened to the public during the French Revolution. Beyond that is Place Vendome, one of the most fashionable sections of Paris. It is home to several luxury hotels, such as the Ritz, as well as many famous design houses and jewelers, including Dior, Louis Vuitton, Chanel, Valentino, Cartier, and Van Cleef & Arpel.

"Coming up on our left is the beautiful Musée d'Orsay. This building was originally a Beaux-Arts railway station, the Gare d'Orsay, finished in time for the Universal Exhibition of 1900, which took place here, in Paris. The station was one of the major terminals in Paris until the late 1930s when it became obvious that the station's platforms were too short to accommodate the new, longer trains that were now fashionable, at which time it was converted to a station to handle suburban train traffic. By 1970, the d'Orsay had slowly fallen into disuse and was scheduled for demolition. The Ministry of Cultural Affairs opposed the move. Finally, in 1974, a plan was put forth to convert the former train station into a museum. The Musée d'Orsay now contains the largest collection of Impressionist and Post-Impressionist art in the world."

Nicki pointed to the converted railway station. "Let's make sure that we go there sometime this week," she said to Sissy, who nodded in agreement.

"If you look a little ahead on the right, you should see the ornate Baroque dome de Invalides. The structure was originally designed to serve as a residence and hospital for elderly and ill soldiers. The complex also housed a royal chapel for the king called, Eglise du dome, or Church of the Dome, referring, of course, to the exquisite golden dome inspired by St. Peter's Basilica, which crowned the chapel. To this day, the building is still used as a retirement home and hospital for veterans. It also contains the national military museum of France. But, without a doubt, the most famous site is the tomb of the Emperor Napoleon, whose remains were interred in an elaborate sarcophagus located directly under the dome.

"Please direct your attention straight ahead to the magnificent bridge, the Pont Alexandre III, which I mentioned earlier in our tour. Like the Musée d'Orsay, the Pont Alexandre III was constructed to help accommodate visitors to the Universal Exhibition of 1900. The bridge was named in honor of Tsar Alexander III of Russia as a symbol of French-Russian cooperation. The opulently decorated structure has long served as a favorite setting for many famous novels and films, including two Academy Award winners: 1952s *Moulin Rouge* and 1954s *Anastasia*. More recently, it has been showcased in the 1985 James Bond movie, *A View to a Kill*, and the 1997 animated hit *Anastasia*. Finally, Adele's 2011 video, *Someone Like You*, was also filmed here.

"As we approach the Eiffel Tower in the distance—and the end of our tour—let me invite you to sit back and enjoy the remainder of our cruise. Please feel free to ask me any questions you may have. Also, remember that our refreshment bar will remain open for the next 20 minutes. Thank you for choosing Vive la Ville Tours.

Bonsoir et bon séjour!"

They returned to the dock and, along with the rest of the passengers, thanked the crew for a wonderful tour as they disembarked. The air had definitely turned cooler, and the hours were finally taking a toll on the girls. They made their way across the bridge decorated with powerful horses at its entry to find the nearest Metro station. The traffic didn't seem to slow as the girls dodged across the street, pausing once more to look at the Eiffel Tower, now twinkling in champagne- colored lights against the charcoal night sky.

15 | CALLING IT A DAY

They walked up a steep incline that led to the front of Cité de l'Architecture et du Patrimoine on the Palais de Chaillot opposite the Eiffel Tower. Angela paused at one of the benches as she attempted to get her breathing under control.

"Who told you that I wanted all this exercise in one day, Jane Fonda?" she jokingly asked Sissy, referring to the exercise queen of the eighties.

"Don't think that I'm not suffering, too. All those stairs up and down the Metro station have me huffin' and puffin'." She took a seat as they waited for Nicki to catch up.

"Just keep moving," Nicki said between gasps of air. "If I stop for one of these park benches, I won't get up again until morning."

The street traffic picked up in pace, and pedestrians of all ages, shapes, and sizes moved like ants on a hill going in every direction, signaling the end of the work day.

"What time do you have, Nicki?" Sissy called out.

She looked at her watch. "It's only five p.m., and look how dark it is. I thought it was later than that."

"Yeah, I thought it was more like nine in the evening," Angela commented. "I can't believe we've been up since five this morning when they gave us that so- called continental breakfast on the airplane."

"When they flicked on the lights and their food carts rambled down the aisle, I thought it was feeding time at the zoo," Nicki retorted.

"Yeah, I felt nasty," Sissy frowned, "as though the stewardess said 'OK, it's time to feed the animals.'" They busted out in shrills of laughter, a much-needed distraction to the next hill they had to climb before reaching the Metro.

They paused outside the entrance, composed themselves, then descended the stairs to catch the next train. As they waited on the platform, Sissy took several pictures of some of the artwork inside the terminal. She put her camera away as the train pulled in and finally slowed.

When they entered the car, they tried to

stay as close as possible. It was rush hour, as people pushed and shoved their way into the crowded cars, not wanting to wait until the next one. All were in a hurry to get home.

"So this is what it feels like to be in a sardine can," Nicki said sarcastically.

"Just as long as someone doesn't say, 'Pass me some Ritz crackers and mustard,' I'm all right," Angela chuckled, causing another English-speaking passenger who overheard their comments to laugh along with the group.

They exited on Boulevard Saint Michel to visit Notre Dame Cathedral. This would be the last stop before they returned to the hotel. The church stood out like a beacon, its lights glowing from the upper level. It seemed to call out, "All sinners, all those who are lonely or in need of rest, come in."

Even in the waning hours of the day, crowds continued to mill around the famous West Façade of the cathedral, cameras flashing away. Sissy followed a small group of worshipers as they scurried to the entrance to attend the last Mass that was about to begin.

Angela stared up at the bell tower. "Isn't this the place where the Hunchback—"

"Quasimodo," Nicki said.

". . . took that chick—"

"Esmeralda," Nicki replied.

". . . up to the bell tower?"

"That was in the movie, not real life," Nicki said sarcastically as she hurried to join Sissy.

Angela used her 300mm camera lens to stare at the hideous gargoyles that served as water spouts. The creatures reminded her of an episode from the cartoon, *Johnny Quest*. She shivered at the sight of them. When she turned to tell Nicki how horrible they looked up close, she realized that she was alone and ran to the church entrance to catch up with her friends. Pushing through the dark, wooden doors just as the Mass started, Angela scooted into a vacant seat near the back of the church and stared at the two priests who stood at the altar. They were dressed in striking shamrock-green vestments. Cream-colored pillar candles cast a soft, angelic light throughout the nave. A sense of reverence filled the entire area. Angela stared at the large statue of the Virgin Mother, her arms open wide. She appeared to be watching over everyone who entered, encouraging them to pray.

As the Mass continued, the voices of parishioners echoed "Amen" in response to the prayers of the priests, while curious visitors wandered along the roped-off perimeter of the nave, viewing the magnificent stained glass, statues, and carved woodwork that graced the interior. It all seemed surreal that she should be here, giving thanks to God for this opportunity of travel with her friends. She pulled her jacket tighter as a cool draft rushed over her. She closed her eyes and bowed her head.

"Sortez pas ce portail, madame, merci."

With a start, Angela straightened in her seat and turned to see an usher a few rows behind her as he encouraged people to exit the church through a side entrance.

"Must have dozed off." She yawned as she took a peek at her watch. "Has it really been an hour since we came to the church?"

Since the usher was only one row behind her now, Angela stood up, stretched, and lazily joined the group of stragglers heading toward the exit. She turned and noticed a few bold souls who tried to rush to the altar rail in an attempt to offer up some last-minute prayers. The weary ushers were having none of it and blocked their path.

When she stepped outside, Angela saw Sissy and Nicki waiting for her beside the door.

"Hey, Sis, did you see those people who got shooed out when they tried to pray at the altar?"

"Yeah," Sissy laughed. "The ushers were like, 'Don't even try it!'"

"I know! The look on the ushers' faces reminded me of a quote I read about prayer: 'Give it to God and go to sleep!'" Angela giggled.

"Speaking of sleep," Nicki hinted.

"I know, I know; let's head back to the hotel," Sissy said.

"Amen to that!" Angela shouted as she led the way to the Metro.

***

They climbed up the last flight of stairs, pushing against an incredible wind pressure as they exited the tunnel and found their footing on the sidewalk. Neon lights flashed with the names of shops, restaurants, and cafés beckoning tourists into their businesses. Newsstand owners hawked their newspapers, magazines, postcards, and small selection of souvenirs. Streams of cars passed up and down the narrow streets until the traffic lights turned red, allowing the girls to make their way through the crosswalk. They faced the café they'd passed earlier that morning, now bristling with customers.

"Hey," Sissy called out. "Before we call it a night, let's have a drink."

"As cold as it is out here?" Angela balked.

"Oh, girl, live it up. You're in Paris! Who knows when you'll ever come back again," Nicki pleaded.

"OK, OK, stop whining. Besides, I thought you said you were sleepy."

"Well, I was until—"

"Yeah, yeah, yeah," Angela grumbled. "Let's get this over with," she said while entering the café's terrace.

Just as they seated themselves at an empty table, a waiter stepped up and greeted them, took their order, and sped off.

"I wish we could have snagged one of those seats," Angela said, pointing at the benches with the heating elements hanging over them.

"I like it here," Sissy retorted as she looked around at the other customers.

The busy waiter returned with coffee, tea, and three forks to share the dessert they'd ordered, and then disappeared just as quickly as he'd appeared.

The tired group munched silently on their late-night snack, watching the pedestrian traffic along the busy sidewalk. For a while, each woman settled into the moment, lost in her own thoughts.

Angela finally broke the peace and complained as she gently stretched her lower back. "I don't know if I'll ever walk again."

"You'll be fine," Sissy reassured her.

"I know how Ms. Thang feels," Nicki moaned. "My knees are killing me, and my lower back feels like someone has worked me like a pack mule."

"Ladies, ladies," Sissy said, holding her hands up in protest. "We are here, *in Paris*. I think we can endure a little pain in exchange for all of the beauty and culture that this place has to offer."

"Humph," Angela snorted.

Sissy continued, "And just think how sexy all this walking will make you."

"You mean dead from a heart attack," Angela snipped. Sissy gave her the eye.

"All right, I'll stop complaining, but you have to remember, Jane Fonda, to take it down a notch for the non-exercising crowd."

"Agreed," Sissy said while stifling a yawn.

"Sounds like you're finally ready for bed," Nicki laughed.

"Yes! And thank God the hotel is only three doors down." Sissy smiled.

After the group had slowly made their way down the block and stepped inside, Nicki took the lead and walked up to the front desk. "*Bonsoir*. We checked in earlier, but our rooms were not ready. The names are Nicki Cole, Angela Thomas, and Sissy Bakersfield."

"*Oui, mesdemoiselles*. Your rooms have been set aside." The clerk reached under the counter and pulled out three small packets; each one included a map and a key card. "You are in rooms 503, 504, and 505."

"*Merci*," they said in unison and headed for the storage closet to retrieve their luggage. They rolled their items to the elevator and were surprised when the doors opened and the small space presented itself.

"OK," Angela said. "This elevator is big enough for three small children—not three large sisters with luggage, too!"

"You go first, Angela," Sissy said. "Let's meet at seven in the lobby tomorrow morning."

"Seven!" Angela protested.

"Sorry, but we have a full day of tours scheduled."

Sissy and Nicki pushed the complaining Angela into the elevator, gave her a quick hug, and pressed the button. A few last-minute expletives issued from Angela's mouth as the door slammed in her face.

"Lord, have mercy!" Nicki grimaced. "Do you think we'll be able to survive a whole week in Paris with Angela?"

"I don't know. What was that prayer she told us at the cathedral?"

"Give it to God and go to sleep!" They laughed in unison.

16 | CALLING IT A NIGHT

It took Sissy a few minutes to realize that the same key card to open the door had to be placed in a slot by the doorframe to turn on the lights. Hopefully, Angela would figure it out before tearing the room apart, looking for a light switch. The room was quaint. The walls were covered with a brown, gauzy fabric overlaid with a gray, black, and white rosebud pattern. She had seen this style before while scanning decorating magazines for her home. The name finally came to mind—Toile. Sconces that looked like twisted vines stood out from the wall. The full-size bed was a welcome sight as she pulled back the covers before sitting on its side to remove her shoes. Sissy drew the tote bag that lay open on the bed toward her and removed an ink pen and her journal. She sprawled across the bed like a lovesick teenager and began a quick note.

Whew, what a day it has been! Land in Paris, run to the bathroom, run to catch a subway. Run here, run there, run everywhere. I feel like the Gingerbread Man. Seriously, I still can't believe that I'm here, in Paris, France, with my girls. We did it! We made a plan, stuck to it, and now we're celebrating the beginning of a new and healthier lifestyle.

I watched as Nicki struggled to climb the stairs at the Metro stations. There are very few elevators and escalators in these places. I must admit, all that walking was getting to me also, but I couldn't say it aloud. I feel somewhat responsible for placing them in this situation and must keep my complaints to a minimum. One thing is for sure—we should come back a few pounds lighter! Bonsoir.

***

Nicki was grateful that Sissy told her about the light switch; otherwise, she would have had to rely on the dim hallway lights to find it, and she was far too tired for a nighttime game of hide-and-go-seek! The tiny, contemporary-styled bathroom was a welcome sight, and Nicki couldn't wait to take a shower and rub down her sore muscles.

She walked over to the French-door-styled casement windows and pulled back the sheer curtains. Notre Dame, illumined by artificial light, glowed in the dark sky. The muted lights gave the appearance of a soft halo hovering over its two towers. She cracked the windows open, allowing the cool air to drift over her and fill the room. A rectangular planter filled with ivy perched on the outside ledge caught her attention. She leaned out the window to examine the plant, and then let her gaze wander across the rooftops that spread out across the city. She smiled and began to sway back and forth as she thought of Mary Poppins, Bert, and the chimney sweeps, singing and dancing the night away, jumping from one building to another. Nicki cleared her throat and softly began singing in her out-of-tune voice.

"Chim chiminey. Chim chiminey. Chim chim cher—ouch!"

A sharp pang in her calves brought a swift end to her impromptu solo.

"I guess it's time to throw in the towel," she giggled as she headed to the bathroom and turned on the shower.

***

"Those heifers could have shown me how to turn on the lights," Angela fumed.

She propped the door open with her

suitcase, allowing the hall light to guide her until she reached the telephone to call the desk clerk.

"Yeah, *Bone Swar*, to you, too. Look, I can't turn my lights on. Huh? Oh, OK. Thanks . . . um . . . I mean, *Mercy*."

"Shoot, where's that stupid card? Oh, here it is." She shoved the card in the little slot and looked around the now-illumined room.

"Not bad . . . but not good, either," she complained as she threw her suitcase on the luggage stand and tossed items haphazardly around the room.

"Maybe a little entertainment will get me going," she murmured as she picked up the remote and pointed it at the TV.

". . . le colibri mâle est généralement plus petit que la femelle, et. . . ."

"Oh great! Everything I've ever wanted to know about the hummingbird but was afraid to ask." She tossed the remote on the table and moved to the bed.

Angela grimaced as she bent over the mattress and laboriously began checking for bedbugs. *"Long Live France!"*

***

Nicki turned out the bathroom lights and walked over to the bed after checking the door locks. She snuggled under the fresh sheets and thick covers with her journal and ink pen. After a deep yawn, she began her entry.

I have no idea what time it is. My mental clock is so thrown off. This was one of those crazy, busy days that didn't want to end. After landing in Paris early this morning, we've been on the go ever since the plane touched down. We toured the city and walked till I can't feel my feet (I think they fell off somewhere between the Eiffel Tower tour and the last subway home). We got lost, went through several Metro stations, and prayed at Notre Dame before finally returning to the hotel.

My senses are in overload, and my body aches like crazy. I'll be glad when this Advil kicks in. I hope that I'll be able to keep up with Angela and Sissy this week. It's no wonder Parisians are skinny; they walk everywhere and eat very little. I brought a pocket notebook with me to keep track of what I eat. We didn't drink much today because bathrooms aren't as prevalent as they are at home. Some of the restrooms require you to pay to enter. Yikes! I hope I don't come back with a bladder infection.

Bonne nuit!

.

17 | OH NO, HERE WE GO AGAIN

Angela, twisted in the bedsheets and in a deep sleep, stirred due to a faint sound in the room. Still in some form of REM sleep, she turned onto her left side. "Paul," she whispered. "Baby, stop."

The pounding on the door became louder. "Paul," she said aloud while reaching out from the comforter.

"Angela, wake up," the voice shouted through the door.

"Paul, hold on; here I come." The next thing Sissy and Nicki heard on the other side of the door was "Ouch" and a few colorful words. When it finally opened, a half-awake, mean-faced woman greeted them in pale-pink, silk pajamas and a scarf pushed up like a misshapen crown on her head while a bedsheet hung limply in her right hand. The funky, leopard-print eye mask was pushed up on her forehead.

"What happened to you?" Nicki asked.

"Daylight and you guys pounding on my door." She limped away and returned to bed.

The girls, still dressed in their pajamas underneath their robes, stepped inside and closed the door.

"Ooh, I like the colors in your room," Nicki said after looking at the burgundy-and-red country pattern on the wall. "And this is a nice dresser set," she said after gliding her hands over the walnut top.

"I know you did *not* wake me up for a decorating Q&A session on French furnishings," Angela said while pulling the sheets over her head.

"Pull that thing off and listen," Sissy said as she sat at the foot of the bed.

"What now," she mumbled.

"It's seven in the morning, and we need to get started. We have an appointment to visit the Opéra Garnier."

"The what?" Angela asked, pulling the sheets down to reveal her eyes.

"The Opéra House," Nicki chimed in. "Remember when the tour guide spoke of it? The grand staircase, chandeliers—"

"Oh, that place. Well, I was thinking of skipping that."

"What?" Sissy said while staring at Angela. "The tour has already been paid for. We have to be there by two o'clock. By the time we catch the Metro, shop for souvenirs, and walk over—"

"I just don't feel . . . well, I'm just . . . I'm—"

"Spit it out; what's wrong with you?" Nicki asked.

"I'm embarrassed to say this, but it's this whole bathroom thing." Sissy and Nicki looked at each other, then back at Angela.

"I never told you guys this before, but ever since my gall bladder surgery, my bowels have never been the same."

"Ewe! Do we really have to talk about this before breakfast?" Nicki asked.

"Yes, we do, since you're all up in my business. Anyway, this bathroom thing in Paris is bothersome. I have to be careful about what I eat. If the food is too greasy, in thirty minutes or so, I have to—"

"We get the picture," Sissy interrupted.

"Maybe I should have brought some of those adult diapers with me."

"Yuck," Nicki cried out. "TMI! Too much information!"

"Look, everyone, calm down," Sissy insisted. "Angela, you must be doing something right because this is the first time you've mentioned this problem to us."

"Sissy, back home, we have plenty of bathrooms I can run into: department stores, grocery stores, restaurants, gas stations, even rest stops along the highways. We're so spoiled in the States, but you don't notice it until you lose it."

"Yes, you're right about that."

"I may not show it, but I'm so worried, I carry a change of underwear, cleaning wipes, and slacks with me in my backpack just in case. I try not to drink too much water for fear of not finding a restroom."

"A *free* bathroom," Nicki said.

"Yeah, a free bathroom," Angela said like a senator on a campaign trail. "The U.S. Consulate will hear from me."

"Oh my goodness," Sissy giggled. "I don't think we have to go that route."

"Our plumbing is precious," Nicki insisted.

"Look, ladies, we can't let this spoil our plans. Angela, whenever we see a public bathroom, just force yourself to use it, whether you really need to or not. Continue to sip during the day. Once we return from our tours, drink plenty of water at the hotel. As far as food choices are concerned, we'll snack on fruit, bread, and things that are gentle on your stomach. Dinner will be our splurge so you're close to the hotel in the evenings."

"And who knows," Nicki added, "we'll all lose a few pounds with all the walking we've been doing."

"So, what do you have to say now?" Sissy asked.

"I guess I need to kick you two out of my room so I can take a shower and get dressed. I'm hungry," Angela said with a slight smile.

18 | THE BOYS BACK HOME

Robert closed the door of the trailer to his makeshift office. As he pulled the key from the lock and turned around, he almost knocked the shapely female who stood behind him down the stairs.

"Candace! What the hell are you doing here?"

"And hello to you, too," she purred while stepping backwards down the stairs.

"You need to be careful who you walk up on in the dark."

"It's only six fifteen in the evening, and besides, I know a few self-defense moves to protect myself." She pretended to jab and kick like Bruce Lee, sound effects included.

Robert shook his head. "That won't get you very far. Anyway, why are you hanging around my job site?"

"I thought we could grab a bite to eat."

"That wouldn't be cool. We aren't a couple anymore, or did that slip your memory?"

"So, what, we can't be friends? You know,

hang out, talk, or have a drink?"

He didn't answer and chose to keep walking in the direction of his car. She followed him, refusing to give up so easily.

"We still have to figure out what to do about the house."

Robert cringed at the mention of the home that was built for the future he thought he had with Candace. Images of the brown-stucco, two-storied, traditional-styled house flashed in his mind. Together, they'd picked out the furniture, the pictures, the carpet—everything. He remembered how they haggled over kitchen cabinet styles. He wanted her to be happy and relented on the design of the master bathroom. The landscaping was his baby; he'd had a blast working with a consultant on the design. So many memories raced through his mind.

"What about it?" he finally responded as the thoughts faded like wisps of smoke.

"Well, do you want to keep it or should we sell it? After all, part of your money is tied up in it."

Robert opened the car door and paused before stepping in. "I told you before. I don't care what you do with it. You can continue living in it or sell it. Just send me the paperwork either way so I can move on." He slid behind the wheel, started the engine, and shut the door, hoping that she'd get the hint that the conversation was over.

Candace stepped up to the window and knocked on the glass. Robert sighed and finally pushed the button, rolling the window down halfway.

"What now?"

"How are you and what's her name getting along?" Candace asked with mock interest.

"Her name is Sissy, and we're just fine. She's currently in Paris with her friends."

"Paris!" she said slowly and sensuously. "*You know* that Paris is home to the most romantic men in the world . . . and oh, what men!" she teased.

"Look, Candace, you're not going to put any wild ideas in my head. My girl is having some fun with her friends and that's all. I'm tired and I need to get some sleep, so why don't you just walk your narrow hips back to your car so I know that you're safe and go home."

"*Oui, monsieur,*" she teased and seductively switched back to her car.

***

Paul reared back in his office chair. He felt

a tension headache coming on and paused to rub his temples. Working on two projects at the same time was draining, and he was ready to call it a day.

"Night, Paul!" Colleagues saluted him as they passed by his open door, hurrying to leave the office and taste freedom once again.

Paul stared at the city's landscape through the broad, plate-glass window. He chuckled to himself as he leaned forward and rapidly typed on his computer. When he clicked the search button, an image slowly filled the screen: Patrick Roger Boutique in Paris brought wonderful memories to mind. It was one of the buildings he told Angela to look up during her trip. The iconic chocolate store was more like an art gallery than a food store. The impressive exterior, inspired by nature, consisted of a series of emerald-green, curved, aluminum tubes representing a forest full of trees. The interior continued the forest theme with floor-to-ceiling aluminum tubes that spanned all three floors of the structure. No less impressive are the intoxicating aromas and eye-catching, life-sized chocolate sculptures found throughout the store. While Angela wouldn't be able to see the 32-foot chocolate Christmas tree that the talented Monsieur Roger had constructed a couple of years ago, she would, no doubt, find plenty of smaller treats to tempt her palate. In fact, the boutique has been likened to a jewelry store, as clerks lovingly handle the confections as if they were precious diamonds and emeralds. How decadent it would be to place one of those dark chocolate bonbons oozing with a pear-flavored, caramel filling between Angela's ruby-colored lips, and then—

"Paul? Paul?"

He spun around, the office assistant's voice catching him off guard. "Sorry, I thought everyone had gone home," he mumbled.

"No," the non-descript, slender brunette said through a slight smile. "Mr. Holbrook is just as much of a workaholic as you. In fact, he asked if you were still in the building and wanted to speak to you."

"Of course," was all he said and shut down his computer before joining his senior manager in an impromptu meeting.

***

Robert stepped into Brown Lee's Bar and Grill. The out-of-the-way hideout was located in the area known as the "Bottoms" on the Missouri side of Kansas City. The brown brick building was a well-known haunt for construction workers, police officers, and firemen, to name a few. It was the kind of place where a man could come and relax and not feel pressured to dress up to impress a woman. He grabbed a table near the big-screen TV, dropping his jacket in the chair next to him.

Robert ordered a steak sandwich, fries, and a side salad. "Could you add a gin and tonic and bring it before my meal?" he asked the waiter before he stepped away from the table.

Robert gazed blankly at the baseball game on the TV while his mind ran wild with Candace's parting remarks: "*You know* that Paris is home to the most romantic men in the world . . . and oh, what men!" He tried to shake her words, but they stuck like a fly on adhesive paper. He reached for his cell phone and with one slide of his finger, unlocked it. No messages. Robert let out a deep sigh, closed the phone, and stuffed it back into his pant pocket. Just as he stood to walk over to a pool table, his drink arrived. He tossed the drink back with two gulps and sat down again, staring at the big-screen television, his thoughts wandering.

Why hasn't she called me again since that first night in London? Maybe she doesn't miss me as much as I miss her. Idiot! She's in Paris! There's a thousand things to see and do there; she's just busy having fun. Yeah, but who's she having fun with?

Robert leaned back in his chair and closed his eyes, but all he could see was the Eiffel Tower.

19 | A BUMP AND A FALL

At 37 Rue de la Bûcherie, Nicki fidgeted, Sissy tapped her foot impatiently, and Angela—who decided to cop a squat on the nearest bench—filed her nails. On the banks of the Seine across from Notre Dame, they waited outside the doors of the famous bookstore, Shakespeare and Company. Several people were ahead of them, chatting away like drug-induced cats, making Sissy want to scream.

"Tell me again, Nicki, what's so special about this little bookstore?"

"Well, first, this isn't the original bookstore. That was located down the street at 12 Rue de l'Odéon. Anyway, the store was started in the early 1920s by Sylvia Beach, an American bookseller and publisher who lived in Paris. She was deeply involved in the cultural life of Paris at that time and knew all the major figures in literature: T.S. Eliot, Andre Gide, Ernest Hemingway. . .." Nicki sputtered to a stop as Sissy stared at her blankly.

"Yeah, and what else?"

"Well, she's probably best known for having published Joyce's *Ulysses* in 1922 . . . you know, stream of consciousness?"

The look on Sissy's face let Nicki know that she was getting nowhere fast, so she decided to speed her little history lesson forward by a few decades.

"Yeah, uh, anyway, the original Shakespeare and Company closed during World War II. But then, after the war, an American named George Whitman opened this store in front of us in 1951, and Sylvia Beach called it the 'spiritual successor' of her original store. The bookshop was first called Le Mistral but was later renamed Shakespeare and Company.

"Go on," Sissy said tolerantly.

"Well, I don't know every detail. . .." Nicki scoured her brain for something— anything—to humor her unimpressed friend.

"Um, he started the store with his own personal collection of one thousand books. Actually, he didn't even have a store to begin with; he just kept the books in his apartment. His door was left open all day long, and anyone could come in and take a book whenever they wanted. He was a free-spirit type. Before he moved to Paris, he lived a sort of hobo lifestyle, hitchhiking all over the States, Mexico, and Central America. Besides that, he—"

"Sounds like you, Sissy," Angela chimed in, unceremoniously cutting off Nicki's ramblings.

"I see you've finished filing your nails. And I *don't* hitchhike across America. I drive, thank you very much, Ms. Smarty-Pants."

"Same thing, different style. In the meantime, while you little bookworms comb the shelves for the next big thing, I'll be across the street, taking some pictures." She walked off before either of the women could comment. Sissy turned to Nicki and said, "Continue."

Nicki grimaced as she tried to recall more interesting tidbits. "One time, in the Yucatan, he got sick and was treated by some Mayans. He used to cook pancake breakfasts for guests on Sunday mornings. There's one of his quotes somewhere in the bookstore about strangers and angels—"

"Enough!" Sissy called out. She stepped out of line to gauge the length and gratefully noted that they were only three people away from the doorway. She couldn't understand why she was so restless and berated herself for being short with Nicki.

"I wish I could be a Tumbleweed," she heard her friend mutter.

"A tumbleweed? Now why in Heaven's name would you want to be some dried-up plant that gets blown around by the wind?"

Nicki snickered, then said, "You nut! Tumbleweed was a term George Whitman used to describe the many writers, artists, and intellectuals who visited his shop over the years. In fact, they say that around 30,000 people have slept or hung out here. To qualify as a Tumbleweed, you have to read a book a day, help out in the bookshop for a couple of hours, and write a one-page autobiography that is placed in the archives that George Whitman began. Oh, you also have to be cool with the fact that this is a communal project."

"What, no privacy? Like you have to share beds and stuff?"

"Share and share alike."

"I don't think so!"

Just then, a rail-thin male with a pale complexion called them to enter. His dark-blue jeans were slightly wrinkled, but the black-and-blue plaid dress shirt looked presentable. A black knit cap hid the majority of the thick, blond hair that stuck out from the back of it and grazed his shoulders. Sissy wondered if he'd borrowed the ratty tweed jacket with leather patches from his father—or maybe even his grandfather. It would be a fitting complement to the chicly run-down interior that greeted them once they crossed the threshold. Maybe he was one of those Tumbleweeds.

"Sissy, look, there it is," Nicki said while pulling her friend near the bookshop's doorway: "Be not inhospitable to strangers lest they be angels in disguise."

Before Sissy could comment, Nicki had taken off to the left with an audible creak of the wood floors betraying her moves. As she watched her friend navigate the extremely narrow aisles, she understood why it took so long for people to get in and out of the bookshop. Every possible cranny was crammed tight with books. Some of the bookcases looked precariously close to toppling over, like some literary Leaning Tower of Pisa. With her curiosity piqued, Sissy strolled off in the opposite direction, letting her hand trail against the tightly packed book spines, glancing at titles, all the while admiring the quirky charm of the shop. Several times, she had to plaster herself flat against a shelving unit to allow another customer to pass through the narrow corridor. She stooped to pull out large folios from the lower shelves, and then stood on tiptoe to spy out tiny, elegantly bound volumes with titles embossed in gold. With each new discovery, she decided that the long wait outside had been worthwhile.

Thirty minutes later, the two rendezvoused at the checkout counter with their selections.

"I decided to go with *The Hunchback of Notre Dame*," Sissy said, holding up a paperback-sized book bound in leather. "Considering that the church is just across the street, I felt it was an appropriate choice."

"Would you like our complimentary stamp?" a dark-haired clerk asked as he scanned the barcode on the book.

"I'm sorry, I don't know what you mean."

He smiled and began to explain. "In France, tradition states that we ink-stamp the title page of any new book with the booksellers' hallmark."

"Oh, how nice! Please do."

Sissy took her book from the clerk and moved to the side while she waited for Nicki to finish at the register. Finally, the two stepped outside, maneuvering around the newly formed line of book lovers who waited to get inside.

"Look!" Sissy said, opening the cover of her book, displaying the newly stamped mark.

"I know," Nicki smiled, admiring the round stamp that featured a fuzzy picture of William Shakespeare surrounded by the words 'Shakespeare and Company.'

Nicki and Sissy started down the sidewalk and moved along the bridge that crossed the Seine.

"Thanks," Sissy said. "That was a fun little history trip. I was a little peeved at first, but the more I got into it, the more I liked it."

"Right?" Nicki agreed. "You should always be open to new experiences; you never know what you'll run into."

The pedestrian light flashed and they made their way across the street, still chatting about the shop. Just as they stepped on the curb at the corner of St. Michel, after spotting Angela in the crowd, Nicki let out a squeal as her package went up in the air and she stumbled forward, landing on the back of a total stranger. It appeared that the two adults were engaged in a piggyback ride as his hands flew backwards, grabbing her in the process. He stumbled forward, with Nicki in tow while yelling, *"Aidez-moi! Aidez-moi!"*

It was a comedy of sorts as Sissy and Angela pulled on their friend's jacket to prevent her from crushing the poor guy into the sidewalk. When everyone was finally in an upright position, they moved to the side so that the amused onlookers could continue traveling along the crowded sidewalk.

Nicki apologize profusely to the attractive man. "Oh, I'm sorry! No, I mean, *excusez-moi! Je suis dés . . .* uhh."

Embarrassment written all over her face, she tried once more to apologize in French—without success—and looked to her friends.

Sissy stepped up to the rather tall, dark-blue-eyed man and said, *"Merci beaucoup. Nous sommes Américaines. Nous ne parlons pas très bien français."*

The man nodded his head. In an amusing, baritone voice he said, *"Oui.* Your friend, is she all right?"

Nicki nodded her head as she looked

around frantically for her package. She spotted it near a vendor's stall and rushed over to retrieve it. When she returned, she looked at the stranger and stuck out her hand. "I'm sorry about that. Someone shoved into me and the next thing I knew, I landed on your back while holding on for dear life."

"Ne vous inquiétez pas. That means, don't worry," he said, squeezing her hand. "You should all check that everything is in your purses and backpacks. Street thieves like to distract their victims in order to grab money and credit cards. Bumping into unsuspecting tourists is one of the oldest games around."

The girls checked their items and let out a sigh of relief.

"I hope I didn't hurt you," Nicki offered.

He let out a hardy chuckle. "Me? No, not at all. In fact, I am the better for it. I have bumped into three beautiful Americans, and the most beautiful of them all almost went home with me on my back!"

The three women laughed and waved goodbye. *"Au revoir,"* they said, as they turned and began moving quickly down the crowded sidewalk.

"Mesdemoiselles!" a voice called out. The girls turned around. The stranger scrambled

to catch up with them. "Would you join me in a cup of tea? My nerves are still rattled, and I need something to settle them," he lied. Looking directly at Nicki, he added, "I'm sure you feel the same."

Nicki was startled, unsure how to respond. Angela answered for her with a resounding, "Yes, why not! I know I could use a drink about now."

"*Monsieur*, we don't want to intrude. Besides, we don't even know you," Sissy said somewhat apprehensively.

"And I could say the same about you."

"Touché," Angela said, glaring at Sissy while tossing a lock of auburn hair over her shoulder.

"If you would permit me, I would like to offer you tea, and then you shall know my name. It will be safe. There is a café just across the street." He pointed in the direction of a little establishment nearby.

"Allow me to help you," he said as he stretched out his hand.

Angela stuck out her well-manicured hand but was stunned when the tall stranger grabbed Nicki's hand and led her down the sidewalk, leaving the other two women behind. Nicki looked back helplessly at her two friends with a slightly panicked look in her eyes.

"Well, I'll be!" Angela huffed.

"Now, now, Ms. Thang. You can't have *all* the men. Learn to share with your friends."

Angela stood, fuming, hands on hips. Sissy grabbed her by the hand and pulled her across the street in the direction of the café.

***

The group settled into their seats around a small table, grateful that the café was not very crowded. After a quick look at the menu, they placed their orders, then all eyes focused on the handsome man sitting next to Nicki.

"I know that you are wondering who is this strange man," he pointed to himself, "who keeps intruding on your vacation." The girls stared at him expectantly, and with a brief delay, he continued with a smile. "Allow me to introduce myself. My name is Ermenegilde Degaré Leclercq."

"I'm Sissy. This is Angela, and the young lady whom you so graciously rescued is named Nicki."

"*Enchanté*," he bowed slightly. Then, turning to Nicki, he added, *"Je suis ravi de faire votre connaissance, Mademoiselle Nicki.* Ah, forgive me. It is natural that I speak in my native tongue, but I will try to remember to speak in English."

"And what a tongue he has," Angela whispered to Sissy, who gave her friend a playful kick under the table.

"What does your first name mean?" Sissy asked.

"It comes from an old Teutonic word which means 'all-giving'."

Angela inhaled deeply and flashed a salacious glance in Sissy's direction.

"Don't even start," Sissy muttered under her breath.

"And your second name?" Nicki asked shyly.

"My second name means 'strayed' or 'lost.' However, I assure you that I am neither," he laughed.

"So," Nicki began, "you weren't lost or straying when I ran into you on Boulevard St. Michel?"

"Not at all! In fact, I was coming from work. I'm a professor at La Sorbonne. It's not far from where we met."

"You mean, like, *the Sorbonne*?" Sissy asked in amazement. "It's one of the oldest universities in the world."

He smiled and nodded. The waitress returned with their drinks. He prepared his tea with cream and several packets of sugar before continuing, "I'm a professor in Human Studies and Languages. The Sorbonne is part of the University of Paris and dates back to the 13th century. It's known for its history of rich culture, tradition, and top-of-the-line researchers," he said with a touch of pride.

"We're sorry if we kept you from your classes," Nicki said after taking a sip of her tea. She nibbled on part of the brioche on her plate.

"I was finished for the day and was in the area, settling some business. Your landing on my back was a pleasant surprise."

Nicki winced, then choked on part of her brioche.

"Are you all right?" Ermenegilde asked as he patted her back.

Nicki raised her hand, signaling him to stop. She took a swallow from her water glass and, for the first time, looked straight at him. A breath escaped her. His clean-shaven face was framed by a head full of dense, raven-black hair, which perfectly highlighted his ivory complexion. Narrow, sapphire-blue eyes glinted beneath a pair of thick eyebrows. Ridiculously long lashes, a strong jaw, and an off-center aquiline nose completed the picture. She estimated that he was easily six feet tall, and his black wool jacket couldn't conceal the broad-shouldered, trim physique that lay beneath it.

Ermenegilde took another sip of tea before speaking. "So, *mesdemoiselles*, where are you off to now?"

"The Panthéon was next on our list," Sissy answered.

"But if you have any suggestions, we'll be happy to listen," Angela chimed in.

"Ah, the Panthéon! I know it quite well since it's near the Sorbonne. It has a rich history. Originally, it served as a church dedicated to one of France's patron saints, Saint Genevieve. Now, however, it functions as a mausoleum for many of France's most famous citizens. Victor Hugo's remains are in the crypt, as well as Pierre and Marie Curie and Alexandre Dumas."

The girls looked at each other and broke out in laughter.

"What's so funny?" Ermenegilde asked with a puzzled look.

Rather than answer him, the women picked up their knives and, with outstretched arms, crossed 'swords' in the air, chanting, "All for one and one for all!"

"Ah, I see! The Three Musketeers."

"It's sort of the motto for our trip," Sissy explained, laughing.

"Would you like to join us?" Nicki asked. The words were out of her mouth before she realized what she had done.

Ermenegilde turned to face her; his smile brightened, causing his eyes to crinkle around the edges. "A fourth musketeer would not be, how do you say in your language, a side thorn?"

The girls giggled. "You mean a thorn in our side? No, you are most welcome to join us as the Fourth Musketeer!" Sissy joked as she gave him a courtly bow.

"*Merci beaucoup*!" he responded, returning the gesture before draining the rest of the tea from his cup.

"And now, to take care of the check," he said while pulling a sterling silver money clip from his pocket and depositing some bills on the table.

"Oh, no, Monsieur Leclercq, we'll pay our share," Nicki said as she and her friends rummaged through purses in search of coins.

"Please, do not insult me!" he replied in mock offense. "It was my offer so I must pay. Put your money away. Besides, I am the Fourth Musketeer, am I not?"

"Touché," Nicki laughed.

"*Et maintenant, en avant mes amies!*" Ermenegilde shouted as he grabbed Nicki's hand and marched down the street.

"I guess that means 'forward march' or something," Sissy said, turning to Angela.

"I don't know about all that," Angela replied as she and Sissy jogged to catch up with them, "but I *do* know men, and if I'm not mistaken, it looks like he wants the Four Musketeers to become the Two Musketeers!"

20 | REGRETS

As the click-clack of Candace's high heels on the rosewood floor bounced off the living room walls, she swore that she would have kicked her own butt if she could just reach back behind her. It was nearly a year since she'd broken off her engagement with Robert—and she regretted it.

"How stupid could you have been, Candace!" she chided herself. "And for what? Lust and money. OK, maybe not in *that* order," she confessed. "After all, you can't buy a pair of Jimmy Choo's with lust."

Anyway, Chad Honeycutt was the last person on earth who would have reprimanded her for putting money before love. The wealthy, spoiled executive of Cisclean Electronics had promised her both—and he delivered. Life with Chad was a non-stop merry-go-round of fun, impromptu weekends in Chicago, ski trips in Colorado, and wild nights at the casinos in Vegas. And the shopping! She enjoyed sprees at YSL, Prada, Dolce & Gabbana, and

DKNY. Chad never skimped on anything . . . except his promises. Candace found that out the hard way. How could she forget.

"Hey, babe," he'd crooned over her cell phone, "can you come over to the penthouse? I have something for you."

Candace remembered how she raced to his apartment, confident that the "something" was that spectacular diamond engagement ring that they'd looked at a few weeks earlier. And she wasn't mistaken. She could still remember how he met her at the door, kissed her, and then told her to hold out her hand. She gasped as he slid the gorgeous stone on her finger . . . and then casually turned around and walked back into the apartment, leaving her standing in the doorway, staring at boxes stacked on top of boxes, half-filled packing crates, and rolls of bubble wrap.

"Sir, do you want the bed placed in storage with the other furniture that we moved yesterday?" asked a stout man, standing near the bedroom dressed in an Allied Movers uniform.

"Yeah, that would be great," Chad answered cheerfully.

"Honey . . ." Candace began with

trepidation, trying hard to keep her voice from trembling. "What's all this?"

"Oh nothing. You know me; I've got to keep the creative juices flowing. I thought a change of location would do me some good, so I'm moving back home to Burlington, Ontario. That's where it all started, Cisclean Electronics, in my parents' garage all those years ago!" he reminisced happily.

"You're moving back in with your parents!" Candace was beginning to lose it.

"Nah! I'll have my own place, of course, but I just thought that a simpler lifestyle might do me good, get back to my roots!"

"And what about us? This ring?" she asked, waving her hand in his face.

"Yeah, I saw the look you had on your face when you showed it to me in the jewelry store a few weeks ago," he grinned. "I knew it would be the perfect going- away gift for you!"

"What? Chad, I don't understand! Aren't we getting marri . . .?"

Candace's sentence died in midair as Chad bent down and gave her a quick peck on the forehead.

"Hey, babe, look. I'll call you from Ontario. I have a couple of meetings to get to before I catch my flight."

Chad grabbed his car keys from the top of one of the packing crates. "The ring looks great on you, babe!" he shouted as he waved goodbye and disappeared down the hall. The man-child was gone.

The next few weeks were a blur for Candace. There were tears, lots of them. So what if they were more for wounded pride than for lost love. Candace wasn't the kind of girl who was used to being played. Besides, this little excursion had cost her Robert.

"Ms. Rice?" a female voice echoed throughout the house.

Candace turned from the bay window and stared at the realtor. She had forgotten that the woman was even there.

"I've completed my inventory of the kitchen, the guest room, office, and bathroom. I'll work on the living room last. I'd like to see the upstairs now. This is a beautiful home. I'm still amazed that you want to sell it."

"My ex-fiancé and I have decided to let it go. There are too many memories. We want to sell the property and split the profit."

"I'm sorry to hear that," the older, pear-shaped woman replied. Her brown knit skirt stretched across her backside and thighs, causing it to pucker at the seams. "Would you mind leading the way?"

Candace moved up the carpeted staircase like a woman going to the gas chamber. Memories flooded her mind as she stepped onto the landing, then moved aside as Ann— at least that's what her name tag said—made her way to the master bedroom.

"Oh my," the woman exclaimed. "What wonderful light!" She scribbled in the spiral notebook that she held in her hands. When Ann moved into the master bathroom and opened the shower door, a squeal of delight could be heard. "You have one of those shower heads that makes it seem like you're standing in a rain shower! And these double sinks will be valuable for couples."

Candace remained in the master bedroom, her back pressed against the cool, bare wall as Ann scurried back and forth, clucking like a hen. Robert was so proud of the house; after all, he had designed it and supervised the construction. Right here—pressed against this wall—he'd leaned over her and whispered in her ear that he'd poured all of his love for her into it. Then he proved it. But that was before Chad.

"You fool! I could kick myself!" she half-shouted.

"What's that?" Ann called out.

"Nothing, Ann. I'll meet you downstairs," Candace answered.

"Girl, you messed up royally. And now he's with that little nursey," she fumed as she slowly descended the stairs.

"And there's nothing you can do about . . . it. Paris, huh? How long did he say she'd be there? A week or two?"

Candace grabbed her cell phone and pulled up Robert's number.

21 | RETRIEVAL

He punched the redial button on his cell phone and waited for the long-distance number to finally kick in. After four rings, the mechanical voice stated that he was unable to reach his party and to please leave a message. The phone beeped and he did as instructed.

"Hey, babe, I miss you. Wish you would call so that I'd know that you're safe. I guess I'm just a little lonely without you. Later."

He clicked off the line, then tossed the phone on his desk. It slid across, coming dangerously close to the edge, when his assistant, Colin, caught it in his hand. "That could have been costly, boss."

"Yeah, right," Robert mumbled while reaching for his hard hat on top of the metal file cabinet.

"I take it that you haven't heard from your girl."

Normally, Robert didn't discuss his personal life with his employees, but he and Colin had worked together for five years. To an outsider, they seemed like brothers. Their relationship was built on mutual respect and a shared work ethic.

"Naw, it's like she forgot all about me. Probably found some Parisian and hooked up with him. At least that's Candace's take on the situation."

"Oh, speaking of your ex, she left a message for you to call her." Colin passed the pink slip of paper over to his boss, along with his cell phone.

"I have to oversee the men on section seventeen," Robert said while stuffing his things into his orange vest pocket. "Women," he huffed as he began to pull the trailer door closed behind him.

"Brrrng!"

Robert pulled the phone out of the vest pocket and saw Sissy's number.

"Hey, Colin, you go ahead. I have to take this call."

"Sure boss," Colin grinned as he left the trailer.

Robert's hand shook slightly as he clicked on.

"Hey, can you hear me?" Sissy shouted into the phone.

"Yeah, babe, I can, but take it down an

octave," Robert laughed. "It sure is great to hear your voice, Sis!"

"Sorry, I had to step outside. The traffic and noise is crazy around here."

"I hate that I had to bust in on your party, but I've been kind of worried about you and the girls. You haven't called in a couple of days and, well. . .."

Sissy didn't know what to say. Her mind hadn't really been on Robert. Besides, she reasoned, Candace, aka *the beauty queen*, was probably keeping him company. "Well, it's been wild around here. First, there's the time change. And then, we've been trying to maneuver the Metro while reading everything in French. We've managed not to get too lost during our trips; still, it's been a little hectic and . . . um." Sissy wasn't sure how many more lame excuses she could come up with.

"No worries. It's just that I miss you so much, but I'm glad you're having fun. I wish I had the time to travel with you."

"And I'm glad you *don't* have the time," she whispered under her breath. Immediately, she berated herself. *I'd better end this call before it turns ugly,* she thought.

"Well, sweetie, I'd better get back inside

before the girls think I've run off with some sexy French man."

"What was that comment about?" Robert wondered. "Better let it pass and move on," he decided. "OK, well . . . um . . . have fun. I know the rates are high, but give me a call when you can." ·

"Sure. Today we're at the Panthéon. It's fantastic and so huge. It would have warmed your engineer's heart to see it! Well, stay safe out there. Miss you!" Why did she lie like that? He was the furthest thing from her mind right now.

"Miss you too. I can't wait to hold you in my arms again."

"Same here. Later." She quickly clicked off before he could say anything else.

"That story should hold him for a while," she said to herself while jerking the door of the Panthéon open and stepping back inside. "Out of sight, out of mind," she grimaced as she jogged across the hall to join the girls.

22 | DANGER AHEAD

The Johnston & Murphy black calf Moc shoe pressed down on the gas pedal. The orange needle on the speedometer jiggled from sixty-five, to seventy, to eighty, to eighty-five.

"What the . . .," Robert started to say as the roar of the engine filled his ears. "Oh, that's me." He smiled ruefully as he realized that he was the source of the noise pollution. His foot lifted from the pedal, and the needle settled down to a nice, stable sixty-eight. Inside, however, Robert felt anything but stable. That conversation he'd had earlier with Sissy left him feeling off-kilter. And now, on top of everything, he had to deal with Candace again.

"I need you to come by the house to pick up the rest of your stuff in the basement. Plus, we need to discuss a few things before I start work with the listing agent."

It sounded reasonable, but you could never tell with Candace. Anyway, it would be easier to just go over there and get everything taken care of, once and for all. She lucked out that this had been a short day for him. Earlier, he'd met with the corporate tenants who would occupy the building currently under construction. Robert had reassured them that the work was on schedule and that he and his men could pull off the job in time. With the successful completion of this contract, it would move his construction company into the top bracket with the other big names in the industry in the Metro area.

Yeah, that meeting turned out OK, he thought, *but what about the one I'm about to have with Candace?*

***

He rang the doorbell, and at the sound of the soft chime, all of the old memories surrounded him. Robert looked around his old neighborhood. Across the street, the Patterson's open garage no longer displayed the old, navy-blue Plymouth Voyager with the familiar dents and scratches. A Subaru Forester in quartz-blue pearl had taken its place.

And to the right of them, it looked as if Mr. and Mrs. Barker had acquired a few more birdhouses since he left. The two trees—one in the front yard and the other to the right side of the house—seemed to be loaded down with feeders of every shape and color.

He stared at his own empty yard. The ghost of what should have been taunted him—the crushed-stone path leading to the arched arbor in the back of the house wrapped in a burst of morning glories, or was it clematis that they had decided upon? Anyway, what does it matter; the whole thing came crashing down when Candace discovered Chad Honeycutt's deep pockets.

"Good evening."

Robert turned around, startled, and stood gazing at Candace through the screen. Her shoulder-length, brown hair had been pulled up in a soft topknot; whispers of bangs covered her forehead. Her large, dark eyes teased him as she tilted her heart-shaped face slightly and turned up the corners of her mouth in a calculating smile. He hated to admit it, but she still looked as sexy as ever.

"Well, are you going to come inside, or do you need this screen to shield you?" she smirked.

"That depends on you."

She pushed the screen open and made a slight bow.

"Wow, this feels strange," he said as he crossed the threshold and moved to the living room.

"It shouldn't. After all, it was your home, too," she said after joining him. "Won't you sit down?"

Robert ignored her invitation. "So, what's the hurry with me moving the rest of my stuff out, and what did you have to discuss with me?"

"I just wanted you to know that I'll be moving forward with obtaining a listing agent so that I can place the house on the market."

"You could have told me that over the phone. Besides, I told you that you could do whatever you wanted with the house; it's all yours."

"It used to be all *ours*."

"*Used to be*. And we both know whose fault that is."

Without replying, Candace stared at him enigmatically.

"I'm sorry, Candace. That was uncalled for. It's just that seeing the old neighborhood and coming through these doors again brought everything back."

"Haven't I already apologized for all

that?" She took a sip of the Merlot she held in her hand. He hadn't even noticed the glass until now.

"Yeah, you did, but . . . could I get a glass of whatever it is you're having?"

Candace moved like a cat to the oak bar and poured him a glass. Just as she turned to walk back, she almost came crashing into his broad chest. "Oh!"

"Sorry, I didn't mean to startle you," he said, taking the drink from her hand and downing half the glass.

Candace eyed him silently.

"What made you decide to give up the house?"

"When the agent was here making notes about the rooms, going on and on about what a find the house was, well, I naturally thought about you. You designed the place from top to bottom. Do you really think I could stay here, seeing you in every little detail, yet knowing that you'd never be here with me?"

Robert gazed at Candace, trying hard to decipher the expression that she wore. Her beautiful face was made up flawlessly, as usual—not that she needed it—and she was wearing the hell out of that coral wrap dress!

He turned his eyes to the wine glass, tossed down what was left, and darted over to the staircase, taking the steps two at a time.

"Hope you don't mind," he yelled back. "Nature calls," and slammed the bathroom door immediately.

"No, I don't mind at all," she said in a low voice. "I have you just where I want you." Candace placed her glass on the bar, adjusted the neckline of her dress, and then climbed the staircase.

***

Robert stepped out of the bathroom and looked to his left. It was all just as he had designed it: the guest rooms, the nursery, the boudoir he'd created so that Candace could have her own private space. He moved a little farther down the hall and stopped. There was the master bedroom. The door was open and the room was empty. He felt Candace's presence behind him and spoke without turning around.

"You never slept in here?" he questioned. "No furniture?"

"It just didn't feel right anymore. You know. . .." They stood in silence before she cleared her throat and continued, "I used one of the guest bedrooms."

Robert moved forward and entered the room. He walked over to the windows and looked out into the backyard. He had loved this room. He had loved the woman he'd designed it for.

"Robert," Candace called out.

A chill swept over her arms, and she quickly wrapped them across her chest. Beneath her feet, she felt the vibration of his footsteps on the carpet as they moved toward her. Robert towered over her, and for the first time, she could not and did not anticipate his next move. It took her breath away when he grabbed her arms, raised them and pinned them against the wall where she stood. A moan uttered from Candace's gaping, pink-tinged mouth.

Robert leaned in to her left ear and whispered, "Why?"

The moisture from his breath glided and tickled the outer surface of her delicately shaped ears. That single word slid inside and down her eardrum while vibrating throughout her brain. Candace's stomach tightened, releasing a desire that began to fill her.

"I loved you so much." He said each word with such deliberation. "I would have given you anything."

"Robert, baby . . . I'm so sorry."

"Save it," he yelled.

Before releasing her arms, he moved his mouth from her ears to her lips. It hovered there for the slightest second before he licked his own lips ever so slowly and deliberately.

"Remember how we made love?" he asked while releasing the tie that held her dress closed. His right hand expertly parted the opening. He looked down and noticed the plum-colored, padded bra and matching lace, hipster-styled panties.

"Yes," she answered. Her chest heaved up and down while tears spilled across her cheeks. She longed for his touch and parted her legs slightly.

"Good. I hope you never forget." He stuck out his tongue, touched her upper lip, then pulled it back into his mouth as he traced the top of her breasts with his fingers. He sucked her top lip slowly and listened to her sweet, soft moans. Then he released it and said, "Now I'm going to get my things and go." He removed his hands from her arms and walked out of the bedroom without looking back.

Candace slid down to the floor and drew her knees up as her head fell forward. She cried out with all her strength, "Robert! Baby, I'm so sorry!"

***

He loaded the last of the storage crates in the truck, closed the garage door, slid behind the wheel, and backed down the driveway. Before pulling away, he looked up at the house. He could see Candace's outline, standing at the living room window, then he tore down the street. Candace's voice echoed in his ears, *"Robert! Baby, I'm so sorry!"*

Robert turned on his blinker and moved to the right to take the ramp that would put him on the interstate. Going to the house had been a bad idea; he wasn't over Candace after all. And what about Sissy? She seemed to be getting tired of him. Was she going to be another Candace? He pressed down on the accelerator and tried to hurry away from Candace, Sissy, uncertainty.

Candace backed away from the living room window with a satisfied smile on her face. She moved thoughtfully back to the bar, picked up her glass of Merlot, and raised a toast— "Act One, Scene One, Robert."

***

Sissy looked up from the little tour pamphlet that she'd picked up at the information desk. She silently gazed at the massive stone-and-marble neoclassical structure surrounding her: seemingly endless rows of elegant Corinthian columns, floors of intricately patterned inlaid marble, spacious vaults, and the crowning glory—the triple-shelled dome, rising 279 feet from floor level and decorated with a mosaic of St. Genevieve. Sissy shook her head and laughed to herself, "Who would believe that all of this is a 'thank-you gift' to God from Louis XV after a successful recovery from a bout of gout!"

"Hey, Sissy, over here," Nicki and Ermenegilde waved. "Look. Aren't they beautiful murals of Saint Genevieve, the patron saint of Paris?" She searched her pamphlet and pointed to the paragraph. "Several artists painted the actions of the saint's life, highlighting the ideas of sacrifice and resistance."

"It is said," Ermenegilde began, "that because of her prayers, she saved the city from invasion when it was being attacked by Attila the Hun."

"Speaking of attacks, I'd better find Angela. You know she'll go ballistic if she thinks we've gone off and left her here alone," Sissy joked as she moved off in search of her friend.

After spending several minutes ducking in and out of side chapels, she was surprised to find Angela standing stock-still, right in the center of the building under the large dome.

Sissy snuck up beside her, "Boo!"

Angela jumped and glared at Sissy, "Girl, stop!"

"Whatcha looking at, kid?"

"Can't you see? It's Foucault's Pendulum."

"Please enlighten me, Madame Scientist," Sissy smirked as she examined the stunning object, solemnly swinging back and forth.

"Well, that large, white circular band surrounding the pendulum is marked with numbers in military time. The numbers represent the 24 hours in each day, and hash marks show the quarter hours. A smaller table inside the band indicates the minutes. And in the center of that big circle is a pendulum. That golden sphere is the bob of the pendulum; it's a 61-pound, brass-covered lead ball. The sphere is hanging from a 220-foot-long steel wire suspended from the dome of the building."

"Yeah, it's real pretty," Sissy responded,

duly unimpressed.

"Well, hold on, Ms. Smarty-Pants; let me tell you what it does."

"Please, enlighten me."

"The thing was created by this French scientist named Leon Foucault. He wanted to prove that the earth rotates on its axis. No, that's not right. Wait a minute." Angela hurriedly scanned her little pamphlet. "OK, he wasn't trying to prove that the earth rotates; everyone had already known that for a long time. What he was trying to do was provide a public *demonstration* of the rotation," she pronounced proudly.

"Sooo, how did he do it?" Sissy asked, suddenly intrigued.

"Well," Angela continued with an air of importance, enjoying her role as a wannabe Brainiac, "when he first conducted the experiment in 1851, instead of the big, white circular band, the only thing beneath the pendulum was a large circle of wet sand. You see that pointy thing at the tip of the sphere? That's called a stylus. When they set the pendulum swinging, the stylus traced a perfectly straight line in the wet sand. A quarter of an hour or so later, as the pendulum continued to swing, the line that was being traced in the sand was no longer a single straight line. Instead, the line began to fan out, clockwise, more and more from the original line. As time progressed, so did the movement of the line."

"Oh, I see! The line fans out because this building that we're standing in is attached to the earth, and the *earth* is moving beneath us!" Sissy exclaimed triumphantly.

"Exacto!"

"Well, I'm impressed with you, Angela! This is a far cry from the conceited, self-centered woman whom I know and love."

"Excuse you! As they say, you can't judge a book by its cover. Besides, with Nicki glued to 'Mr. Paris,' I knew we'd be stuck here for a long time. What else was there to do other than stare at this darned pendulum and try to figure out what's going on."

"That's my girl! I knew the real Angela was lurking somewhere."

"Sis, I've had enough culture for today. Can we get out of here?"

Sissy quickly turned to glance at Nicki and Ermenegilde; the couple still appeared to be engrossed in conversation.

"Well, we haven't seen the crypts yet, Angela."

"You know I'm not interested in any crypt. Neither are you. You're just trying to give the *love bug* some extra time with her man. Well look, I didn't come to Paris to play matchmaker to Nicki, and besides, I need—"

"Yeah, yeah, girl, I hear you," Sissy said consolingly as she pulled the complaining Angela down the stairs to the crypt.

***

Ermenegilde stole a glance at Nicki as she continued to examine the impressive murals adorning the walls. The rich, brown color of her flawless complexion fascinated him. Her long, dark lashes brushed the tops of her round cheeks when she looked down to read her guidebook. He wanted to reach out and caress that pretty face, but, of course, that was out of the question—for now. It's true, she's much heavier than any woman he's dated in the past, but there's a certain seductiveness about her, a strange mixture of shyness and sexiness. She reminded him of the generously proportioned, big-breasted nudes that Rubens is famous for. A Baroque beauty, he mused.

"Degaré." A faint voice caught his attention. He shook his head to clear it of his present thoughts. *"Oui?"*

"I was asking if you were all right. You seemed so far away, lost in thought."

"*Je suis parfaitement content!* I am perfectly happy, especially because you appear to be enjoying yourself. But we should, perhaps, find your friends. I do not want them to think I have captured you for my own pleasure."

A warm sensation passed through Nicki. It had been at least five years since a man had even looked at her, let alone flirted with her.

I must be nuts to think that this guy wants me. He's just being nice. If I could only lose another fifty pounds, OK, sixty pounds, then maybe I'd stand a chance, Nicki thought.

"Shall we?" Ermenegilde smiled, extending his hand.

"Sure," Nicki replied somewhat demoralized, letting him take hold of her hand.

Ermenegilde squeezed Nicki's hand and moved toward the stairway leading to the crypt.

"Let's bid Saint Geneviève *adieu*," he joked as they passed under the mural.

Nicki smiled faintly, looked up at the painting, and prayed under her breath, "Dear Saint Geneviève, if I stand even half a chance, please let him ask me out again!"

23 | ALL'S WELL

"You're positive that you can find your way back without using the Metro?" Ermenegilde asked.

"Yes, thank you," Sissy reassured him. "The Best Western is just three blocks away. Besides, the walk will be good for us."

"*Mademoiselles*, it has been wonderful to spend time with you. My day has been so bright because of it." He smiled as he shook hands with Sissy and Angela. When he reached out to take Nicki's hand, he gently raised it to his lips and lightly kissed it as he stared intently into her eyes.

"Well, excuse me," Angela said under her breath. Sissy jabbed her elbow into her mouthy friend's rib cage.

"Ouch!" Angela yelled while rubbing her side.

"I'm sorry?" Ermenegilde asked, turning suddenly at Angela's outburst. "You are OK, *mademoiselle*?" he asked.

"Sure, swell," Angela murmured. "I mean, thank you for the wonderful dinner at the Hippopotamus." She smiled while brushing a few strands of hair over her shoulder in an attempt to steal the attractive man's attention.

"Yes, an interesting name for a restaurant, considering our size," Nicki commented ruefully.

"Your size?" Ermenegilde said slowly. "I don't—" Then, glancing around at his companions, he blushed deeply and hastened to add, "Ah, *Mademoiselle Nicki*! I assure you, in no way did I mean to suggest that . . . I mean, the meals there, they are filling . . . ah non! I mean, the prices, they are very *reasonable* . . .," he stuttered, turning redder by the second.

"There is no harm taken!" Nicki smiled, patting him on the arm. "I was just making a joke. Probably a bad one, at that."

His smile returned before he said, "Unfortunately, *mesdemoiselles*, I must depart. I have classes at eight in the morning, and the hour is late for me." He reached inside his suit jacket, pulled out a silver case, and presented his business card. "Please do not think I am bold, but only concerned. If you should need some assistance while in Paris, would you please call me?"

Angela stretched her hand out confidently, but it was in Nicki's palm that the card was delicately deposited. "I hope to see you again," he said, staring directly at Nicki.

"*Bonsoir*," he added, finally turning to the other two.

"*Bonsoir, monsieur*," the women said in unison as they began to walk away.

He watched them cross the street to the next block. Just as he was about to depart, Nicki turned suddenly and waved. Ermenegilde raised his hand high, returning the gesture with a smile. He dropped his arm when she spun around and ran to catch up with her friends just as they turned the corner past the pharmacy.

***

Sissy and Angela tapped on Nicki's door. When she opened it, the two women looked like the Cheshire cat from Alice in Wonderland.

"What's wrong with you two?"

Angela strolled in, followed by Sissy. They paused in front of the bed and began their act.

"Let me take your hand, Princess Dark and Lovely," Sissy began.

"*Oui, Oui*, Ermenegilde, you handsome devil you," Angela said as she sputtered the remainder of her lines between fits of laughter.

"Whatever!" Nicki said, waving the two off before heading into the bathroom.

"And what possessed you to invite him to join us?" Sissy yelled while leaning against the door.

"Do you mind?" a muffled voice said before a flush of the toilet could be heard. Sissy stumbled as the door opened, and Nicki went back to wash her hands.

After righting herself, Sissy said, "You have to admit, he was somewhat drawn to you."

"He was being nice. Now if you two alley cats don't mind, I would like to go to bed so I can get up in the morning." And with that, she picked up her tube of Icy Hot, squirted some of the cream in her hand, and began to rub it over her knees.

"Let me out of here. Grandma is about to stink up the place," Angela shouted as she headed for the door.

"Sweet dreams, Princess Dark and Lovely," Sissy teased as she closed the door behind her.

Nicki changed into her pajamas, then walked over to the window and opened it slightly. She returned to her bed and stuffed a couple of pillows behind her back before reaching inside the bedside table to retrieve her journal. She began to write.

Paris 2014

What a day this has been. If I had wanted to find a man, it would not have been this way. Who would have thought that my falling onto the back of a stranger on a Paris sidewalk would mark my grand entrance into the world of romance? And what a handsome stranger he is! Ermenegilde, that's his name, has made my heart jump so much that it thinks it's in the Olympics. He's a professor at the Sorbonne and he's a gentleman—at least he appears to be.

I can't believe that I, Nicki Cole, invited him to join us on our tour to the Panthéon. The girls were stunned that I said anything. I can't get over the fact that I was so bold. Maybe Angela is having an effect on me! Just the thought of him makes me feel like a schoolgirl. All right, all these emotions are so stupid and crazy. Why would this man be interested in me? Anyway, I had so much fun today and learned a lot from our trip. I even fulfilled my dream of visiting a Parisian bookstore, Shakespeare and

Company, and picked up a few things.

All this walking should have knocked off two or three pounds. We've managed to stick to grazing on bread, fruit, cheese, and pastries during the day. In the evening, we have a decent dinner and then hydrate until morning. I can tell my legs are getting stronger with all the stairs that we have taken up and down inside the Metro station, since it's rare to find an elevator or escalator. My back and legs—especially my lower back—hurt, but I know I'm working different muscles. Right now, I need sleep before the next adventure, so I bid you adieu.

***

Angela dug through her carry-on bag until she located her journal. She carried it and her backpack to the bed and pulled out various folders and pieces of paper. "If the girls saw this, they would laugh." She placed the tickets from the Eiffel Tower tour, the bus ride, and riverboat and tucked them in-between the lined blank pages. Even the little paper menu from the restaurant found its way into her makeshift scrapbook. Angela sat on the side of the bed and scribbled out an entry.

What a day! Besides the countless steps

and blocks we had to walk, the craziest thing happened today. Who would have thought of all people, Nicki, yes Nicki, caught the eye of some man? And it wasn't the eye of any man but a Parisian! I couldn't have done any better if I tried, and boy did I try. Mr. Handsome was so busy checking out Nicki that I didn't have a chance to throw my charms at him. The punk made me mad!

I guess I shouldn't be jealous, but I can't help it. My ego is at stake. Apart from that, I will admit that I'm having a great time. Paris has really opened my eyes to a lot of things, and one of them is life. I've decided to extend my ticket and stay a few more days. There is so much to learn that will benefit me in regards to my job. Paul will be so impressed with all the new things I've absorbed, but even if he's not, I will be proud of myself.

***

Sissy looked at her portable alarm clock and cringed. It was nine p.m., and the sandman was calling her name. She felt better after her shower, but soon her eyelids felt like shutters as they slowly closed, causing her to yawn. "Just one quick note," she muttered while digging under her pillow for the leather journal.

"Toto, I have a feeling that we're not in Kansas anymore," as Dorothy said. This was apparent in several things. I shopped in a French bookstore, Nicki fell onto the back of some man, and I fell in love with the Panthéon. My body aches and my heart feels empty.

For Nicki, I'm happy. Ermenegilde seemed smitten with her, and I have to admit that it was great for her ego. He's handsome, intelligent, and oh so French. Even if she should not see him again, maybe this was the kick in the butt she needed to stay on track and continue to believe in herself. I love that girl, and I want to see her healthy and happy.

As far as Red/Robert is concerned, what should I do? I still care for him, but who's to say what's going on behind my back with Candace. After all, she is a very attractive woman and they have a past. Oh, well, I can't think of that now. I have Paris and my friends, and that's all that matters.

24 | FEELINGS NOT SO DEEP

As expected, the admission line into the Musée d'Orsay was long, to say the least.

"I told you we should have come sooner," Angela complained after settling behind a young Asian couple holding hands. The crowd, dressed in outerwear of various colors, reminded her of a mosaic print tile that she used in the kitchen of one of her clients. Angela tried to make out the countries that the strangers were from as she eavesdropped on their conversations: Russia, Britain, and India for starters. The cool morning air whisked by, causing Angela to tug on her scarf to cover any exposed areas on her neck. She watched the couple in front of her pull away after a deep, affectionate kiss, then turned to Sissy and said, "Well, wasn't that sweet?"

"What are you talking about?"

"Did you not see that little show of affection? Doesn't it make you think of someone?" Angela said in an overly endearing voice as she stepped aside just as the couple completed another lip-lock.

"No, not particularly. Besides, I can't stand it when people do all that mess in public." Sissy turned her head to the right and noticed the activity behind the glass walls of the building.

"What, public display of affection?"

"Yes! Take that mess back to a hotel."

"Didn't it make you miss Robert?" Angela huffed.

"No, it did not. Look, I don't care to discuss my love life—or lack thereof—in public."

"Well, excuse me, Ms. High and Mighty." Angela reached inside her jacket pocket and pulled out her cell phone. A pair of orange earphones dangled from it. She hastily gathered the cord in her right hand and pushed the buds into place. After a few taps on the screen, she made a music selection, then turned her back on her friends.

"That's just great," Nicki whispered as they continued to move with the crowd.

"I didn't start it, but I'll finish it."

"You haven't spoken to Robert in a while. Would you mind telling me why?"

"Look, I'm in Paris and he's in . . .," she paused, turned to make sure the people behind her could not hear their conversation, and said, "he's in Kansas. I'm trying to enjoy my time with you and Cruella and not think of some guy."

"Some guy!" Nicki screeched.

"Would you cool it," Sissy hissed.

"No, I won't. I don't want to see you mess this relationship up. Robert has been good to you and doesn't deserve to be treated like crap."

Before she could reply, Sissy found herself standing in front of a cashier who asked, "May I help you?"

After purchasing their tickets, the trio proceeded to the coat check window to turn in their backpacks. Nicki lowered her voice and said to Sissy, "We'll finish this conversation later."

There was an audible gasp when they entered the first floor. Huddled together, they turned, pointed, and chattered like magpies while admiring the vastness of the interior. The great quantities of light streaming in through the windows highlighted the white marble statues and architecture, giving the grand hall a sense of opulence. Once they gathered their senses, Sissy held up a floor map to the museum so they could plan their next move. Nicki pointed to the back of the map and said, "I want to see this, *Galerie Impressionniste*."

"That's fine as long as I can check out the paintings of Toulouse-Lautrec," Angela countered.

"I should have known," Nicki began. "His works *are* something you can relate to."

"And what's that supposed to mean?"

"Well, after all, you are experienced in showing the men your petticoats, bloomers, and legs just like the Moulin Rouge dancers."

"Don't be jealous, Nicki, just because I can reel them in," Angela scoffed as she attempted a high kick with her left leg. Shortly, a sound like that of a sea lion echoed in the main hall followed by a slight whimper.

"Oh, my thigh!" As Angela began to lower her leg, her fingers rubbed the top and sides of her leg. "I guess I'm a tad bit out of practice."

"I'll say," Sissy laughed. "Could we stop with the cabaret show and move on?"

They made a pact to meet in the main hall in an hour, giving each one a chance to seek out their favorite areas. "You see that big, gold clock?" Sissy asked, pointing behind her.

"It's gorgeous!" Nicki said. "Look at the ornate work and the intricate details like the small crown on top—"

Angela interrupted. "Could we focus, please?"

"Yes, ladies, please. As I was saying, in one hour, let's meet in this area." Sissy made a circular motion with her hand to show the information desk and mini gift shop. "So, Angela, you go and hang out with your man Toulouse-Lautrec, and Nicki and I hear the ghost of Claude Monet calling our name."

"I didn't know *Comedy Central* was in the house," Angela sneered. "Peace out, chicks." She turned left and headed down the granite stairs.

"See ya later, alligator," Nicki waved and walked in the direction of the escalators to the middle level.

"Let the games begin," Sissy whispered as she turned and pointed her lens in the direction of the grand clock, snapped a photo, and began to explore.

***

Built to serve as the heart of rail life for Paris, the former train station almost met its demise in the 1970s as plans to demolish it were set in motion. This was not the first time such sadness came upon the structure. It had been birthed from ashes when the former Palais d'Orsay burned in 1871 during the Commune.

In 1900, the eve of the Universal Exposition, the government gave the Orleans Railway Company permission to construct a train station on the site of the ruins. Victor Laloux used the most advanced technology of the time to build such things as elevators, ramps, electric traction, and a 370-room hotel to surround the station.

Edouard Detaille called it a "Palace of Fine Arts." It provided the canvas for other great train stations around the world, including the Grand Central Terminal in New York and Union Station in Washington, DC. This was the crown jewel, providing service to Southwest France for forty years.

As rail service continued to grow, the station no longer met the demands of the modernized trains and over the course of many years served in different capacities, including a film set for the adaptation of Kafka's, The Trial, by Orson Welles. Soon, critics lobbied to save the building as a historical monument.

After its inauguration in 1986, the new home for Impressionist works and other collections continued to grow as they became instrumental in the history of contemporary art.

***

Sissy found her way along the first floor, which contained the work of artists during the period of 1848 to 1870. Although not as well-known as the Impressionists, this was the work of new artists who did not follow the guidelines of the Salon (the official exhibition of art that the French government sponsored). She felt unsure, at times, of her knowledge regarding fine art and how it impacted history. Sissy took a seat momentarily along a partition and noticed the light that poured throughout the building. Incredible designs, textures, and materials surrounded her.

How foolish I am to have waited so long to spread my wings, she hastily wrote in a compact journal that she kept in her purse. ***This is why I have to be alone a little longer. So much beauty and education I've yet to learn. Every Metro stop takes me to a new part of town, and like a child, my eyes widen to all things new.***

She closed the notebook, sighed deeply, then rose to her feet to continue her journey.

***

Nicki studied the two Realist paintings—*The Gleaners*, by Jean-Francois Millet and *The Gleaners Return*, by Jules Breton—feeling drawn by the former, although it received much criticism. She moved through the crowded area to find other paintings of the same theme. *The Picnic*, by Claude Monet, was full of light and color balance, while Edouard Manet's, *The Picnic*, seemed flat, dark, and uninteresting. And what was the purpose of the woman sitting naked in the grass next to two fully dressed men, while another naked woman in the background splashed about in Manet's work? These were questions that seemed to challenge her intellect, causing Nicki to realize she had sheltered herself from the world for far too long.

To her left, she noticed a small crowd and made her way in that direction. What a surprise when she found herself standing in front of the famous portrait by James McNeill Whistler. Although she had always heard of it referred to as *Whistler's Mother*, she read, for the first time, the correct title on the little plaque next to the painting, *Arrangement in Grey and Black No.1 or The Artist's Mother*. The height and width of the canvas were incredible and caused Nicki to realize how *tangible* everything in the gallery was. She was no longer just glancing at photographs of art as she flipped through one of her schoolbooks. She was now confronted with genuine artifacts—gobs of precious pigment smeared onto real canvases and three-dimensional marble statues that were cool to the touch as she surreptitiously grazed her fingers against one—artifacts of incredible value that defied being labeled with a price tag.

She glanced at her watch and realized she needed to head downstairs. "An hour is nowhere near long enough!" she sighed as she passed through the exit. Just as she reached the staircase, she quickly glanced to the left and a group of familiar faces stared straight at her. "I remember that picture from my middle school humanities book, except it was in black-and-white back then!" She laughed. "Now it's in living color," she mused as she eagerly approached Renoir's *Bal du moulin de la Galette*. The beautiful pastel palette, lively brush strokes, open faces, and energetic silhouettes of the dancers reeled her in. Oh, why did she let her eyes wander! "I have a feeling I'll be just a wee bit late," she smiled, allowing herself to be entertained by her old friends.

***

"Poor Toulouse-Lautrec," Angela sighed when she gazed upon his incredible work. She stared at the painting, *La danse au Moulin Rouge* by the young artist with a brilliant mind, extraordinary talent, and a disfigured lower body. The painting focuses on a couple dancing the "cancan" in the midst of a crowded dance floor. The woman's red-stockinged leg is raised high as she begins to seductively circle it under her raised skirts. Her partner, hands on hips, swings his leg energetically toward her. Angela smiled bitterly as she continued to stare at the dancers, recalling how a genetic disorder would prevent the painter from ever being able to dance the cancan himself; he could scarcely walk without being in excruciating pain. A fractured right thighbone that he suffered in a fall at the age of 13 refused to heal properly, despite repeated medical treatments. A similar fate befell the left leg the following year. In the end, his legs stopped growing. The result was a young man with a fully adult torso and the legs of a child. He stood only 4 feet 8 inches as an adult.

Art became his life. He eventually settled in Paris and established himself as one of the most important late 19th century Post-Impressionist artists in Europe. His innovative skills as an illustrator and lithographer, as well as his detailed depiction of the Bohemian nightlife of Paris, gained him fame even during his lifetime.

Angela moved on to the next painting, *Jane Avril dansant.*

"Funny how many of his paintings featured dancers!" she wondered aloud. "I guess he was fascinated, looking at people doing something he would never be able to do," she answered herself.

The young woman in this picture was in stark contrast to the other that she'd seen. This one, Jane Avril, was dancing all by herself and didn't seem to care. Her thin frame was dressed very discretely in shades of white, gray, and black. A black hat covered her red hair, but it was the delicate face that caught Angela's attention. She strained to try to get a better look at it. The very pale complexion, thin cheeks, and small red lips were plain to see, but the eyes looked half-closed and sad—almost as if she were trying to forget her surroundings, and herself.

"How sad for Toulouse," she murmured. "He was probably like Jane, always trying to forget. Forget about his legs, forget that he could never find true love. The only difference is that instead of using dance to forget, he used alcohol and prostitutes."

As she moved around the room to view more of his work, she paused to check her watch. "Almost time to go," she whispered. Angela stopped long enough to glance at a sentence on a plaque that contained a brief biography of the artist. "An alcoholic most of his life who contracted syphilis and died months before his 37th birthday, it was reported that his last words were, '*Le vieux con!*'"

"The old fool!" She repeated the translation aloud. "No, Toulouse, not a fool. Just someone who needed love like we all do—like I do."

***

"Well, I'm here but where's Nicki?" Angela asked, breathless from rushing to meet the group.

"I have a feeling she's still upstairs."

"Figures."

"No sweat. Let's just go up there together and pull her away before she becomes one with the paintings," Sissy joked.

Once they stepped through the entrance, they knew they were doomed. "Wow," Angela said. "This is a huge collection of artwork."

"No wonder she lost track of time," Sissy agreed.

After ten minutes, they found her standing in front of a painting by Renoir. Sissy leaned forward and cleared her throat in Nicki's ear.

"Oh, yikes, I'm sorry. I, I—"

"Yeah, I know," Sissy interrupted.

Angela leaned down to read the painting's title, *Les baigneuses*.

"It's called *The Bathers*."

"And why are you looking at a bunch of naked women?" Angela asked with a cocked eyebrow.

"Don't even go there," Nicki warned her. "I was just thinking I was born at the wrong time. Back in Renoir's time, artists loved painting big women with all their softness and fat rolls."

"In classical painting, large women were seen as models of fecundity, prosperity, and well-being. Renoir also liked the way the rolls and folds of their skin responded to the light when he painted," Sissy said. "In fact, I read that a woman's buttocks were his favorite feature."

"I know that's right," Angela said after striking hers with the palm of her hand.

"Anyway," Sissy continued, "a well-rounded, broad-hipped woman was his definition of beauty."

"Like I said before, I was born in the wrong time period."

"Hey, I want to pick up a few things at the gift shop, and then could we grab something to eat? I'm starving," Angela whined.

"Sure. I wanted a few souvenirs myself," Sissy agreed.

The three weaved in and out of crowds as they navigated back toward the front of the museum where they took an elevator to the upper level. They snapped a few more pictures, this time of the monumental clock that could be seen from a large window on the top floor. The black, metal hands and large Roman numerals allowed a fabulous view of the Paris skyline.

After a visit to the gift shop, their next stop was the museum's beautiful first-floor restaurant. The girls stood in the entrance for a few moments just to take in the gorgeous setting: arched doorways, high, frescoed ceilings, white walls with gilded embellishments, tall windows, sparkling chandeliers, and two monumental mirrors located at either end of the salon to reflect the dazzling scene back to all who were lucky enough to dine here.

The hostess greeted the group, then guided them through a maze of tables before stopping at a large one located in the middle of the room near a counter full of desserts. Before they could settle themselves, a waiter approached them as though he were on a timed assignment and asked if they were ready to order.

"We were just seated and haven't looked at the menu," Sissy explained.

He gave a curt nod and walked away.

"Dang, I just got my butt to fit into the chair, let alone pick up a menu," Angela said with agitation.

"Oh, I think I see what I want," Nicki started just as a short, stout waitress approached the table.

"Are you ready to order?" she asked, pen poised like an efficient secretary.

"No, not yet," Sissy stated with annoyance. "We've just been seated. But I have a question about the lunch menu."

"That is no longer available after three. You may select from the salads, appetizers, and drinks," she said while pointing on Nicki's menu. "I will return in a moment," she said with all the manners of a prison guard, disappearing before a word of response could be uttered.

"If I weren't so hungry, I'd say let's get out of this place," Angela huffed.

"True that," Nicki said while giving her friend a hand slap.

When the waitress returned, the women agreed to split two of the salads and ordered coffee and tea. After the waitress jotted down their orders, she turned and from a small cabinet area pulled out a platinum container filled with bread and butter and practically threw it on the table.

"Why, that hussy!" Angela snapped. "I ought to throw one of these rolls at that 1960s bouffant hairdo."

"Be quiet and calm down," Sissy whispered when she noticed a woman being seated at a table next to theirs.

"All I know is she better get in check before I give her a taste of American pie with my fists."

The other two women stifled a laugh as they sipped their drinks and admired two milky-white statues—one of a nude bather, the other of a boy in the position of a sprinter about to take off—each positioned at different ends of the hall.

When their food arrived, they dined quietly, each lost in their own thoughts of what they had seen. As they neared the end of their meal, the same waitress returned and whisked away the dishes while asking if they wanted dessert. They refused.

"Could we have the bill, please?" Nicki asked.

"Wait," the woman said and rushed off to care for a large party behind them.

"OK, Angela, you hold her down and I'll punch her," Nicki huffed.

"I'm right there with ya, girl," as they pretended to get out of their seats.

"Sit your behinds down," Sissy laughed. "We'll trip her on our way out the door." They watched as the woman completed the orders and drinks behind them. Then she asked a gentleman at another table, in French, if he wanted dessert, as well as the woman at the table beside them. After serving them, it seemed like a week had passed by the time she returned to their table and finally gave them their bill. After Sissy looked it over, she took out her credit card and watched as the woman swiped it on the mobile card machine. She handed the slivers of paper to Sissy. The whisper of "*Au revoir*" was barely off her lips before she rounded the corner of the table in a different direction.

"Don't you leave her a tip," Angela sneered while picking up her packages before heading for the door.

"Yeah," Nicki agreed, "or I'll beat you." She walked out behind Angela.

"Yikes," Sissy said before signing the receipt and running to catch up with her friends.

"I hope you enjoyed your luncheon, *Madame!*" the hostess chimed as Sissy approached the exit.

"Let's just say that it was memorable, *mademoiselle!*"

25 | GROWING, LEARNING, AND WANTING

After they exited the building, Angela asked to borrow the cell phone from Sissy. "Give me a minute. I'll pay you back for the call." Sissy waved her off. She and Nicki descended the museum staircase, pulling out their cameras to shoot some photos.

The phone rang three times before a male voice, groggy from a deep sleep, shouted, "Hello?"

"Hi, Paul, it's Angela. I'm sorry to have awakened you."

He righted himself in the bed and clicked on the bedside lamp. The glare temporarily blinded him when he tried to focus on the clock. Once his eyes adjusted to the light, he noticed the time. It was six in the morning. He took a deep breath before speaking. "Well, hello stranger."

"Please forgive me," she apologized. "I haven't gotten this time change thing down yet."

"No worries. I should've been up long

before this. Are you in town?"

"No, I'm still in France, so I can't stay on the phone long."

"Sure, what's up?"

"I plan to extend my trip by three more days. Paris is great, and I'm learning so much."

"Wow! I knew you would enjoy it. I don't foresee a problem with the extension. If I remember correctly, you're two weeks out on both of your projects. Not being here won't affect them that much. I'll keep an eye on things. Besides, you and Marie could use a little time apart." The image of Angela pretending to choke the famous chef behind her back resurfaced, causing him to smile. "Don't forget to have fun while you learn new things. I'll see you soon."

"Oh, I will, unless one of these Parisian guys tries to hit on me, and then, baby, watch out!"

Paul didn't want to entertain that thought and quickly changed the subject. "I look forward to hearing about your adventures when you return. Tell your friends hello for me."

"I will. *Bonne journée!*"

"Who taught you to say 'Have a good day'

in French?" he asked in amazement.

"Sissy and her little language book. Well, I better get a move on before the girls leave me."

They said goodbye before she disconnected the call. "I wonder what else she's learned since she's been there," Paul said as he swung his legs over the side of the bed. With his eyes closed and his head bent, he envisioned Angela sipping a glass of merlot with some dark-haired stranger. Leaning against his muscular frame, she released a throaty laugh into the mystery man's ear. Whatever he said to Angela triggered her cat-like movements against his skin. Just as she turned to kiss the lips of the dark-haired stranger, Paul yelled out, "NO!"

His eyes flew open. "I must be losing my mind." His body jerked upright. He paced the bedroom floor as his hands raked through his hair. "Yep, I've lost my mind," he repeated before storming off to the bathroom.

***

"Please read chapters eleven and twelve for our discussion with a possible pretest on our next meeting," the schoolmaster announced as he made his way back to the front of the classroom.

"*Monsieur Leclercq*," a female student called out.

He paused in front of his desk, turned, and searched the sea of students until he located the lone arm waving back and forth to gain his attention.

"*Oui, Mademoiselle DuFour?*"

"The chapters are quite detailed in history. May we instead study each alone for better understanding and then proceed with the test next week?"

He blinked twice, frowned, then asked the class, "Is this the consensus of the rest of you?"

Immediately, hands filled the space of the auditorium, silently answering his question.

"You have *Mademoiselle DuFour* to thank. It is as you wish. Class dismissed."

The once-silent room now roared to life with endless chatter, laughter, and the sounds that come from desks being moved and feet hustling across the floor as students made their way into the hallway.

Ermenegilde gathered his notes, stuffing them into the burgundy leather portfolio. He felt the presence of Mlle. DuFour to his left as she paused at his desk.

"*Merci beaucoup, Monsieur Leclercq,*"

she said.

He turned and looked at the fair-skinned lady, who appeared to be twenty-two. Her face had not wizened to the cruelties of the life outside of the Sorbonne. *She is pretty enough*, he thought, as he noticed whispers of light-brown hair protruding from a black knit cap. *"Mlle. Du Four,"* he began. "If you have not considered a degree in politics, I think you should. At the very least, even an avocet. Many times, you have been the voice of the people." He smiled afterwards.

"I will keep it in mind, *monsieur*." She blushed, then hurried out the door to her next class.

Ermenegilde watched her depart. *It's students like Mlle. DuFour that keep me from my daydreams of Nicki,* he thought. He gathered the remainder of his belongings, then walked out the door, down the hallway, and through the double doors into the fresh, midmorning air. He passed the statue of Victor Hugo in the courtyard, took in a deep breath, and released all the tension within as he headed to his favorite café.

***

Madame Léa Yount beamed when her favorite customer strolled through the doors of Paper & Tea. With her arms outstretched, Ermenegilde walked into them and placed affectionate kisses on her cherubic cheeks. They chatted as he made his way to his favorite table near the window. He spoke of his day, and she updated him on the latest news regarding her grandchildren, whom she adored. She scuttled away, returning ten minutes later with a tray filled with a cup and saucer, a carafe of hot water, and a tea chest of assorted flavors, all of his choosing.

He placed his order of la poire and le pain chocolat, then settled into his seat after preparing his cup of Earl Grey. How he adored the space around him —the exposed brick on one side of the room and cream walls on the other. As he looked toward the back of the room with its bookcase brimming with new and used books, he made a mental note to bring in his completed novels to add to the collection.

This was the best time to come and relax before his next class. The morning rush of patrons heading into work was over. It was the regular crowd, with a sprinkle of new faces, who found Paper & Tea to be that comfort spot to meet friends, study, or have time alone with a good read. The space was long and able to seat at least twenty. The glass, refrigerated cases showcased Madame's best tarts and layer cakes, baked fresh every morning. Another waitress restocked the pastries of fruit fillings and croissants. To the right, meat sandwiches awaited the afternoon lunch rush sure to come. This was the place to be, offering a warm setting, good food, and fine company. His mind drifted back to Nicki. Just as he began to imagine kissing her lips, he was startled when Madame Léa placed his order in front of him.

"You were deep in thought, Ermenegilde. Is it bad or good?"

"Oh, very good," he said with a smile, then picked up a slice of pear and popped it into his mouth.

"You are a sly one, *Monsieur Leclercq.* Your smile is full of mischief."

"I will tell you why if you have time, Madame Léa."

"I will make the time." And with that, she sat across from her friend as he recounted the chance meeting of Nicki.

At one point, her eyes widened with merriment when he told her of the 'piggyback' ride. She let out a laugh so high pitched, it startled the other patrons for they had never seen the reserved shopkeeper in this light before. She was holding her sides, and by the end of the story, Madame Léa dabbed the corners of her eyes with the end of her apron.

When he completed the story of the Panthéon tour, she placed her hand atop his and said, "You mustn't let her get away."

"But she is an American and will leave soon."

"Use your French charms! In matters of the heart, my son, you cannot leave such things to chance. Send her some flowers from the market with a note."

"Madame Yount, are you sure?"

"Sure I'm sure, foolish boy!"

He reached for her hand, ignoring the traces of flour that laced her fingers, and kissed the back of it. "A wise woman you are."

"You flirt," she chastised. "I must check on my cookies. I'm making Madeleines II. My new baker is still learning the art of such things. I'll bring back a Langues de chat for you," she said as she stood to leave.

"You have my heart, Madame Léa Yount," he said while grabbing at his chest. "When are we to marry?"

"After I divorce my husband of twenty-seven years!" She laughed, then disappeared around the counter through the swinging doors leading into the kitchen.

26 | COMING TO JESUS

With bulging backpacks resembling tortoises' shells, the girls set off on their next adventure. The village of Montmartre, located in the 18th arrondissement, would be a step away from the Paris they had become accustomed to. Full of character, charm, and history, this area—whose name means "mountain of the martyr"—never disappoints.

"Tell me again why we're going to this church and sleeping there all night?" Angela grumbled after stepping out of the subway car.

"One, it's a very famous church," Sissy began, once she knew everyone was accounted for. "Two, it sits at the highest point in the city, and—"

"And three, everybody needs a little church in their lives," Nicki added with a chuckle.

"OK, laugh if you want to, but don't come running into my room if Jesus taps you on the shoulder and says, 'Rise and walk with Me.' Besides, I can't help it that we missed church services yesterday."

"That's all right," Sissy reassured her while patting Angela on the shoulder. "Now you can be one with the Lord and tell Him all about it."

They reached the turnstiles to exit the Metro station and placed their tickets into the slot holder, but the bars would not turn. As the tickets popped back into their hands, they observed other people at nearby turnstiles, making sure they were doing the right thing. After several attempts, they moved to another bank of machines, but they, too, failed to work. A crowd began to gather, and soon people took it upon themselves to climb or leap over the arms of the turnstiles.

"Oh, I know you're not expecting me to hop over that thing?" Nicki squealed.

"What are you whining about?" Angela sniffed. "I picked a fine time to wear a dress!"

Sissy looked up and down the rows of machines and said, "There's no other way. The system is down, so either we crawl or we return to the hotel and lose our reservations at the basilica. Hold my backpack." She shimmied out of the straps, then faced the protruding silver arms. Sissy lifted one leg, then placed her foot on the spindle and attempted to hoist her body up and over—to no avail. The girls got behind her, shoving and pushing until she finally landed on the other side of the machine.

They handed their backpacks over, trying to repeat her moves, but Nicki wound up with a bar between her legs while falling backward. Angela, on the other hand, battled with her dress as it became twisted in the silver arms.

"Just crawl underneath," Sissy called out while strangers stood by, watching the crazy Americans put on a show.

Nicki finally managed to get on her knees and slither underneath. Angela's butt and plum-colored panties wiggled back and forth in the air, giving the French men a show they would never forget. This continued until she was free from the turnstile's grasp.

"Rick Steves, the travel guru, failed to mention this in his television series," Nicki quipped.

"I'm going to send him my dry-cleaning bill," Angela complained as she swiped at the dirt on the lower portion of her dress.

The men who watched intently now clapped and cheered as the girls gathered their belongings, turned, bowed, and waved goodbye as they proceeded up the street. The harsh street lamps pierced the evening sky, exposing the gritty side of the town. Although dirty and trashy, people continued to move up and down the sidewalks, one after another. The red glow of cigarettes flickered in the darkness before being tossed into the street as vendors and shopkeepers vied for local, but mostly tourist, trade. Doorways were packed with carousals displaying berets, postcards, scarfs, aprons, magnets, tote bags, and a whole assortment of items. These enticements were lures to pull one farther into the small shops where more merchandise like sweatshirts, T- shirts, suitcases, and other knickknacks awaited your money.

"Oh man, look," Nicki called out as she dodged around a group of strangers to cross the street to a nearby cookie shop. The doors stood wide open with soft, muted-colored walls welcoming her in. It was the type of store even the tooth fairy would love.

Bulk cookies, which varied in size, shape, color, flavor, even smell, were laid out in large display cases. Metal tin cans—round, rectangular, square, tall, and short—were designed with motifs of Paris, merry-go-rounds, spring, and other designs, brightening the shop even more.

After noticing Nicki's pleading eyes having a love feast over the display cases, Sissy offered an intervention.

"Why don't you wait until tomorrow when we have more time to shop and make purchases before we return to the hotel? Right now, we need to keep our reservations before the nuns close the check-in desk for the evening."

Nicki asked the clerk what time they opened in the morning and reluctantly agreed to wait as she gave the cookies one last look before they continued their trek to Rue Foyatier to board the *funiculaire*.

They paid the clerk for their tickets and then stepped into the glass car on the cable railway. As it moved in a slow, persistent pace, Angela tried not to stare at the interracial couple on the opposite side of the car. She felt a slight stab of pain in her chest as she watched the white male—angular, attractive with a slight hint of a beard, glasses, and curly, dark hair. He wore a nubby-brown wool jacket, dark slacks, and shoes. He displayed such honest affection for the beautiful, black female who stood by his side. Her features still young and fresh, she looked to be 24, possibly 25. The young lady carried herself well and seemed to blush during their conversation. He appeared confident as he took in every word she spoke. Angela wondered how long the couple had been together as she tried to read their body language.

I wish someone were as enamored with me as he is with her, she thought. The car came to a stop at the top of the steep hill. When the doors opened, she watched as the couple disembarked after he gathered her hand in his.

"Why couldn't that have been me?" she sighed as thoughts of Cody replayed in her mind.

"Angela! What are you waiting for?" Nicki called out.

Reality kicked in as she dismissed the thoughts and exited the car. The skies darkened even more as the trio approached a long staircase. "Not again," Nicki stated, her voice full of weariness.

"Don't wimp out now," Sissy began. "After six subway stops, the turnstiles, and hills, I'm sure you could make it to the top to the cobblestone streets and the most photographed building in the world."

Before she could continue, they were startled by several male voices. In the guise of the surrounding bushes and darkness, the men were partially hidden. The girls could make out their shapes but not much else. Although their words were in French, the tone, sprinkled with a few whistles, was unpleasant. Fear gave them the energy needed to climb the staircase to safety.

On the final landing, they paused to catch their breath. The scene that lay out before them was not as expected. On the street below the beautiful, white, Romano-Byzantine Church were street vendors, utility vans, and bright spotlights with thick cords snaking out behind them. Up and down the staircases, people sat, drinking and merrymaking into the late evening.

"Why do I feel sinful all of a sudden?" Nicki asked as she tried to avoid tripping over a man who lay across a set of steps.

"Look at that skyline," Angela pointed out while kicking an empty soda bottle from her path.

"This is the highest point of the city at 425 feet above sea level," Sissy said, digging through her jacket pocket for the reservation papers. "Let's get going. I think," she paused to read the directions with the help of the blaring spotlights, "I think we go to the left. Look for this number on the building or gate," she pointed.

They moved through the thinning crowd to a softly lit area on the side of the building. Sacré-Coeur (Sacred Heart) was built as a memorial to the 58,000 French soldiers killed during the Franco-Prussian War. As one of the most photographed images in the city, it took 46 years to build and was completed in 1923 at a cost of 40 million francs.

After a few missed twists and turns past three semi-trailers parked along the side of the building, Nicki found the wrought iron gate to the entrance. "Here it is," she called out. "It says 3335. She pressed a button on a console on the outside of the fence and spoke into it. The gate flung open. They followed a short pathway that lit up with the use of a motion detector and then stepped into a building made partially out of glass. They were greeted by two French-speaking nuns who stood behind a desk dressed in their traditional habit from head to toe.

"Why is this bringing back memories of Catholic school," Angela whispered to Nicki who let out a giggle.

"*Bonjour,*" Sissy began. "*J'ai fait une reservation,*" she tried to explain while showing them her confirmation paper.

"Ah, you speak English," the first nun said with a heavy French accent.

"Yes, all three of us," Sissy answered.

They welcomed the trio, then asked a few questions to verify their booking. The layouts of the rooms were explained after the payment was complete. "The restrooms are down the hall from the cells—"

"Cell, Cells?" Angela stuttered.

"Rooms," the nun clarified. "Checkout is at seven. We must have time to prepare them for the next scheduled guests. Here are your keys." The large, old-fashioned skeleton keys with an oversize, heavy bob in the shape of a bell gave the impression that they actually were staying in prison cells.

"Before you go," the second nun turned a ledger in their direction, "you need to sign up for your hour of prayer."

"Prayer?" Nicki repeated.

"Yes, everyone who visits must take a turn. Here, we pray for the souls of the dead, 24 hours a day, ever since 1885."

Nicki and Angela stared at Sissy as she gave

a sheepish grin, taking the ink pen from the nun's hand and scribbling her name in the midnight time slot. Nicki chose 11:00, while Angela joined Sissy for the same time. After receiving directions to the inside of the church and their sleeping quarters, they headed out.

"I ought to crown you with the bell on this key ring," Nicki screeched as they moved down the hall. "What is this, a scene from the movie *Sister Act*? Do I look like Whoopi Goldberg to you?"

"Shush and calm down," Sissy said as they passed a sign that read 'Toilettes.'

They turned down a white hallway with numerous doors that resembled closets.

"What in the world?" Angela asked.

"Will you guys keep your voices down? Other people might be here."

"I don't care. Why didn't you tell us we had to conduct prayer services? I was ready to kick my heels up and call it a night."

"Amen," Nicki shouted.

Sissy grabbed the women by the arm, shoved them into room 104, and pressed against the door to make sure it was closed. "What is the big deal, you guys? Why are you freaking out?"

"So, Sister Sissy Mary Frances, what are we supposed to do while we wait to go upstairs?" Angela huffed.

"How about meditate and give thanks or, better yet, take a little nap?" She gave them their keys. "Angela, you take 105 and Nicki 106."

"Let me check this mess out," Angela said, stepping from the room and crossing the hallway to her door. She plowed the odd-shaped key in the lock, turned it to the left, and pushed on the handle. After pressing the small panel on the right side of the wall, the room brightened as two wall sconces came to life. "You have got to be kidding," she said after standing in the middle of the room. Her friends followed.

The clean but modestly furnished small room had textured white walls, a radiator in the corner, and an unpretentious lightwood trundle bed against the wall that took Angela by surprise. A silver-and-blue bedspread gave the room some color. A single teakwood desk and chair sat on the opposite side of the room.

She pointed at the white porcelain pedestal sink with two plastic-wrapped cups and a trash can below. Angela walked over and pulled back a curtain that revealed a shower.

"All the comforts of home," Sissy joked as the two women turned and glared at her. "Well, what else do you need?"

"Look you. There are a few choice words I'd like to say to you right now, but I can't while Jesus is staring at me," she said, pointing at the crucifix on the wall behind her.

"Good. In the meantime, I'm going back to my room, turning on the heat, and catching a few winks before my prayer session." And with that, she turned on her heels and shut the door behind her.

"Remind me to murder her later," Nicki said. Just then, she looked in the direction of the crucifix. "Forgive me, Lord. I forgot that you were there." She said goodbye to Angela. "Prayer duty starts in ten minutes."

She left her friend standing in the middle of the room, hands on her hips while she shook her head. "No television, radio, or Internet connection. It's going to be a long night."

27 | A WICKED NIGHT

Nicki closed the door to her cell. Just saying the word made her shiver. She unpacked her few belongings for the next day—jeans, a T-shirt, and sweater—and hung them in the tiny closet. Then she pulled out her journal. "Just a quick note," she said and took a seat at the desk.

Once again, Sissy has outdone herself. We are spending the night in a modest room at a church in Paris. And it's not just any church but a famous one that requires a person to pray for an hour! I guess it really can't hurt anything. Besides, I have a few things I need to get off my chest anyway, so this is the perfect place to do it.

Regarding my weight, I think I'm really shaping up. I don't have a scale to prove it, but my clothes aren't as tight as before and my pants sag a little in the butt. I feel better but still get winded when I take the stairs.

I wish that I could see that guy, Ermenegilde, again. He's so handsome and smart. What a package! Well, I better go. Sissy is knocking on the door, which means

it's time for prayer duty. Later.
***

Sister Sissy Mary Frances told me to take time to meditate while I'm here awaiting my turn inside the church. I can't believe people find this little room comfortable. I'm a big girl, and I need room to move. Maybe that's my problem—my size. Someone forget to tell me that we would be walking as much as we do. If I haven't lost at least five pounds from this trip, I know I've done something wrong.

From my window, I can see the Bell Tower. When I was reading up on this place in my tour book a few minutes ago, it said that it holds one of the heaviest bells in the world, weighing 19 tons, and resonates with a high C note. On the last part, I don't need a demonstration! I better take a catnap before it's my turn to pray. Cells and prayers; what a mess!
***

Well, my friends aren't very happy with me, but they'll get over it . . . I hope. Sacré-Coeur is glorious! It stands like a beacon, reminding me of a lighthouse. I read that it is built of travertine stone that exudes calcite. This almost guarantees that the basilica will remain white despite pollution and weathering.

I haven't spoken to Robert in a few days. I guess I should call him, but I don't feel like it. I don't know what's wrong with me. I will admit that I like the way some of the men look at me or give me an occasional wink. I feel sexy, so alive. Better yet, my clothes are becoming looser as my leg and thigh muscles get stronger. Like the song by Right Said Fred, "I'm Too Sexy."

***

Midnight came too soon as far as Angela was concerned. She wanted to throw her shoe at the door when Sissy knocked on it but decided not to, considering Jesus was looking down on her. She snatched the door open and stared at her friend.

"Don't give me that look," she said.

"I'm really not feeling this, but let's go and get it over with."

"That's not quite the attitude to take before going before the Lord in prayer." Sissy turned to walk out the door. Angela raised her fist in an attempt to bop her friend in the head but decided against it. After all, she had enough sins to atone for, and she didn't need one more thing on her plate.

"You better take your jacket or blanket. Nicki said it's chilly up there."

They walked down the hallway, their footsteps echoing in the silence. After they stepped inside the elevator, the slow, chugging sound caused the women to look at each other and wonder if they would make it upstairs. The doors took forever, it seemed, to open, and they were glad to be free of the metal box.

"This way," Sissy said, pointing in the direction of the hallway. Its stunning, arched, glass windows set the tone of the building. They walked through heavy oak doors and stepped inside the church. Although illuminated by the dimmest of lights, the site was breathtaking. A Byzantine mosaic of Christ shimmered in the vault of the chancel, causing Sissy to stop breathing for only a moment before she finally released a breath.

"Let's go up front," she told Angela as she zipped up her jacket and pulled the hood over her head.

"Hey." Angela took hold of her arm. "I want to sit in the back. You go ahead. I'll be all right."

They departed as Sissy found a place in the dim light near the front. She made the sign of the cross and began to pray.

Angela was surprised at the small group that dared to show up at such a late hour. *I guess they couldn't sleep*, she thought, and made her way toward the back of the church that was shadowed in the last fringes of light. She was glad that she brought her blanket, draping it over her shoulders and head to fend off the draft inside the building.

The architecture was fantastic and immense, making her feel insignificant. *Paul will be impressed when I tell him about this*, she thought while scribbling some notes and drawings in the pocket journal she brought with her. Angela watched as people moved silently in and out of the church. Outside the building, she could still hear the rabble-rousers with their merriment as bottles crashed to the ground against the blaring music. On occasion, a howl from a dog or two would add to the distraction.

"Someone needs to remind them that people are trying to pray in here," she whispered between her own prayers. "But I'll leave that to You, Lord."

Sissy shifted in the pew, trying to find a comfortable spot. Occasionally, she would look back to make sure Angela was awake.

She pulled out her journal to make a prayer list—anything to fight off the drowsiness that crept in.

Another forty-five minutes, she thought after checking her watch. "Come on, eyeballs," she pleaded, "don't fail me now."

As her body rocked back and forth, Angela fought to stay awake, but her eyelids were like shutters, attempting to close. The blanket felt like a cocoon, protecting her from the cold as she snuggled deeper into its folds. She looked up at the ceiling and then at the carvings on the walls. The cherubic faces were sweet and lifelike. They seemed to be talking to her, but that couldn't be. They were wood, not the real thing. Angela turned her head to the left and jumped when she looked into the eyes of an angel, a statue recessed in one of the softly lit arches.

"Get a grip, girl; he's not real." But when her eyes dared to look again, she was sure the angel was speaking to her. "Don't you dare close your eyes," he seemed to say.

"Fifteen minutes to go," Sissy moaned as she continued the battle to stay awake. Her prayer list became unintelligible and led to doodling. Her eyes fluttered and were about to close when she heard a bloodcurdling scream from the back of the church.

28 | YOU BETTER WATCH OUT

"No! Please don't! I'm sorry," the woman's voice cried out. "Don't come any closer."

People stood, one woman fainted, a few made the sign of the cross over their bodies, while others turned to see what was going on. There was another scream. A pair of hands were flailing in the air. Sissy jumped up and ran to the back of the room. It was Angela!

She grabbed her by the shoulders. "Shush, girl! What is wrong with you?"

"Him, it's him! He's coming after me. Leave me alone." She yanked the blanket over her head as muffled, unrelenting screams continued while she pointed in the direction of the cherub protruding from the wall.

"Angela, wake up. It's not real; it's a carving." Sissy snatched the cover from her friend's head, forcing her to look at her attacker. "See, it's not real. You must have dozed off and imagined it."

"No, I saw him in the light, dancing and pointing at me." Angela clutched Sissy's shirt so tightly that she began to choke.

"Let go of me," Sissy squeaked out while prying Angela's hands from the collar of her shirt.

After a few deep breaths, she looked around the nave and realized that the flickering candles cast a sense of movement on the innocent figure. Sissy tried to reason with Angela, to calm her down, when she noticed a nun running—at least the best she could in her habit—toward them with her finger pressed against her lips.

"Mademoiselles, silence s'il vous plait!" As Sissy held Angela in her arms like a child to quiet her, the nun stepped inside the pew to help. She appeared to be fairly young, maybe in her late twenties, and very petite in size. *There is softness in her demeanor for someone so young,* Sissy thought.

"Your friend, she is unwell?" she asked.

"I think she fell asleep and had a bad dream. I will take her back to her room. *Excusez-moi.*"

The nun nodded in agreement, then went about the task of settling the other parishioners so they could return to their prayers.

Sissy pulled the cover away from Angela to allow the coolness of the room to assist in waking her. She gathered her belongings while helping her up.

"Come with me. I need to get my notebook and blanket." She didn't dare let go of her friend's hand as she made her way to the front of the church. Afterward, Sissy made the sign of the cross, then hurried out the door with Angela in tow down the hallway leading back to their rooms.

When Angela was more awake, she meekly said, "I'm sorry. That was so embarrassing."

"I think you need some sleep. Are you going to be OK?"

"Yeah. I was so exhausted that after a while, the walls and statues seemed to come alive and have this major conversation with me."

"Wow! That's freaky."

"You're telling me? Let's get out of here."

As they returned to their sleep quarters, Sissy watched as Angela crashed on the bed, still dressed in her clothes with the blanket wrapped around her. Before Sissy could say "good night," her crazy friend was asleep.

"What a night," Sissy muttered when she pulled the door to Angela's room closed. "Please, Lord, let's not have a repeat of that scene again," she said as she headed to her room for some much-needed sleep.

29 | REALITY

A warm sensation fell across Angela's face, cradling it gently.

Maybe it's Paul, trying to sneak up on me, she thought, her eyes still closed. *I'll show him.* With arms outstretched, she gave the imaginary body a shove and found herself immediately on the floor. Was it a dream?

"What the . . .," she mumbled while dragging the blanket from her head and face. Angela's eyes flew open as she looked around the room, until they rested on the crucifix on the far corner of the wall. Then it all came rushing back, like a movie after the replay button had been hit. She moaned at the memory, dropping her face into her hands.

The church, the screams, then being attacked by the figures hanging from the walls. What a mess. She gathered her blanket, stood, and looked back at the figure. "OK, Jesus. You have some explaining to do."

***

The knock on the door was so soft, Sissy

thought she had dreamt it.

"Yes?"

"It's Nicki. Are you up?"

The door swung open, and she was greeted by her matted-haired friend. "Rough night?" she asked after stepping into the room.

"I had to deal with the wild child last night," she said and continued with the details. Nicki let out shrills of laughter, shook her head, settled in a nearby chair, then busted out in fits of laughter—again.

"Are you sure there wasn't some sort of exorcism going on?"

"Maybe," Sissy said while holding up her toothbrush and paste. "Well, let me get dressed. You know we have to be out of our rooms in an hour."

Nicki headed to the door. "I'll make sure Her Highness is up."

"Would you?" Sissy's eyes held a pleading look. "I'm not ready to deal with her after last night."

"No worries, chickadee. I've got it all under control."

***

Angela jumped at the pounding on her door. Was it the hammer of death that God was wheeling after her comment to Jesus?

"Go away," she yelled.

"Don't make me send the angel of the Lord after you," Nicki called out. The door flew open, and the two women looked at each other. "What's wrong with you?" she asked.

"Bad night."

"So I've heard. You're lookin' kind of rough this morning, like the *Creature from the Black Lagoon*."

"I've got your creature. Why don't you go and harass someone else?"

"I have already. Remember, we only have an hour left before checkout."

"All right already. Go."

"Fine. Don't make me call up Barnabas Collins from that show *Dark Shadows* to put you in check." Nicki laughed at her own joke, then shut the door behind her.

"Everybody wants to be a clown," Angela snorted as she made her way to the shower stall.

***

Daylight was a welcome relief as they stepped from the confines of the church. Gone were the crowds of the night before as street cleaners picked up the last remnants of the rabble-rousers' trash.

"You would have thought they were still celebrating the wine festival with all that noise," Sissy said. "The way I was feeling, I could have used a drink from one of the hundred bottles of wine they auctioned off from their collection."

"I know," Angela chimed in. "I could hardly keep my focus to pray because of all that. . .." She caught the girls staring at her. "What?"

Nicki shook her head. "Girl, you shouldn't play like that." Then she pulled out her camera and started shooting photos of the basilica's ovoid dome, the second-highest point in Paris.

"Ooh, I can't stand you guys." She turned and whipped out her cell phone to photograph the city skyline before the sun's full blaze crested the horizon.

The photo shoot continued as they captured rich details of the statues and architecture. A black, wiry-haired dog caught their attention as it chased a ball thrown to him by a young man. It leaped and barked after retrieving it.

"I wish I had his energy," Nicki quipped as the trio made their way to the steep staircase at the base of the church to walk into the town of Montmartre. In the light of day, they could take their time and appreciate the lampposts and deciduous trees that lined the path.

"*Cinq*," a male voice called out.

"*Deux*," another yelled. Then the sound of dice being shaken and the mutterings and yells of the winner were heard. When the girls walked by, they were appalled at the group of men gambling in front of the church. "Have they no shame?" Angela asked.

"Obviously not," Sissy said. "It's only nine thirty in the morning. I guess they have to hustle up some breakfast money. They almost sound like the guys we passed by yesterday."

"Hey look," Angela called out, "it's a carousal." The top of it peeked out from the bushes that hid it.

"I wish I could ride one of these," Nicki said while shooting a close-up of the cream-colored horse with flared nostrils. Angela photographed Sacré-Coeur from this vantage point before they continued.

"I need to get a few things," Nicki said while leading the group to a nearby shop. "This is the one that had the postcards I wanted."

"They all look the same to me," Angela mumbled.

"See, Ms. Smarty-Pants, you don't know everything. His shop sells twelve postcards for two euros compared to the other guys." She pointed at the signs of other shops. "That's a bargain."

Angela held up her hand. "I stand corrected." They stepped into the narrow gift store before the merchant had a chance to set out his outdoor display. The girls gathered not only postcards, but magnets, berets, and other trinkets. Sissy chose a crossbody bag that had the word Paris embossed all over it. "Let me get out of here before I hurt myself," she said and moved to the front counter to pay.

When they reached the sidewalks into the heart of the village, Nicki crossed the cobbled street without warning. "The cookie store is open," she yelled back to her friends, then darted inside.

"I hope she doesn't plan to have a love affair with those things," Angela huffed.

Sissy grabbed her friend's hand and pulled her along. "It's intervention time, hurry."

***

They stood on the platform, awaiting the subway. "I thought you were going to buy out the store," Angela said between bites of a dark chocolate cookie that left crumbs on her coral lipstick.

"I would have if you guys hadn't stopped me. I love my tin; look." She showed them for what seemed like the fifteenth time the gray-and-gold box that read, 'La Cure Gourmande.' The embossed theme, Paris Exposition Universelle 1900, a colorful scene, was stamped on top. The hinged tin box made her feel like a child hiding a treasure buried within. There were so many cookies, or biscuits as they were called, to choose from that Sissy and Angela had to calm her down so she could focus.

"The train is coming. Put that thing away before you lose it and we have to go back for more," Angela said. Nicki reluctantly placed the tin inside the bag and climbed aboard.

"You guys might as well have a seat because we have several stops ahead before we reach ours," Sissy said.

"Where are we going today?" Nicki asked.

"Saint-Ouen Flea Market in Porte de Clignancourt. It's one of the paid tours we signed up for."

"You mean that *you* signed us up for," Angela said, then looked out the window.

"When you see something that catches your eye and you want to buy it, don't buy it since you didn't want to be here," Sissy shot back.

"Ladies," Nicki called out. "All boxers back to your corners." They rode on in silence.

30 | FINDERS KEEPERS

Twenty minutes later, the trip was shortened by an abrupt stop. The girls looked to one another, then to the other passengers who began to disembark.

"Oh," Nicki said while pointing upward at a sign posted on the door, "they're working on the rail system today."

The police directed the girls out of the subway car. They entered the Metro tunnel, an enormous space echoing with loud voices. More officers, dressed in yellow vests, answered numerous questions thrown at them from people crowding around. Other policemen, sporting orange vests, were directing the core of human bodies toward the staircase where city buses awaited, free of charge, to transport the crowds to their next destination.

When the women finally climbed out of the bowels of the dank underground, they were taken aback. It was a side of the City of Light they hadn't seen before—real life with few tourists. The magazines, movies, and tour books forgot to point out this gritty side of town. As they moved to the top side of the landing, Nicki stepped back to avoid two mattresses on the ground that were still occupied. Autumn-brown leaves and trash swirled along the concrete ground. People rushed past, either oblivious or accustomed to such sites as they tried to make their next connections.

"Nicki, come on," Angela called out as she crossed the street.

"Did you see them?" she asked after catching up with her friends.

"Yes, but it's no different than what you see back home," Angela reminded her.

"I guess," Nicki answered reluctantly while looking back.

The women stayed together as they awaited the next bus that pulled up. People shoved and pushed their way to the front door, causing the girls to get pushed back. A police officer took control of the crowd and pointed at the second bus that pulled up. The women ran and stood in front of the door until it opened, climbed aboard, and took their seats. They said nothing as they watched the sights that passed before them.

The neighborhoods looked like beaten bodies in a gang fight. Dirty sidewalks and graffiti written on walls were common sights. Some of the storefronts had not yet opened their gates, blocking off the awaiting shoppers.

Butcher shops touted bright-red cuts of beef, links of sausages, and fresh fish. The prices, hastily scribbled on chalk signs, remained upright in beds of chipped ice alongside the raw samples. Next door were Oriental shops with colorful displays of fresh fruit and numerous cartons of eggs, stacked on the opposite side. Bright packages of noodles, and other unpronounceable items, spilled out onto the streets.

Various bakeries were seen throughout crowded businesses that lined the sidewalks, displaying trays of brioche, croissants, tarts, and crusty breads that stood like swords within their baskets. Doors to the boulangerie swung open as customers clutched bags in one hand while jamming their free hand inside a coat or jacket pocket to fend off the chilly morning air.

"We'll have to walk the rest of the way," Sissy said after they disembarked. She pulled out her pink binder, reread the printout sheet, then guided the girls down the sidewalks, occasionally calling out the street names, confirming that they were going in the right direction.

Nicki tugged at her scarf, then reached inside her trench coat pocket, removing from it a pair of gloves. "I hope the sun comes out," she said while pulling them over her blanched fingers. "These gray clouds are depressing."

"Hey, let's stop at that place, La Boulangerie," Angela called out. "Is that how you pronounce it?"

"Check you out," Sissy said in amazement.

"Well, I couldn't let you be the only one who knew a thing or two," she said before crossing the threshold of the shop.

A few minutes later, they stepped from the bakery with bags filled with au pain sucre and au pain chocolat. "I think with all the changes on the transit lines, we're still early," Sissy said after chewing a bit of the warm bread. They continued their walk until they crossed the street in front of a McDonald's.

"If I had known we would end up here, I would have waited," Nicki huffed.

"Our guide should be here, and who's to say we would have had time to sit and eat," Sissy said while looking about for someone wearing the Discovery Walks pink vest.

A woman, who appeared to be in her mid-fifties with chestnut-brown hair cut in the style of a mushroom cap, ruddy cheeks, and baby-pink lips slowly approached the trio. Her cotton candy-pink jacket was zipped tight to the neck, while a khaki-colored skirt hung below her knees, exposing a pair of heavy, pale legs in brown ankle socks and sensible brown walking shoes.

"You wouldn't happen to be a guide?" Sissy asked.

"Oh, dear me, no," she smiled broadly. "I'm to take a tour of the flea market. How about you?"

"The same." Sissy introduced herself and the girls. "Our guide seems to be a tad bit late."

"Probably because of the rail system," the woman said with a twang in her voice. "People back home call me Sally Jean. I'm from Wichita Falls, Texas. I'm settling a bet my friends made that I wouldn't come to Paris alone." She let out a hardy laugh and said, "I guess each one of those suckers will owe me $100.00 when I get back. That will round out to about, I'd say, $600.00, which is just about the amount of spending money I used here." She laughed some more as the girls joined in.

They were comparing notes of places to visit and tours to take. Fifteen minutes had passed when a slight man, 5'11" in height with unruly, light-brown, curly hair and morning stubble across his chin, ran up to the group as his pink vest blew in the wind. The stranger was panting as he stood before them. Once he gained control of his voice he said, "*Bonjour*!"

31 |ALVERÉ

He was almost comical, dressed in mauve corduroy pants and a light-colored, button-down, cotton dress shirt. He dropped his messenger bag on the ground while stuffing a brown bomber jacket between his knees and began removing the pink vest.

"Hey, so sorry I'm late. The subway—"

"We know," Nicki interrupted.

"Oh, so you had to deal with it, too. Well, my name is Alveré, which means elf counsel. As you can see, I'm far from being an elf, but I am your guide today to the famous Saint-Ouen Flea Market."

He stuffed the vest into the messenger bag and pulled on the jacket. Alveré ran his hands through his hair, then slung the carrier over his body, rummaging inside of it for his paperwork. Once settled, he asked each woman where she was from and shook their hands. Then his mood changed. It was all business at this point, as he began a casual introduction of Paris history. He pointed at a map posted in the area, describing the various arrondissements. Just as his presentation got underway, he turned and stared at several youths who had begun to hang about the area they were standing in. He spoke to the two boys in French, causing them to slowly walk away. Alveré continued as though nothing had happened.

"The business of collecting had been a staple in Paris for years, no matter if it were metal, clothing, or so forth. "Biffins" were the rag-and-bone men, and "crocheteurs" were known as pickers. These groups would set out through the Paris well-to-do areas to find what was available to barter with during the day. They soon were pushed out of the city by the end of the 19th century by those who wanted to clean up the capital. The Biffins and crocheteurs soon set up camps between the fortifications and early houses built in the village of Saint-Ouen. After a while, dance halls and cafés opened their doors to the people of Paris who would come to the area for untaxed white wine."

Angela couldn't seem to stop staring at their attractive guide. *Maybe it's those green eyes of his,* she thought while looking his body over. *I need my men with a little more meat on their bones, but those eyes and that sexy French accent would be a start.* She shook her head slightly, took a deep breath, and tried to focus on what Alveré was saying.

"Soon, the press, during 1905-14, became wise to the area and wrote colorful passages about it, driving more visitors in its direction. After the first World War, businessmen purchased land, paved the roads, installed electricity and water, and began to rent out stalls for a cheap price. By the 1920s to 1991, indoor markets came to be. During the late 90s, you had urban development."

He instructed the women to walk with him. They paused at a street corner as horns blared. Cars seemingly piled up on one another as they tried to beat the traffic lights, blocking oncoming cars in the other direction. Pedestrians weaved in-between and around the group as he continued. "In 2001, the area was named, 'Zone de Protection du Patrimoine Architectural Urbain et Paysager' because of its unusual atmosphere."

They crossed the street, and soon men— some old, some fairly young—paraded up and down the sidewalk. *"Bonjour, Madame,"* they would say while approaching the women, waving watches, socks, handbags, and an assortment of knickknacks while yelling out prices for their goods.

Angela looked at the so-called name brand items for sale. "Where do they get this stuff?" she asked while peering down an alley where several trucks with goods lined the street.

"I don't know," he began, "but I would question the quality of those iPhones," he chuckled. "We are not in the actual area. These are the hawkers who try to sell their cheap wares." The women asked a variety of questions as they continued to walk between more cars in long lines of traffic as motorcycles bullied their way along the sidewalks, then back onto the streets. Alveré slowed his pace when he noticed his charges were not able to keep up with his long stride and apologized.

"Forgive me, ladies. I walk so much that I forget to slow down when I have company. This is a city that is so easy to get around in if you know how to ride the rail and bus system. In fact, in 1908, with the help of the Metro station, the market became a popular attraction, drawing hundreds of Parisians each week." They stopped on a block that was filled with pedestrians. "We are now in the area known as Saint-Ouen Flea Market. It is filled with at least 2,000 stalls and around

16 markets that spread out in several directions and streets."

There were small and large shops and booths of various sizes. It seemed as though every era you could imagine was represented. They peeked into windows of the very expensive antique dealers, artists, and artisans. He spoke of the best area to find film memorabilia or shabby chic.

"The rule of thumb regarding the market is to go early in the morning, and don't be afraid to bargain. The prices can be high, but if you want it, try to talk them down on the price. If they won't move on it, walk away. You're bound to find it elsewhere. Most of the shopkeepers will work with you to sell an item."

Their tour began down avenues and side streets as he interjected a bit of history about the neighborhood. "If you want to purchase silver," he paused by a nearby shop, "look at the boxes on that serving fork." The women nodded. "Those two boxes hold the information you need regarding that item's worth and history."

He waved at some of the shopkeepers and they at him, a familiar face. They climbed the stairs to other buildings and, once again, passed by windows of other shops. Their guide paused, allowing the women to look about. Angela stepped inside a booth that carried old movie posters, music albums, and 45s. Sissy was drawn to anything related to travel, while Alveré assisted Sally Jean as she haggled over a beautiful old brooch just two doors down. Nicki snapped away at the activity in the area on her camera. Once they met up, Alveré mentioned that there weren't many toilets in the area and suggested where they could find one.

Soon they were on their way again as he stopped by some of his favorite cafés, pausing to speak to the proprietors while informing the women of the family history of that business. He stood outside of buildings, pointing out the artwork painted on the side. Alveré enlightened them on the meaning, origins, and his love of "Gypsy Jazz." The women were engrossed with his insight regarding the political histories of each neighborhood, for example, if they were Jewish or African. They turned corners that hid entrances to other workshops that built or designed over-the-top objects for stage productions or eccentric buyers. He introduced them to owners of booths with a quirkiness for hand-carved items, or where one could find the best bargains on vintage clothes or unique artwork.

Two hours later, they returned to the entrance of the market. Alveré informed them how to find their way back to the main road before he said goodbye. "You may stay as long as you like, but I would advise not being here in the late evening. It could get a bit dodgy down here. It's time for me to leave. Enjoy yourself and have fun shopping. *Au revoir.*"

The women tipped their Bohemian teacher before he left. They stood for a moment, trying to decipher their scribbled notes to match up the avenue to the booths they wanted to go back to for purchases.

"Well, girls, it was a pleasure," Sally Jean said while shaking each woman's hand. "I'm going in that direction," she said, pointing to her right, "because I can pick up a thing or two before I head back to my hotel. I'm flying back to Texas in the morning so I can pick up my dough." She laughed once more, waved, and walked away.

"Well, ladies," Nicki began while imitating Sally Jean, "I'm a heading in that direction because I saw a thing or two that I wanted." They chuckled, then turned left to start their search for the booth with the antique keys that Nicki noticed earlier during the tour.

After several twists and turns, they finally located booth 138. Nicki rummaged through the small box of rusty skeleton keys as the girls looked about. She held two of them in her hand and stared at them when Sissy walked up. "What do you want with that old thing?"

"I don't know. Maybe I'll place them in a special bowl on my desk to remind me of our trip. You have to admit, there is something mysterious about them."

"Mysterious?"

"Yeah, like did they open the doors to a famous hotel, or did they belong to someone's home?"

"OK, Agatha Christie, let's get going."

The shopkeeper's son—who spoke a fair amount of English—explained after being asked about the history of the keys that they came from many places. "He, my father, was a key smith many years ago. As a hobby he collected old keys." She purchased the keys before they made their way back to the Metro station and then the hotel for the unexpected.

The women were chattering, talking over one another, when they stepped inside the hotel lobby. They paused long enough to say *"Bonjour"* to the desk clerk before heading to the elevator.

"Excusez-moi, mademoiselles."

They spun around to face him. *"Oui?"* Sissy said.

The clerk turned, then sat a tall, slender glass vase on the desk. An explosion of color—yellow, pink, and orange in the form of Gerbera daisies—brightened the room. *"J'ai des fleurs pour Mademoiselle Nicki."*

Before Sissy could call out her name, Nicki ran back, snatched the vase up with both hands, buried her face in the colorful blooms, then, like the Cheshire cat with a wide grin, said, "From whom?"

The clerk handed her a sealed pink envelope with her name written on it.

"Merci," she said and carried the card in her left hand while cradling the vase in her arms.

"Don't mind me while I carry your

packages upstairs," Angela said, picking up the dropped items.

"Oh, sorry, thanks. I just can't imagine who would have done this."

"You know who," Sissy said when they reached Nicki's room.

"No way," she muttered while carefully tearing the sealed envelope. She read the card and then sat in the nearby chair.

"Well, what did it say?" Angela asked in anticipation.

She looked at it again and read it aloud. *"My beautiful Nicki. These flowers reminded me of you. I would like to see you again, if it is possible, this evening. I will ring your hotel room at five."* It was signed, Ermenegilde.

The other two women sat at the foot of the bed. "Just like in the movies," Sissy sighed.

"I know you're not going to see this guy," Angela said.

Nicki was taken aback by her tone. "And why not?"

"We're in a foreign country, he's a stranger, and he's white."

"What?" both women shouted.

"You heard me."

"Hold up," Sissy said as she jumped off

the bed. "What does his skin color have to do with anything?"

"I'm just saying we have enough fine, intelligent *brothers* back home who would be more than willing to date Nicki."

"Oh yeah? Where are they? Because it seems to me that black men have forgotten that black women exist. Why should my happiness be placed on hold for a *brother*?"

"I never knew you felt this way about crossing the line, Angela," Sissy said with disbelief.

"Well, I do. Haven't you noticed that all the men I date are from the chocolate variety box?"

Nicki laughed. "Oh, you mean those tired trolls you go out with?" She began to count on her fingers. "Let's see, we have the stand-up comics, or the I wanna be a player, or—"

"Well, at least I can get a man!"

Nicki and Sissy stared; their mouths fell open. "I know you didn't cut her down like that," Sissy said. "How dare you!"

"I know the truth hurts baby girl, but deal with it." Angela turned and started for the door. Nicki sprung from her chair. She grabbed a hunk of the auburn- streaked hair, balling it into her fists.

"Let's see how much *this* hurts," Nicki screamed as she pulled tighter.

Angela cried out in pain as she tried striking Nicki on any part of her body that could be reached. Sissy ran over, slapped her hand over Angela's mouth, and yelled at Nicki.

"Let go before they kick us out of here!" Moans and wails of pain slipped from Angela's mouth as Sissy readjusted her hand to quiet her.

"NICKI, LET HER GO!" Sissy took her free hand and struck Nicki in the chest until she finally came out of what seemed like a trance, while releasing Angela's hair.

Angela held her head, tears streaking her makeup. With the back of her blue-striped shirtsleeve, she wiped away the mucus that teetered on her upper lip. In a low, unrecognizable voice she said, "I will kill you if you touch me like that again. Do you understand me?"

Nicki pointed her finger. "Don't you *ever* disrespect me again, Angela. I'll kick your—"

"Hey!" Sissy yelled. "Shut up, both of you! Angela, get out of here!"

She snatched up her belongings. The

mangle-haired Angela turned the knob, opened the door, and stepped out. She looked back at the two women, then slammed it.

Nicki fell into the nearby chair, shaking her head as uncontrollable tears gushed from her eyes. "My worst fears have come to life," she said between sobs. "I'm not attractive. I'm too fat. Ugly and fat. No man wants that," she cried.

Sissy took a deep breath, not believing what had just taken place. She walked over to the casement windows, pulling the doors open to fill the room with fresh air. After wiping her forehead with the back of her hand, she went into the bathroom, turned on the cold water, and splashed her face until her composure returned. She moistened the lower end of a bath towel and handed it to Nicki. "Clean your face," she said.

They sat in silence for what seemed like forever before Sissy spoke. "I don't know what and why that started, but I have one question," she said while looking at Nicki. "Are you going to go out with him?"

"I don't know. I mean, I was all for it until Ms. Thang opened her mouth. Maybe she's right. Why bother when I know I'll be leaving soon. Besides, I've never dated outside of my race, and I'm not ready for all the drama that comes with it."

Sissy walked over to the open window and looked at the thick, green ivy plant below the sill. It seemed to stretch as if trying to escape from its container. Her eyes drifted to the other rooftops and windows in the distance as the noise from mopeds and motor cars filled her ears. Farther still, she noticed the spire of Notre Dame and its gray rooftops. "Come here," she said over her shoulder.

She pointed at the structure. "In the 12th century, that cathedral was in ruins before great men decided to replace it and make it better than before—a masterpiece of French Gothic design. It is marveled, loved, and admired by millions of people, every day, every year. You, Nicki, are a marvel. You said you wanted to lose weight, and so you began something that was—and is—very hard to do. Each pound took effort and the belief that you could get rid of it. You said you wanted to travel to London and Paris, and you did, because you believed in yourself. So now there is a handsome, intelligent Parisian who finds you appealing and wants to spend time with you. Would you have ever imagined that to happen?"

"No," she said as a fresh tear rolled down her cheek.

"No, you didn't, but now that it has, are you going to allow someone to take that opportunity away from you?"

Nicki turned and looked at Sissy. "I think I'd be stupid to let it slip away."

"Yes, you would."

Just then, the phone rang. Nicki gawked at it. When it rang a second time, she ran over to it. Sissy looked out the window as bits of the one-sided conversation filled her ears. Shortly, Nicki returned and draped an arm across her friend's shoulder.

"He's coming by at six. He said that we'll just eat at a place in this area so I wouldn't be too far from the hotel."

"How considerate."

"Ermenegilde said he didn't want you guys to think he was trying to kidnap me."

"He has a point there."

"I love you, Sissy."

"I love you, too." She straightened and kissed her friend on the cheek. "You have a date to prepare for. Stop by the lounge area downstairs so I can check you out before you leave."

"I will."

Sissy walked to the door, turned, and gave her friend a thumbs-up before walking out.

"That's my girl," Nicki said before heading to the shower. "My sister girl."

***

She didn't mean to do it, but somehow when Nicki pulled her cup from its cardboard drink holder, it caused all the other drinks to rain down on the hot asphalt.

"Nicki Renee," her mother's shrill voice called out. "You stupid little—"

"Hey!" her father's voice boomed. "Watch your mouth." He walked over and gave the blue-and-yellow bag he was carrying, full of burgers, fries, and onion rings, to his wife. "You and the kids get in the car while I get this." With tears streaming down her face, Nicki picked up the paper cups and handed them to her father. "Daddy, I'm sorry."

"Don't worry about it; just get in the car. I'll be right back."

Her mother turned around in the passenger seat and waited until her husband's body disappeared inside the diner. She stared at Nicki. "You fat little . . . can't you do anything right?"

Her father returned and passed everyone their cups. She was fearful of drinking hers, replaying not only the spillage, but the hate-filled, painful words. Her wails began again.

Her mother turned around in her seat. "Shut that noise up before I shut you up."

Nicki tried to stop the tears and wiped her face with the back of her chubby hand as her parents argued. She sucked up a deep breath of air and held it briefly, then slowly released it. They continued to argue. It was her fault. If she hadn't dropped the tray, if she hadn't cried, if she were not fat.

She placed the straw in her mouth, like a pacifier, to stop the tears, to stop the pain. The cold, frosty, chocolate flavor could not be felt on her tongue. It was something to keep her quiet, and eventually her parents would be quiet, too.

"It started with words, a mistake, then food," Nicki said while looking at her reflection in the mirror as the memory floated away. She held the makeup sponge full of foundation in her hand. "I will be slimmer and healthier in time." After her declaration, she continued to prepare for her date.

***

"What do you think?"

Sissy placed her bookmark inside the mystery novel she was reading and looked at the black, tasseled dress pumps and critiqued Nicki from the pant leg up. "Black dress slacks; fits just fine. Yellow-and-blue, splash print, pullover dress shirt. Very nice. The color looks good on you."

"Will you stop being so silly. You're making me nervous. I feel like Coco Chanel is looking me over."

"Now we must get this right," Sissy continued, her voice in a mock, haughty tone.

"Dress jacket, black, of course, hip length. And what is that in your hand? A fashion accessory? I believe they call that a clutch. Love the jeweled colors, darling," she drooled.

Nicki pretended to be a high-priced fashion model as she twirled, then pivoted, in the empty lounge area. She tossed a lock of the fall piece she was wearing over her shoulder.

"Your makeup is flawless, darling, simply marvelous," Sissy said, pretending to be a fashion photographer while using her imaginary camera.

"Look at me," Nicki called out. "I'm on the catwalk." She shimmied, turned, and threw out her arms. "Take my picture," she laughed. "Hey, what's wrong with you?"

All Sissy could do was point. Nicki turned, only to find Ermenegilde standing behind her with a sexy smile plastered on his face.

"I did not realize I was taking out Nicki, the famous French model," he joked.

"Oh, I . . . um . . . didn't know—"

"Well, it's time for me to hit the hay," Sissy said loud enough to cause the doorman to peek around the corner of the lounge. She gathered her book, shook Ermenegilde's hand, and ran out of the room.

"This is so embarrassing."

"Why? I find you most attractive. Are you ready to have dinner with me?"

She nodded her head. The doorman returned to his post and held the door for the couple as they approached. Ermenegilde guided her to the right. "The restaurant is two blocks away. Will you be all right if we walked?"

"Just as long as it's not an all-out sprint," she teased.

"And if you should break a heel, I will be honored to buy you a new pair of glass slippers."

"My, you are a charmer."

He quickly switched places, making sure she was on the inside of the sidewalk as they turned the corner.

33 | A HOT MESS

"Angela, you might as well open this door because I'm not going anywhere until you do." This was Sissy's second and final attempt to speak to Her Highness.

From the other side of the door came a click and then the jarring of a handle before it glided open slowly, and then halfway, it began to go in the opposite direction to close. Sissy grabbed the handle and stepped inside, closing the door behind her. Angela was strewn across the bed on her stomach, legs bent, feet pointing toward the ceiling. She was engrossed with the Paris edition of *Vogue* magazine. Sissy looked around the room and noticed the suitcase sitting open on the luggage stand, her clothes hanging out of it. She pulled out the chair near the desk and turned it to face Angela, who was ignoring her up until then.

"What do you want?" she asked while turning another page.

Taken aback by the directness of her question, Sissy plunged in, "What's your problem?"

"I don't have a problem."

"Oh, so that little smackdown highlight that happened in the other room was just a qualifying demonstration for the WWE wrestling judges?"

"Whatever!" She waved off Sissy's comment and continued to turn the pages of the magazine.

"Excuse you! I'm speaking, so at least have the courtesy of putting that—"

"All right, already." Angela pitched the one-inch-thick magazine across the room, causing it to land right at Sissy's feet.

"Girl, you better get a grip and tell me what is going on with you."

Angela jerked upright in the bed and stared in Sissy's direction. "I can't believe that of all people, Nicki caught the eye of that Parisian hunk of a man. It's not fair."

"Hold up." Sissy said as she bolted out of her seat, kicking the magazine out of her path. "Please *do not* tell me that you're jealous?"

With her arms crossed, Angela's bottom lip began to quiver.

***

They were seated at a booth on the back wall of the restaurant, away from the screaming baby whose mother's attempts to silence the infant failed miserably. Once they were settled, Ermenegilde ordered two glasses of Riesling.

"I'm very happy that you decided to dine with me this evening," he said after returning his gaze in her direction.

"I must admit that I was surprised by the beautiful flowers and invitation. I love the bright colors."

"They reminded me of you as I stated in the card—bright and full of such pleasure."

She raised an eyebrow.

"What I mean is . . .," he stammered. "I meant to say they remind me of your happiness and kindness." His cheeks blushed into a rosy hue.

"I understand what you meant," she said with a smile while picking up the menu. When the waiter returned with their drinks, Ermenegilde ordered their meals. Nicki relaxed in her seat and listened to the melodic cadence of his voice. For a brief moment, she imagined that she, too, spoke his native tongue and that they flirted and teased one another in a seductive interlude. How pleased her boss, Mr. Stevens, at Amalgamated Shipping would be that she was fluent in French and would raise her pay because of all the help she'd be during the Paris transaction.

"Nicki?" A brief pause. "Nicki?"

She looked at him with a silly grin, then realized that she had been daydreaming. "I'm sorry. You were saying?"

"I was saying how stunning your eyes are. Is everything all right?"

"Just perfect," she said and began to ask him one question after another about life in Paris.

***

"Well? I'm waiting, Angela." Sissy's voice was stern and unforgiving.

"Maybe. Kind of. After all the stuff I've been through, I deserve a little happiness."

Sissy paced back and forth in the small space and shook her head. "And don't you think Nicki has a right to be happy? It's been a long time for her."

"I know but—"

"But what?"

"I'm so unhappy. The weight, Cody, the surgery—"

"What does that have to do with—"

"I need to be cheered up. I deserve to find love, have babies, and be loved in return. I want someone to call me his sugar bear and—"

"Girl, stop and take a breath." Sissy paced the room again. Before speaking, she shook her head and carefully formed her words.

"Angela, I have to admit that I'm really surprised to hear all this coming from you. I mean, I've only seen you on meltdown once, and that was during the Cody incident. Since then, you've always appeared to have it together."

"Well, *don't always* believe what you see."

In the middle of her pacing, Sissy stepped on the magazine, lost her footing, and released a shrill scream before she landed on the bed and tumbled onto her side. Once her senses were intact, she stared at Angela and said, "Girl, if I had broken something, you and I would be fighting."

"You would be in the hospital," she said sarcastically. "Now back to my problem."

"Angela, you're a mess." Sissy fell onto her back and looked up at the ceiling. "You know you'll have to apologize."

Now it was Angela's turn to pace the floor, stopping long enough to pick up the magazine. "Why should I? I mean it was my hair that she pulled and tried to yank out of its roots."

"Its roots?"

"Don't start with me."

Sissy stifled a laugh and tried to sound serious as she sat up in the bed. "We have several places to visit tomorrow that have been paid for in advance. It would behoove you to put your pride aside and clear the air so we can move on."

"That is so unfair." She threw the magazine into the suitcase.

"And while you're at it, you may want to do some anger management." And with that, Sissy slid off the bed, walked up to Angela, and said, "Get a grip!" She opened the door, crossed the threshold, and never looked back.

34 | NEW OUTLOOKS

The Seine River was exceptionally beautiful, flowing in a northwesterly direction. After the Loire River, it is considered the longest. Before emptying into the English Channel at Le Havre, the commercial and transportation uses of the Seine River cannot compare to the simplistic beauty it holds for Parisians and visitors.

Along its path, Nicki and Ermenegilde ignored the murkiness of the water, instead delighting in the reflections of the street lamps that winked back at them. They strolled the passageways after dinner, careful not to hold hands, a personal gesture. Instead, the quiet moments were replaced with long talks of work, home, books, current events, and desires of the heart.

He impressed her with his knowledge; he was a well read and traveled man. His politeness was so different from what she had remembered from the men of her past. He carried himself so well and dressed in such a polished, understated way.

She took notice of the women who passed by them. They would blatantly stare in their direction, giving him a once-over glance of admiration while showing astonishment that she was with him. Nicki wanted to stick out her tongue and say, "Yeah, he's with me. What about it?" Instead, she basked in the pleasure of the evening as their conversation continued.

When they stopped topside at one of the many bridges along the river, she was surprised at their location. Notre Dame's haunting lights illuminated the building, seemingly transporting it to the time of the Middle Ages. Pedestrians passed by—some in an unhurried pace, lovers holding hands, tourists trying to make sense of their travel guides, and yet others in a rush as they entered the mouth of the Metro station that appeared to swallow them.

"Do you know where you are at this moment?" Ermenegilde asked.

She focused her concentration on her surroundings, then noticed the bookstore, Shakespeare and Company. "Oh no," she laughed.

He shared in her amusement, then said, "It is here that you attacked me. I feared for my life."

"Attacked you?" she huffed while folding her arms across her chest.

"Yes! I thought you were the paparazzi and had mistaken me for a famous American movie star."

"You wish," she teased.

He ran his fingers through the thick mop of hair. "How fortunate for you that my bodyguard was not working that day."

"Your bodyguard?"

"Yes. If he had been on duty, we would not have met when you jumped on my back."

"I jumped on your back? Don't you mean when I was pushed and landed on—"

"Never mind such minor details." He could not keep up the charade and let out a deep, boisterous laugh. When they both settled down, he lifted her hand, kissing the back of it and then her left cheek. He pulled away and looked into her eyes. *"Tu es charmante."*

"Which means?"

"You are enchanting."

"It sounds better in French." They smiled. He guided her arm into the crook of his. "I should return you to the hotel before your friends call the police."

"If you insist. But may I ask two favors of you?"

"Oui."

"First, walk *very* slowly."

"And?"

"And would you teach me a few words in French?"

"Ce serait mon plaisir. It would be my pleasure."

She attempted the sentence as they walked against the flow of the Seine, her broken French echoing in the night air.

35 | HEAVEN HELP US!

Dread covered Nicki as she awakened from a deep sleep. Instead of basking in the memories of her date last night with Ermenegilde, the fight with Angela played loud and clear. Maybe, just maybe, she took the words she said to heart, triggering her violent reaction. It was just that it was tiresome to hear the taunting about her inability to get a man.

After a deep stretch, she dangled her legs over the side of the bed and ran her fingers through her hair. This thick crown of a woman's glory is the very thing she tried to pull from Angela's scalp. After some deliberation, she admitted that it was wrong to try and pull a woman's weave—especially a *black woman's* weave—no matter how mad you are.

"I guess I have to step up and apologize so we can move on," she said aloud after standing and walking over to the desk chair that held her robe. She jabbed her arms through the sleeves, then tugged at the sash and tied it. The frown that covered her face changed when she noticed the flowers in the vase. Nicki touched the fragile petals and let out a sigh.

"He likes me just as I am," she whispered. "He doesn't see me as a fat woman but a woman. He thinks I'm. . .." She paused, trying to recall his words. "He said I am enchanting."

After taking a deep breath and releasing it, she opened her bedroom door. "Let the games begin."

***

"Are you sure you want me there?" Sissy questioned after Nicki asked if she would accompany her to Angela's room.

"Just in case she decides to swing on me, I'll have a witness and a referee."

Sissy let out a chuckle, then took Nicki by the shoulders. "Sorry, kiddo, but this is one battle you'll have to face alone. You and Angela need to get over this wall together and without my interruption."

"But, but—"

"I'll see you later. I have to shower, run to the bakery across the street, and then gather you two for our tour of the Opéra House this morning. You better get going so we won't be late."

Sissy opened her bedroom door and waited for Nicki to walk out. Just as she turned to make her last plea, Sissy closed the door in her face.

"Traitor," she yelled, then turned to take the long walk to her doom.

***

"Lord, help me say the right words and not lose my cool," Nicki prayed before lifting her hand to knock.

It seemed like forever before she heard movement behind the door, and then, "Yes, who is it?"

"It's me, Angela. May I come in and talk to you?"

The door swung open and the person behind it stared at her as though they didn't know each other. "You have a lot of nerve."

"Look, can we discuss this inside?"

Angela looked her up and down, then turned and walked away. Nicki quickly stepped in before she changed her mind.

"Say what you have to, then get out," Angela said in a low, unforgiving voice.

Nicki didn't bother to take a seat; she paced the floor as she pushed on before she lost her nerve. "I want to say I'm sorry for losing my cool yesterday. You have to understand that for a long time, I've had nothing but snide remarks about my weight from everyone—parents, so-called friends, and guys I've dated."

Angela continued to file her nails, not giving Nicki her full attention.

"Out of the three of us, I'm the youngest and the largest. I'm packing almost 190 pounds, and that is way too much for my height."

After a moment, Angela paused and looked up. "So, what does that have to do with what happened last night?"

"Could you, for once, see it from my point of view?" Nicki pleaded. "You have always been able to get a man, go on dates, have a relationship. Try not having any of that for five years. The loneliness at times is unbearable."

Nicki looked at Angela, who resumed filing her nails. She felt stupid and wondered why she even bothered to come to apologize. She started for the door when Angela finally stopped her. "Sit down," she said, pointing to the chair with the fingernail file.

After Nicki was seated, it was Angela's turn.

"I have to admit that what I said was not very nice. In fact, to be truthful, it was spoken out of jealousy."

"Jealousy?"

"Yeah, me of you and old boy."

"Ermenegilde?"

"Yeah, him."

"Angela, what are you talking about?"

She went on to explain her desire to have a long-term relationship and the fact that, of all people, Nicki attracted the handsome Parisian. Nicki shook her head in disbelief.

"I can't believe you. It's as if you don't want me to be happy."

"You can be happy, but why can't it be from a black man?"

"Because a black man doesn't want me," she said out of anger, rising from the chair.

"But you don't know that. You have to be patient."

"I've been patient for five years! I know more about the Turner Classic Movies lineup and biographies of so many actors and actresses that I could sit in for Robert Osborn. I'm tired of working overtime, eating alone, and being a couch potato. I want someone to hold me, say that I'm beautiful, to love me—no matter what color he might be. So forgive me for looking for love in all the *other* places."

"But—"

"But nothing, Angela. And why are we going down this road? Ermenegilde lives here and I live in America. There is no future between us, but in the meantime, could I just have some fun?"

Angela stood and walked over to Nicki. "How about a truce?" she asked and stuck out her hand.

The tension seemed to ease between them as Nicki rose to leave. "Let's try to enjoy the remaining time we have in Paris before you and Sissy leave. Again, I'm sorry about the hair tug."

"Forgiven."

Although it wasn't all hugs and kisses, it was a start, and that's all Nicki wanted—a chance to move forward and enjoy the company of her friends before their departure in a few days.

36 |IN THE DUST OF THE PAST

The tempestuous sky with its low-hanging clouds did not deter the trio. "This will be perfect," Sissy said in a breezy voice as they took their seats on the Metro. "The bad weather will not destroy our tour since it takes place indoors."

She looked at her friends. Although they had called a truce, it was evident that it would take more to bring them back to the level they were at prior to the fight. A conversation between an older woman and a child caught Sissy's attention. The biracial girl, possibly around eight years old, threw her curly, sandy-colored hair back and let out a high-pitched squeal. The woman, who stifled several of her own giggles, tried to shush the child, then said something in French. The girl recited several words, a few that Sissy understood after shamelessly eavesdropping on their conversation.

"*Le jardin potager*," the woman said in a somber voice.

"*La carotte, le radis, le concombre. . ..*"

"A carrot, a cucumber," Sissy mouthed the words to herself.

"*Le chou—*"

"*Oui*," the woman said, encouraging the girl to continue.

"*Le chou-fleur.*" The little girl busted out in complete laughter once again, her cheeks turning red and her eyes twinkling in sheer merriment.

The woman tried to quiet the girl by placing a finger across her lips but failed miserably as she, too, joined in the laughter. Sissy smiled at them and wondered if they were related, possibly a grandmother and her grandchild? Could it be a tutor and her ardent student? She found the distraction a pleasure among all the passengers who read, tuned out with their phones, or looked somber while awaiting their stops.

The train slowed, and the two scrambled to the door. Sissy watched as they held hands and, like magic, disappeared into the crowd. The doors closed, and once again, they shimmied and rocked along the rails in silence until they reached Opéra Grands Boulevards.

***

As the trio approached the immense building, they paused for a moment. A school band attempted to entertain a scattered, small crowd that sat on the staircase. They failed miserably with some of the tunes they were performing, but the crowd was generous with their support of praise and clapped to the beat despite it all.

"I'd fire the band leader and send them back to the practice room," Angela quipped.

"Stop," Sissy whispered while tapping her friend on the shoulder. "They aren't that bad."

"I forgot you're tone-deaf."

Nicki had walked ahead of them and found the side entrance to the building. "Look at the statues," she said between clicks on her camera.

"We better go inside. Our tour is due to start in fifteen minutes." Sissy ushered them to the door.

Once inside, they stared at the paintings and art along the walls. As they approached the desk, a sign stated that the tours were full and that no others would be conducted that day.

"Let me speak to that lady over there," Sissy said as she pulled out her pink poly binder. After playing show-and-tell, since her French was limited as was the clerk's English, with the help of the paperwork, they were able to move into the main foyer to join the other guests awaiting the tour.

"This is the place of dreams, fine men, and women in great ball gowns," Nicki sighed as she gazed at the Baroque design along the walls.

"Think more along the lines of *The Phantom of the Opera* and the inspiration for Edgar Degas's dancer paintings," Sissy said.

"And a way-over-budget dream that took 15 years by a then unknown Charles Garnier," Angela added after reading her guidebook.

A willowy, pale blonde in her mid-fifties in gray trousers, three-quarter-inch black pumps, and a pinstriped dress shirt spoke in the softest voice the trio had ever heard as she stepped forward and introduced herself to the crowd.

"Oh, this is going to be ugly," Nicki said. "I *know* they don't expect me to understand a thing she is saying with a crowd this large."

"We'll have to do the best we can," Sissy answered while pulling out her own tour book from her backpack.

At the base of one of many staircases, Marcella began her tour as people gathered as close as possible to hear her. "Palais Garnier is a 1,979-seat opera house built between 1861-1875. With the occupation of 12,000 square meters, on January 13, 1862, the first concrete foundations were poured. Throughout the building, you will find that the use of real gold leaf, velvet, and multicolored marble inside and out, along with paintings and sculptures from the best in their fields, were one of the reasons the opera house sparked much controversy."

"I'm going to have much controversy if she doesn't speak up," Angela said. She received a pinch on the arm by Sissy.

". . . All work on the house came to a halt from 1870-1871 during the Franco-Prussian

War because of the siege of Paris," the woman continued. "Now let us move to The Grand Staircase."

***

It was the thing of dreams as Nicki had stated. Palais Garnier, one of the most famous opera houses in the world, is consider a symbol of Paris, much like Notre Dame Cathedral and the Louvre. In 1910, Gaston Leroux's famous novel, *The Phantom of the Opera*, with all the adaptations in films and the popular 1986 Andrew Lloyd Webber musical, intensified the mystique of the opera house.

At the base of the Grand Staircase, you'll find multi-figured, elaborate torchères. They highlighted the famous red-and-green marble balustrade, which divided into two extensive flights of stairs. Its center flowed into the white ceremonial staircase like a giant "Y" that led to The Grand Foyer.

With a building as impressive as this, one

must not forget to look up, for the ceiling above was painted by Isidore Pils. Rich, detailed depictions of *The Triumph of Apollo, The Enchantment of Music Deploying its Charms, Minerva Fighting Brutality Watched by the Gods of Olympus,* and *The City of Paris Receiving the Plan of New Opéra* are a wonder to behold.

***

She overheard the whispers, pretending to be oblivious to their words. "How beautiful she is." "She outshines all the other mere women in the area." "I wonder if she is available?"

Poised along the third stair of the grand portion of the staircase, Nicki held her fan slightly below her chin. Her hair was an upsweep of brunette curls, as a few tendrils graced her forehead and cheekbones. Small bits of baby's breath were strategically placed in her hair.

Dressed in a soft, polonaise bustle, it

formed a tiered, draped, frilled train in the back as layers of white-and-gold skirts drew all the male eyes to her size 20 waist. But that wasn't the only thing they were fond of.

A gentleman of great distinction, dressed in a black, double-breasted dress coat, matching trousers, and a brocade waistcoat stood on the platform above and to the right of her. He stroked his chin with his right, kid-gloved hand while holding his beaver top hat in his left. His eyes had taken in the firm, full tops of her breasts, which peeked just slightly above the off-the-shoulder ruffle at the top of her dress.

It was not these men whom she waited for but the one who held her heart—Monsieur Ermenegilde Leclercq. She watched as he paused at the bottom of the staircase, looking at her, a smile crossing his face. How handsome he was; broad shouldered, strong, and intelligent.

She held out her right hand, dressed in

long, white, to-the-elbow gloves. She wanted him to come to her, to show everyone that they belong together. He climbed the staircase like a lion, proud and regal. His hand reached for hers, to envelop and caress it, when suddenly, it was rudely slapped back.

***

"Nicki!" a harsh voice called out.

"Hello? Earth to Nicki."

She shook her head, closed her eyes, and reopened them, only to find herself in the present and not that of 1875. Angela stared at her as Sissy snapped her fingers, "Hey, what's wrong with you?"

"What?" Her eyes scanned the room before she said, "Um . . . nothing."

"Oh, no. Don't tell me you did some kind of time travel thing?" Angela teased.

"We better travel our behinds over to our

group and catch up," Sissy quipped as she did a slight run toward The Grand Foyer.

**

"During its time, The Grand Foyer was considered a sort of drawing room for Paris society. With the length of 59 yards, if a guest wanted to view themselves, it was here that they would come. In the towering mirrors, one could prance like a peacock in all its beauty, as well as show off to anyone of importance," Marcella said.

Breathtaking gilt and opulence filled the room. Chandeliers, multiple columns with ornate carvings at their base, and windows ten feet high draped in the most luxurious fabrics transported you to a time of grace, expense, and exquisiteness. The ceiling, painted by Paul-Jacques-Aimé Baudry, represents moments in the history of music. Opening to the outside loggia on each end are the Salon de la Lune and Salon du Soleil.

"Women were not allowed to leave during

intermissions," she continued. "One day, a female dignitary visiting from another country, unaware of the custom, decided that she wanted to view the paintings and left her area. With her ladies in waiting, she dared to walk the halls, causing a scandal."

"I don't blame that chick," Nicki began. "If my bladder's full, you better believe I'm leaving my seat whether they like it or not."

"And I dare anyone to put their hands on me," Angela interjected. "They'll get a fistful of blackness."

"See, that's why God put you in this time frame and not that of 1875. You would have been beheaded before now," Sissy said.

"How many of you noticed the low tread design of the staircase earlier?" Marcella questioned the group.

A few people raised their hands.

"It was designed that way so that women could climb the stairs in their crinolines without showing their ankles. One must remember that this building was one-third the purpose of the opera and two-thirds a showplace and gossip house. Men would come here to show off their wealth or to conduct business. It was also a hotbed for escapades, trysts in dark corners, or while descending the staircase, a man could confirm with his mistress that he would meet her later." She moved the tour into the next room.

***

The group was seated inside the Italian horseshoe shape of the auditorium, a design purposeful to the seating arrangement to not only see the performance but to also be seen. The stage, which can accommodate 450 artists, reportedly seats around 1,979 guests. Prior to a performance, a common practice for the women of the time was to travel to the bank and retrieve their jewels from their safe deposit boxes. Banks would remain open for the sole purpose of the women returning their precious diamonds, rubies, and other trinkets back into safekeeping afterward.

"The upper boxes were reserved for nobility and women. They sat in what was known as "baignoires"—very large boxes with regal chairs that accommodated the women's oversized crinolines. Unlike what is depicted in the movies, the men sat in the seats on the lower level.

"The working class who attended these functions were not allowed access to the marble staircases and would climb the wooden stairs to the fifth floor, known as the "chicken seats," because of the chicken wire used to prevent them from throwing food toward the stage area since the viewing at this level was poor. This provided the platform the poor used to gawk and gossip about the rich and their manner of dress.

"Look up." Marcella's voice rose one octave higher than it had during the whole tour. "The famous seven-ton, bronze-and-crystal chandelier with its 340 lights was designed by Garnier."

The chatter of excitement echoed throughout the auditorium.

"At the time, its cost was 30,000 gold francs. Many complaints began to surface that it obstructed the views of those who sat in the fourth-level boxes, as well as the ceiling painting by Jules Eugene Lenepveu." With her hands poised in a dramatic, sweeping fashion, she continued, "One of the chandelier's counterweights broke free on May 20th, 1896, bursting through the ceiling and into the auditorium, killing an audience member. This incident inspired one of the famous scenes in *The Phantom of the Opera*."

"You would have thought she was in the play," Angela said after noticing how the guide's head fell forward and her hands clutched her chest.

"She's getting a tad too deep into this for

me," Nicki commented.

Later, the tour began to wind down after two hours as the group traveled through the Library-Museum of the Opéra with its permanent exhibition of 600,000 documents, including books, paintings, drawings, photographs, costume sketches, posters, set models, and historical administrative records.

They stepped into the famous "opera seating boxes" hidden behind locked doors, and traveled the staircase to the temporary exhibition hall while viewing massive stone blocks dating from 1870, as well as the main entrance where servants awaited their masters at the back of the opera house.

Marcella paused at the gift shop to say goodbye to the tour group. The girls slipped inside and looked at the items offered before stepping onto the wide staircase at the front of the building and back into the reality of the day.

"So far, that was one of the best tours yet,

with the exception of the guide not speaking up," Nicki said.

"I thought we would have to leave you in 1875 the way you drifted off," Angela joked.

"In the meantime," Sissy said after snapping a photo of the main façade, "let's find a coffee shop or Starbucks; I'm thirsty. Then we can walk around and find a place to eat dinner."

Angela started singing "We're off to see the Wizard" as they descended the stairs.

The walkie-talkie crackled and popped before a voice boomed through. Robert pulled the box away from his eardrums just before the words, "Hey, boss, we need you on section 12," blared out.

He adjusted the knobs and confirmed the message before turning to the foreman. "Dan, go ahead and finish overseeing the work over there for me." He pointed in the direction of the men pouring concrete. "Don't let those guys go until everything is locked down and the area has been cleaned of any trash. You never know who may drive by to check on the project. I don't want any of my sites to look like a pigsty."

Dan tipped his hardhat while yelling out, "Right, boss." He turned and with the bulk of a wrestler and the dust of the Charlie Brown character, Pig-Pen, the sweat-drenched Dan walked off.

The project was two months out from completion, and so far, with few incidents, the office site would hopefully have its grand opening as planned. As Robert walked over to the section, his mind drifted back to the message Sissy left four days ago. She decided to extend her trip and said that they were having a great time.

"I bet she is," he mumbled to himself. "No words of endearment like, "Baby, I miss you" or "Can't wait to hold you in my arms again." No, she didn't mention any of the things he felt about her.

He turned a corner and climbed a slight incline. *That's all right,* he thought. *I have my work and the gym.* He had to admit that he was really starting to shape up due to his early morning workouts. Exercise beat hitting a bottle of liquor out of frustration.

"If she's not careful, she won't have me to cuddle at all," he said aloud.

He picked up a few rocks in his path and

pitched them like a ball player. One of the rocks hit the back of the helmet of one of his workers. The man turned and hurled a few expletives before he realized it was the boss. His face colored when he stopped midsentence.

Robert ran over and apologized. "Sorry, man." He put out his hand as a form of an apology. "I was venting and didn't mean anything personal."

"Sure, boss." When the man pulled back his hand, a crinkled ten-dollar bill lay in his palm.

"Have a beer on me," Robert said and walked away before the worker could say anything or return the money.

"This woman will have me broke and crazy if I don't watch it," he said before taking off into a jog toward section 12.

***

Paul emerged from the boardroom

mentally exhausted, physically drained, and downright tired. "I'm happy that the boost in the economy is keeping us busy," he said to Lulu, the new assistant and architectural student assigned to him for a month.

"But," he handed her a stack of drawings and notes, "I could use a week of deep, undisturbed sleep."

Lulu smiled briefly, fumbled with her glasses that slid down her nose, then turned right as Paul turned left at the hallway intersection.

"Now, after lunch we need. . .."

He looked behind and to each side of himself. "Lulu?" he called out.

Paul opened the door of the interior design office to see if she had stepped in there by mistake, but he could not find the young student. He closed the door, straightened his shoulders, then continued down the hallway and out the front door. "I guess I'll have lunch alone," he muttered.

***

Paul sat in the shaded area of the café's patio. The fresh air had already brightened his spirits, while the seventy-five-degree temperature melted the frost from his skin after sitting in the frigid boardroom.

He gave the oversized turkey on rye piled with lettuce, tomatoes, black olives, and green bell peppers one more look before he sunk his teeth into it. He crunched on chips and slurped flagrantly on raspberry iced tea. After forty minutes, the hunger that had resided in the pit of his stomach had been evicted as a feeling of satisfaction took its place.

Paul relaxed in his seat while throwing a few chips to the sparrows that hopped about the legs of his table. His mind drifted to thoughts of Paris as he wondered what encounters, if any, Angela had gotten herself into. The creative wheels of his architect's mind wondered if she appreciated the design efforts of Baron Georges-Eugene Haussmann.

Would she know or understand that it was he who took on the overpopulated city center that hosted cholera epidemics? It was this brilliant man who broke the corseted strings of Medieval Paris, turning it into an urban center. Haussmann's designs gave the city symmetry and direction through a geometric grid of east and west, north and south.

Paul wished that he could tell her how Haussmann divided the city into arrondissements (districts), creating sewer systems and new roads that made Paris the beloved jewel of the world. These were just some of the lessons he longed to teach her as he spent time with her.

Spent time with her? "Oh, I must be losing my mind," he whispered. "I am the last person she would consider going out with."

He tossed the remaining crumbs to a few

other birds that joined in the food fight, gathered his trash, and disposed of it and any further thoughts of Angela Thomas.

They were seated in a small booth near the middle of the restaurant with picture windows that allowed views of the foot traffic outside. The waiter handed them menus, and the girls chatted away as they tried to translate the meaning of the listed items.

When the waiter returned, Sissy attempted to order in French without butchering the language too much. He assisted her as best as he could with his limited knowledge of English. Together, they managed to order two hamburgers, medium well, with fries and a cobb salad.

He returned a few minutes later, placing a large bottle of water between them and an open bottle of Coke in front of Angela. "May I have ice for my soda," she asked while pointing to her glass. He gave a quick nod, turned, and walked away.

"Why do I always have to ask for ice for my drinks?"

"They believe it diminishes the taste," Sissy said.

Thirty minutes later, their food arrived and

they began to eat and chat. Nicki pointed out that hamburger buns weren't used; instead, they used hash brown patties. "I'm learning something new all the time," she said, then changed the subject and began to discuss their visit to the opera house.

Nicki pulled out brochures from her poly pink binder of the other places they visited. She popped a French fry in her mouth and held up a booklet from the Musée d'Orsay. "This is one place I wouldn't mind visiting again."

"Pardon," a male voice called out.

They looked to their right and noticed a sedate gentleman, possibly in his late forties. His light, wheat-colored hair grazed his forehead and ended in a trim cut. Sloping, gray eyes smiled at them. "Do you mind if I view your book?" he asked while pointing at Nicki's hand.

She passed it to him. "Are you from here?"

"No, from Pennsylvania. I'm sorry, my name is Porter, *bonjour*."

"*Bonjour*," they said.

"It has been some time since I visited this place," he said wistfully as he turned the pages. "It's such a beautiful building with wonderful pieces. Are you Americans also?"

"We are," Angela answered and went on to introduce the group to him.

"Are you here on holiday?"

"I guess you could call it that," Sissy said with a smile. "And what about yourself?" She noticed that his clothes—at least from the waist up—were casual. He wore a French, blue-striped dress shirt that opened at the collar and a brown leather jacket. A beer mug sat to his right.

"Finishing up business before heading home. I love Paris and take every opportunity to visit. I used to live in the South of France and would come up for holidays like Christmas or New Years. I'm sorry for disturbing your meal." He returned the book to Nicki.

"No bother. We know how to chew and talk at the same time," Angela said.

"Do you like Paris so far?"

"I've learned a lot," Nicki spoke up after a swallow of water. "Such culture, the buildings—"

"The history," Sissy added.

"The walking," Angela chimed in, triggering a laugh all around.

"Yes, you will get your exercise here." A

bowl of clams was placed in front of him, and he offered some to the girls. They turned him down and continued to ask questions about his beloved city. An hour had passed when they realized that they still had some late shopping to do and began to end the visit.

"I'm so glad I sat next to you and felt brave enough to speak," he said as his eyes beamed with joy. The three of you are such beautiful and intelligent women and remind me of my wife, especially you, Ms. Angela."

"Me?"

"Your hair and complexion remind me of my wife. She's from Senegal. We've been married for six years and live in Philadelphia, where she is the curator for the art museum."

"*Oh really,*" Sissy said.

What the hell, Angela thought. *Is there some type of Jungle Fever convention going on that I don't know about? First Nicki, now this guy.*

". . . and I know she would have been excited to meet the three of you," he was saying. "She's so clever and travels a lot because of her job. Sometimes we have to coordinate our schedules so that we can spend time together. I love her so much."

"It's nice to find a man who still talks about his wife like a schoolboy with a first crush," Nicki said, looking in Sissy's direction.

She avoided the comment and picked up the folder to pay their bill. "It has been a pleasure to have met you, Porter. We better get going. Tomorrow we are visiting two château's."

"That's great! Which ones?"

Nicki pointed them out in her binder.

"Vaux-le-Vicomte. A fantastic structure with major historical events that took place there. The saddest part of the story that you'll learn is that its creator, Nicolas Fouquet, was evicted from his home after an intense trial. The final turn of events is a sad one."

"And what about this one?" Nicki asked.

A smile crossed his face. "Ah yes, Fontainebleau. You ladies are in for a wonderful surprise. Wear a good pair of walking shoes. There are around 130 acres of gardens and parklike areas and over 1,500 rooms. You will definitely get a good dose of French history during your visit."

He paid his bill and offered to walk the women to the Metro station. "Ladies, it has been such a pleasure meeting you. I envy your tours tomorrow. Take plenty of pictures and enjoy yourselves. There is only one first visit to Paris, so cherish it wholeheartedly."

"Would you mind if we gave you a hug?" Nicki asked.

"Of course not! You brightened an otherwise boring evening." He hugged each woman and kissed their cheeks. *"Bonsoir,"* he said as they waved goodbye to each other. He turned to leave as the women descended the staircase.

39 | CHÂTEAUX AND HISTORY

Exquisite. A simple word that fills the imagination. A feeling of disbelief is encountered when you visit Vaux-le-Vicomte for the first time. The bus ride from Paris's center places you away from the blare of horns and bumper-to-bumper traffic into a space filled with rows of thick tree trunks and branches displaying dense, variegated leaves. In solitude and 500 hectares—without a thought given to its expanse—stands the baroque, French model for the future Palace of Versailles.

The architectural masterpiece, with its light-beige coloring of stone and charcoal-gray rooftops, offers a moat for emphasis. Designed by Louis Le Vau, the structure will leave you breathless as you approach its gates. Vaux-le-Vicomte was built for Nicolas Fouquet, a financial secretary who was one of the most powerful men around, to display his lavish spending. He spared no expense as designers Charles Le Brun and Andre Le Notre set his plans into motion. The château dominated the grounds on which it stood and represented its master and his power.

Unaware of the jealousy mounting in other court members like Jean-Baptiste Colbert, Fouquet's world would crumble because of rumors of embezzled funds from the French government. It was also said that the landscape and palace were larger and more spectacular than the Sun King's, causing a historical downfall viewed as unfair and tragic. Louis XIV had Fouquet arrested two weeks after his elaborate celebration, which included the king and 6,000 guests.

A trial that dragged on for over three years, Nicolas Fouquet was sent into banishment by the courts. But Louis XIV was incensed with the decision and overturned the court's judgement, imprisoning Fouquet until his death on March 23, 1680 after fifteen years of confinement.

***

"Can you believe that," Angela huffed once they stepped away from the château and headed in the direction of the tour bus. "Poor Fouquet was railroaded into destruction because of someone else's jealousy."

"And to leave such a vast estate and die in

prison," Nicki said, shaking her head.

They stood outside of the bus and waited for the other passengers to gather. Sissy unfolded the tour guide and scanned the drafts of the palace while admiring its layout and design.

"I wonder what it was really like to live in the mid-1600s, but not as a black person," Sissy said. "I'd want to be on the flip side of the coin, you know, in the fine gowns and attending the parties and so forth."

The girls looked at her and began to laugh. "Oh, no cleaning the palace chamber pots or making up the beds?" Angela asked.

"Girl, I would be a lady of Paris society. There is no way I would live under the king's rule at Versailles nor be his mistress. Instead, I'd be known as the hostess of one of the most famous salons in the area. I would only invite the most brilliant and famous artists of the day while quail, various fruits, and cheese were being served to my guests. Entertainment would be provided by up-and-coming singers and musicians."

"It's time to come back to reality, Sissy, and board the bus," Nicki quipped.

"I know you're not trying to crack a joke, Ms. I'm-at-the-opera-with-what's-his-name."

"Ermenegilde, thank you very much." And with that, Nicki stepped inside the bus before another word was spoken.

***

The thirty-minute drive stopped in front of one of the most expansive château's one could have imagined, consisting of 1,500 rooms and 130 acres of parklands and gardens. Considered a one-time medieval hunting lodge because of the abundance of game in the area, the estate was once used by the former kings of France, a sovereign residence for eight centuries. Around 1528, François I had visions of grandeur and set out with a theme of a "New Rome" as he began rebuilding the château.

The girls stepped through the impressive gates, emblazoned with Napoleon's family crest in gold, a bee, into the Main Courtyard. They walked the manicured grounds until they came upon the emblematic center—the famous horseshoe staircase dating to the reign of Louis XIII.

As they were completing their photos, Angela noticed the tour guide waving them over, and they rushed to catch up with her. Once they were given their tickets and brochures, the guide gave the group general directions for the best way to view the rooms, then set them on their way. The trio agreed that they would stay together as much as possible, but should one want to stay back and visit a particular area more, they would meet up later.

***

Over a period of many years, the château went through many phases. The Renaissance section saw the start of the royal apartments and ballroom completed later by Henri II. The Belle Cheminée Wing, an example of Italian Renaissance style, presented the striking double-flight staircase by Primaticcio.

During the 17th century, Henri IV had been given credit as a great builder, adding to the château the Baptistery Gate in memory of the baptism of the future Louis XIII, as well as the Cour des Offices. He added the Diana and Stag galleries. In the 18th century, Louis XV had the Ulysses Gallery replaced, adding a more spacious building.

During the French Revolution of the 19th century, the ravaged château lost its furnishings but the building remained intact. Napoleon I set about to refurnish it and turn it into an Imperial Residence in 1804.

***

The women feasted their eyes on the splendor and opulence of each room, the fine-quality furniture and the fabrics appearing to shimmer.

40 | FRIENDSHIPS

The hour-long drive from the outskirts of Paris back into the noise and congestion of the city gave all the passengers a chance to rest, relax, and like most, sleep. When the guide announced that they had arrived back at their starting point, groggy heads began to move as arms and bodies stretched to bring blood and life back into their limbs.

As the women stepped off the bus, they reoriented themselves and, without much comment, moved in the direction of the Metro station. The trip was a blur as each was lost in her own thoughts.

They arrived at the hotel and parted to their own rooms after agreeing to meet an hour later for dinner. Nicki had just swung her legs onto the bed when the telephone rang.

"Hello?"

"Bonjour Nicki."

"Ermenegilde?"

"Oui. Is this a bad time for you?"

She sat up, placing her back against the headboard. "It's fine. We just returned from the tour."

"I would like to hear all about your adventure if you are not too tired. Would you have dinner with me this evening, in forty-five minutes?"

"No, I'm not tired," she lied. "I'll meet you in the lobby."

"Very well. *Au revoir*."

"Au revoir." After she hung up the phone, she scooted out of bed, rushed into the bathroom, and splashed her face with cold water. "Wake up, girl. You've got a handsome man heading your way!" she said. After a quick look in the mirror, Nicki went about to freshen her hair and makeup.

Just as she stepped from her room thirty minutes later, she turned and knocked on Sissy's door. When it finally swung open, her friend looked, then a smile crossed her face.

"Hot date?"

"Yes. He called. I'm meeting him downstairs for dinner. I just wanted you to know I won't be joining you guys this evening."

"Well, be safe and have a good time. I'll handle Ms. Thang. Just remember, our time is winding down, and I need to have our goodbye dinner before Angela and I leave you all alone."

"Don't worry, we will." They hugged, then Nicki strutted down the hall and turned left to the bank of elevators.

Sissy leaned against the doorjamb, gazing down the empty hallway. She was happy for Nicki, no matter how short the time she had with the handsome Parisian. It was better than sulking in her bedroom as she had been doing. Shortly, Sissy would be returning to her life in Kansas and to Robert, a man who, on the surface, was just what she was looking for but, for some reason, didn't have feelings for—at least for the moment. What happened to change those emotions she wasn't quite sure. The Candace situation didn't help, but it was more than that.

Oh well, she thought, *it'll work itself out one way or another.* She stepped back into the room, then peeked down the hallway once more. At least one member in the trio would be happy tonight. She pulled her head in and closed the door.

***

"She went where?" Angela asked as they traveled from Odeon/Saint-Michel. They crossed the street, 24 Rue Saint Andre des Arts, and down the alley to Pizza Rustica.

Sissy opened the door of the shop and

stepped in before answering. "I don't know where they went, except that she's with that teacher again."

"Him? What's up with that?"

"I guess he likes her, Angela. Why else would he send her flowers and take her to dinner?"

"To get into her *American panties*," she sniffed, then turned to the counter and pointed out the type of pizza she wanted to the clerk. They paid for their food and sat on the bar stools along the slender counter, waiting as the slices were placed into the oven.

"Contrary to popular belief," Sissy began, "not every man in Paris is trying to take a woman to bed. I know it's the city of love, but let's be real."

"If you say so, but eventually it will come up, wait and see."

"Girl, stop." Sissy slid off the bar stool and retrieved their food. After a few bites, Angela spoke up.

"What's going on with you and Robert?"

To avoid answering, Sissy took another bite of pizza and shrugged her shoulders.

"Don't give me that. I'm telling you, chick, don't mess up that relationship. Robert is a good man, and he really cares for you. You'll be whining later about how lonely you are if you let him go."

"Oh really, Ms. Advice to the Loveless?"

"I don't care what you say about me, but don't mess over that man, Sissy. If you don't want him, be woman enough to let him go."

She looked at Angela while chewing her last bite and said, "Where is all this coming from?"

"You have lost a fair amount of weight. With all the walking and climbing of stairs that we've been doing—besides the workouts you did at home—you are looking really good. Knowing you as well as I do, you may get it into your head that a few new boy toys just may be up your alley."

"I don't—"

"Shush," Angela said while raising her hand. "Girl, please. A smaller dress size spells trouble. You've only called him, what, three times since we've been out of the country?"

"So?"

"When you bothered to call, did you tell the man how much you missed him? Did you say, 'Baby, I can't wait to be with you again' or anything like that?"

"No, but—"

"But nothing." They gathered their backpacks and walked out the door. Fifteen minutes later, Angela stopped in front of the window of an upscale clothing boutique. "Check out that scarf on the mannequin."

"So, you're just going to flip the script on me like that?"

"Sorry." Angela pushed her way through the door of the shop and sought out a sales clerk.

"What the blank!" Sissy huffed and went in search of her friend who was standing in front of a three-way mirror.

"No one back home will have a scarf like this," she said while preening back and forth, retying the scarf in another style.

"It's too long, and you didn't finish your comment," Sissy said while staring at the reflection.

"Here's the deal," Angela began while holding one end of the knit scarf in her hand. "You are going to be sorry if you don't straighten up and fly right with Robert. He works hard, makes good money, is fine as I don't know what, and is a gentleman all rolled into one. Mess over him, and you will get your feelings hurt in the end."

"Thanks for putting my business out here in the store."

"Girl, these people speak French and don't know what we're saying." She walked up to the counter and purchased the popcorn stitch, maroon, cream-and-burgundy scarf. With the large-handled bag in the crook of her arm, she joined her friend outside as they continued their walk back to the hotel. Angela picked up where she left off in their conversation.

"Sis, if the truth hurts, so be it. I just don't want to see you all alone like me."

"You're not alone. You have men flocking to you all the time."

"But they're not *the men* I want to spend the rest of my life with." They walked the remainder of the way without speaking another word.

***

"I can't thank you enough, Ermenegilde, for such a wonderful meal and great conversation."

"I needed the company of a fine woman to make it complete."

"Oh boy, you do say all the right things."

He held the door open as she stepped out, and they turned a corner to a long sidewalk full of shops that were still open. They gazed and talked of simple things until they came across a stationery store. "Do you mind if—" she pointed.

"Not at all."

"I know it's a bit old fashioned, but I love pretty writing paper."

"What, no emails?"

She picked up a box of note cards with a whimsical print of an old-fashioned typewriter and a stationery pack of cream writing paper, the top of each sheet designed with water lilies.

"Of course, when I must, like at my job, but I like to surprise my friends and family with a handwritten note every now and then. It's personal, and people actually enjoy it."

He smiled while watching her find enjoyment over the items in the store. "You must promise to send me a letter when you return to your home."

"That may be a while," she said. "Oh, look at this journal. Isn't it beautiful." She carried the thickly bound, soft-leather book to him. On what looked like broken panes of glass, were multiple, brightly colored butterflies. He unwrapped the leather tie and opened it. For a moment, he pictured her sitting at a desk or near a tree, writing her thoughts along the lines inside. "It is very pretty indeed, Nicki. I would like to make this a present to you."

"No, Ermenegilde, you don't have to."

"I want to. It would be my pleasure," and he turned to the clerk, handing the journal to her.

Nicki purchased her items with another cashier. As they walked out of the store, he presented the present in bright-pink wrapping paper with a cascade of soft-pink, curled ribbon to her. "Something to remember me by."

"I didn't need a journal for that."

He moved her away from the crowded sidewalk and leaned in to gently kiss her lips, then pulled away. "I have wanted to do that since the day I first met you."

He repeated the gesture without any protest from her, then stood upright after a deep breath. "Let's take a walk along the Seine." Unable to speak, she shook her head as he gathered her hand in his.

Along the western point of Île de la Cité, they paused at the oldest standing bridge in Paris, France—Pont Neuf. Spanning the Seine River with twelve perfect arches, it was inaugurated under Henri IV in 1607. As the first bridge to be lined with sidewalks, it became, at its time, a famous strolling place.

They paused and looked across the city, and the lights made the moment seem magical. "Nicki." She looked in his direction.

"Earlier, at the shop, I said that you must promise to write me, and you said it may be a while. Why is that?"

"I will not be returning to my home state for a few more weeks. I am to stay and assist my boss, my employer, with a merger of a company here in Paris."

He straightened and looked at her. "You will be here?" he asked, pointing in the air as a large grin covered his face.

She nodded, not knowing what to say. She didn't mean to tell him, as she was unsure of her feelings for him. He made her feel so special and desirable, and yet, a secret lurked in her background that even her best friends knew nothing about.

"Oh, Nicki, this is great news for me." He took both of her hands in his and kissed the back of them. "I would like to ask a question of you," he said after releasing her fingers. "If you would like, may I see you again while you are here in Paris?"

"Me?"

"*Oui*, yes you. Please do me the honor," his eyes pleaded.

"May I think about it and let you know in a day?"

"But of course! I will call your hotel the day after tomorrow, once I am finished with my classes."

"Thank you."

"I must return you to your hotel. Your friends will worry and I must sleep. My students are very smart, and I must be ready for their questions after my lessons." They laughed as he took her arm in his, and they made their way to the Metro station.

41 |A SECRET REVEALED

Nicki's fitful night's sleep was riddled with unanswered questions, made obvious by the rumpled bedsheets and pillows that had been tossed about the room. Her innermost thoughts and fears had taken control of her senses.

She had been dressed for an hour as she leaned out of her bedroom window, staring at the rooftops of neighboring homes and buildings, when a knock on her door caused her to jump. Nicki looked at her clock. Eight thirty. It didn't seem like two hours had gone by, and yet, only one person would be up this early—Sissy aka "Little Ms. Sunshine." Nicki walked to the door, pausing to look through the peephole before opening it.

"What a surprise! I just knew you would be dragging around in your pajamas and bathrobe after your night on the town."

"No, I've been up for a while. I couldn't sleep."

"I wouldn't either if I had a cutie pie of a man like you do."

"Sissy, he isn't mine and may never be." Nicki returned to the French doors and looked in the direction of the partly cloudy skies hovering behind Notre Dame. The faint sounds of a Vespa passing by caught her attention, and she looked down just as a car jiggled down the narrow street below. The click of heels on the sidewalk and the tail end of a coat drifting in the wind signaled the day was just beginning.

Nicki tried to form the words to tell Sissy what she was feeling but found it difficult to say. This was her friend who was more like a sister after so many years, and yet, she worried what Sissy would think after she let her secret out.

"Nicki," Sissy said as she walked toward her. Something was troubling her friend, and she needed to know what it could be. "What's going on?"

She quickly turned and said, "If you don't want to have anything to do with me after I tell you my secret, I will understand."

"What are you talking about? What secret?"

"Have a seat and just hear me out," she insisted. Sissy sat at the foot of the bed, watching as Nicki took in several deep breaths and let them out before she started.

"As you know, Ermenegilde and I have been out a few times."

She nodded.

"He's even stopped by the hotel in the evenings when you and Angela have retired to your rooms. We take short walks in the neighborhood while he teaches me French. Other times, we've hung out in the sitting room just off the lobby."

Sissy's mouth fell open. "I had no idea that—"

"Of course not. After the falling out that Angela and I had, I decided to keep that part to myself."

Sissy was shocked at all the action that had taken place behind her back, and yet, she felt a sense of euphoria for her friend. She encouraged Nicki to continue her story by waving her hand.

"Well, the other night, he kissed me."

Sissy beamed at the news. Just as she was about to make a comment, Nicki raised her hand.

"It was the gentlest, the most beautiful, unexpected thing that has happened to me in years. We had just stepped out of a stationery shop after I picked up a few items. He handed me a package wrapped in the most delicious paper with colorful ribbons draping over the sides. Without the slightest warning, he moved me to the side of the building, leaned in, and kissed me! My heart pounded so hard, I thought I would need a paramedic right then and there. And the way he stared at me, you would have thought I was naked. His moves were so smooth and his hands so gentle the way he cupped my face and then kissed me again. Sissy, although it took me by surprise, it felt so right."

"Well, if it was all as wonderful as you say, then what's wrong?" Her face clouded over. "He didn't try anything else?"

"No, of course not."

"Look, girl, since day one, that man's eyes were like headlights on full beam when he met you," she chuckled.

"But look at me." Nicki's hands flew up in the air. "My weight. I'm still so heavy. I've only lost twenty pounds, and that's before we left town. Who knows what it is now."

"It should be less than that since we've been here, walking and climbing staircases like maniacs. Oh, and let's not forget the hills on some of those tours. Besides that, we haven't eaten the same way we do at home."

"But there are so many women who are smaller and more beautiful than me."

"Stop it right now!" Sissy jumped off the bed and stood in front of her friend. "I don't want to hear this negative mess."

"You'll have to hear that—and more."

"What are you talking about?"

Before Nicki could answer, a thunderous knock on her door caused the two women to jump. She walked over, placed her hand on the knob, and called out, "Who is it?"

"Santa Claus! Who do you think it is?" the sarcastic voice replied.

Before Nicki could fully open the door, Angela pushed her way through like a bulldozer. "You two heifers are gathered in here like spies who are about to make their next move. What is going on in here?"

"Excuse you," Sissy said, a little miffed by Angela's tone.

"I've been looking for you guys downstairs where we were *supposed* to meet to have breakfast at the café. So, I go upstairs and bang on Sissy's door, but there's no answer. Then I find you two hanging out in here without notice about your change of plans. How rude!"

"Oh," Sissy said sheepishly. "I'm sorry."

Nicki shut the door, walked over to the foot of the bed, and sat. "Angela, it was my fault. I was caught up in some stuff I was about to tell Sissy and, well, I forgot about the meeting."

"So what's going on, or am I not to know?" Angela asked while folding her arms across her ample bosom.

"First of all, would you sit down and take that scowl off your face? I'm nervous enough without you looking as though you're going to give me a   beatdown." Angela plopped down in the wingback chair as Nicki paced the floor.

"I was about to share something—a secret, I guess you could say—that I haven't told anyone but I must face. Well, here we go. Do you remember when I used to date Michael some years ago?"

They both nodded.

"And remember after we broke up how I started gaining weight and hiding away from you guys for a while?"

"Yeah," Angela said aloud. "I thought you were preparing for nun hood."

"Angela," Sissy said in a disapproving tone.

"Well, I can't help it. She wouldn't talk to

us or go anywhere for the longest time."

"There was a reason," Nicki began. "While I was dating Michael, I didn't realize he was seeing other women behind my back until it was too late."

"Too late for what?" Sissy asked.

"It was a Memorial Day weekend, and I was really sick. I was battling a fever that constantly went up and down but not away. On top of that, I went through a lot of aches and pains. I blew it off as a 24-hour flu bug. Two days had passed, and I still couldn't shake whatever it was. Michael had spent the night, so I woke him up and asked if he would take me to the ER. He said no because he didn't like hospitals but offered his car, stating that I could take it and drive myself since mine was in the shop for repairs."

"What? I would have kicked his butt," Angela shouted.

"Shush, and lower your voice. Go ahead, Nicki."

"Anyway, I got dressed and went in. After camping out for five hours, the doctor said he couldn't find anything after all the labs they drew and sent me home. The ER doctor told me if I wasn't better in a day or two, I should make an appointment to be seen by my personal physician."

"You mean to tell me that punk didn't bother to call the hospital to find out where you were or check up on you?" Angela interrupted again.

"No."

"When we get back home, I need to track him down like the wild animal that he is and—"

"Would you let her finish?"

"Continue," Angela said with a wave of her hand.

"When I went back to my place, he was asleep. So I climbed into bed, and by morning, he was gone. I wasn't any better after another day, so I made an appointment to be seen later that week." Nicki paused, took a deep breath, and let it out while looking at her friends. Her hands shook visibly. Sissy grasped them into hers to calm her.

"Are you sure you want to tell us?" she asked, her voice full of concern.

"Yes. I need to. This has been festering for so long." After a pause, she continued.

"My doctor ran more tests and returned to the room, stating that he couldn't figure out what was causing my illness. I just happened to mention that I, that I. . .." Tears filled her eyes as she tried to get the words out.

"I told him that something tingled and burned between my legs."

Angela let out an audible gasp, then grabbed her chest as she began to weep.

"He said, 'Oh Nicki,' then asked me to lie back as he performed a vaginal exam, explaining that he needed to take a sample from the fluid he found in one of the blisters." Her hands covered her face as her shoulders shook violently. As each woman sat near her on the bed, arms locked together, they held on to their friend until she could speak again. Finally, Nicki cleared her throat, blew her nose, and continued.

"He said that he needed to confirm his suspicions. He returned with the lab results, stating that he was sorry to tell me that I had genital herpes simplex-2." Fresh tears coursed down her face. She began to fan herself with her hands to gain control. "Who would have thought after all these years, just saying the words, even reliving the memories, would upset me so much?"

"I'm so disappointed that you didn't feel you could discuss this with either one of us while you were going through it." Sissy's voice was somewhat tense.

"How do you tell a person such a thing?" Nicki asked after blowing her nose in the wadded tissues she had been twisting in her hands. "I felt nasty, so dirty. How do you tell your friends that you have a highly contagious infection? When I told Michael about the results, he insisted that he didn't give it to me."

"That hound." Angela noticed her voice was slightly higher than normal and lowered it. You aren't the kind of woman who sleeps around. Remember when we teased you and called you one-man Susie?"

Nicki wiped her nose and tried to smile. "Yeah, but he insisted that he didn't do it. Then the idiot let it slip that the girl he'd been seeing behind my back didn't have it, either. I guess that was supposed to put him in the clear. After I cussed him out, I explained that my doctor said a lot of people don't know they have it because they don't have any visible symptoms, but they are spreading it through their genital tracts."

"What a simpleton," Angela said. "I would have cut off his tool like that Bobbitt chick did to her man."

"Of course you would," Sissy said while trying not to laugh. She looked at Nicki and spoke. "What happened after all that?"

"One of his male friends, Howard, who hung out with us at times, spoke to me in confidence. He said that he didn't like the way Michael was treating me and suggested I find a new boyfriend. Howard didn't know about the herpes, but he knew his buddy had been out several times with this chick who worked as a stripper at a nearby club and called him out on it."

"Good for him," Sissy said.

"Eventually, Michael went to the community clinic to prove he wasn't the one who infected me. When he waved his doctor's report in my face, I snatched it out of his hand. When I read the passage that stated, 'The client, at present, has no visible signs of genital herpes. He states that he has no serious girlfriend and has slept with other women. He states that he is currently having sex with one female partner.' I was pissed because *I was not* that partner."

"I'm sorry to ask," Angela interrupted, "but how long has it been since you were diagnosed, and are you having any symptoms now?"

"No worries. I've been symptom-free for almost six years. The first year was the worst. After the initial five days, my symptoms subsided; the blisters broke open, scabbed over, and healed. In the first year, I had three episodes before I learned how to keep my stress level down, rest, and decrease my anxiety attacks."

"So," Sissy began, "you started to eat out

of control because of this?"

"At first, I ate to subconsciously get through the pain of the infection and disgrace. Then I saw it as a way to heal from the humiliation I felt. You have to remember: herpes doesn't go away. It's with you from that day forward. The more weight I gained, the less attractive I became to men and the safer I felt. No boyfriend meant no lies or worries about if you're the only girlfriend or whatever else he was doing behind your back."

"And nowadays, you have to be careful who you go to bed with. So many men are bi-sexual and don't see anything wrong with it," Angela insisted.

"The saddest part of all is that herpes is the most prevalent of all the sexually transmitted diseases. The last report I read a year ago stated that between 80 to 85 percent of the people in this country don't even know they have it!"

"Oh, baby girl," Sissy said through her tears. "I'm so sorry for all the pain you went through."

"What I can't understand," Angela said while moving to the edge of the bed, "is why all this is coming up now?"

"Because of Ermenegilde. He kissed me last night. Do you know how long it has been since I've been kissed? In fact, do you have any clue how long it has been since a man looked at me not in disgust but as a woman—and an attractive one at that?"

"But we tell you that all the time," Angela huffed.

"No offense, but you're my friends, and that is so different than when a man says the same words. You feel it right here," she said, pointing to her chest. "The sensation is so crazy." Nicki stood, walked over to the casement window, and looked out.

"For the first time in a long time, I felt beautiful when he kissed me. It wasn't the kiss of a lustful, greedy man looking for sex, but rather, a man who wants to devour you with his eyes before touching you, to make you feel every inch the woman you are."

"Oh no," Angela whispered to Sissy. "She's been in Paris too long. I feel like a supporting character in one of those black-and-white movies she's always watching."

"I heard that," Nicki said as she spun around. "I'm nervous! I don't know what to do. Should I tell him about my illness or keep it a secret?"

"I think you're jumping ahead of the story," Sissy said in an attempt to lighten the mood. "It was just a kiss. Who really knows what it means."

"Girl, you know it means that sex is next," Angela blatantly stated.

"Thanks, Masters and Johnson," Sissy said. "Let's just take it one step at a time and see what happens before we continue this soap opera. Maybe he's just feeling you out."

"Then he's going to want to feel you up. I hope you brought some decent underwear."

"Angela!"

"Sissy!" she mocked.

"Ladies, may I have a word? After all, *it is* my soap opera," Nicki chimed in.

"Go ahead with your bad self," Angela smirked, then stood to stretch.

"First, thanks for not judging me about this. I hope I don't lose your respect or friendship. Second, Sissy you're right. I need to calm down and not read too much into this kiss. It's possible that he's just flirting with me."

"With his tongue?" Angela asked.

"There you go being nasty again," Sissy said.

"Girl, I'm just being real. I wish one of these French hunks would flirt with me that way."

"Nasty girl," Sissy said while shaking her head. "Anyway, Nicki, thank you for sharing something that was so deep and hurtful for you. Now that you've shared your secret with us and to yourself again, think of it as a starting point in your life. After all, you've been exercising, eating better, and now released an emotional weight off your heart and mind."

"And," Angela began, "you can really

work on moving your life in a positive direction. No more hiding and beating yourself up over something that you didn't ask for."

"But I should have been safer," Nicki said. "I let my guard down because I loved someone and—"

"That's just it," Sissy interrupted. "He was someone you loved and trusted. We can't carry a portable lab with us before having sex with our partners. I can just see it now, 'Excuse me, baby, I need to take a swab sample before we get it on.'"

"But you can take out a condom and say, 'Hey, baby, before we do the do, I need you to wrap that present,'" Angela said and busted out in laughter. Sissy and Nicki couldn't hold back and joined her until their sides hurt.

When they finally settled down, Sissy gathered Nicki's hands in hers and said, "We love you and will not leave you. We are the Three Musketeers. It's time for you to move forward and stop looking back. It's a brand-new day."

They wrapped their arms, one into the other, and chanted the famous quote by Alexandre Dumas, "All for one and one for all, united we stand divided we fall."

"This is so much fun, so French and ooh-la-la," Nicki chuckled as she polished off the last of her Chamomile tea and tartine toast with jam.

Angela swallowed her hot chocolate. She tore off a portion of the pain au chocolat, pausing momentarily with it between her fingers. "Honey, I've gotta keep the sweetness inside for some lucky guy worthy of my love." She popped the pastry in her mouth and moaned with delight as she chewed.

"She's b-a-c-k," the other two women sang.

"I never left!"

Sissy placed the cup on the saucer and sat back in her seat. The warmth of the English breakfast tea mellowed her as she sat among the locals at the sidewalk café, pretending that Paris was her home. The brisk, partly sunny morning did nothing to dampen her spirits. She noticed a man to the left of her intently reading his paper, while a woman at another table chatted away on the cell phone in her left hand as the espresso cup dangled midair in her right.

People shuffled, rushed, walked, and lingered along the sidewalk, all in a world of their own. The staircase to the Metro accompanied the heavy foot traffic that piled at its entrance. In two more days, she and Angela would depart for home, leaving Nicki to resume the adventure alone. Maybe not, if Ermenegilde continues to show interest as he has in the past few days. Sissy found herself worried about her friend. Is he really sincere and interested in Nicki, or will she fall victim to the charms of a French playboy?

This is so silly, she thought. *One would think I was worried over a child instead of a grown woman.*

"Hey, what are you so deep in thought about?" Nicki asked.

"Huh? Oh, I was just thinking I can't believe that Ermenegilde is taking part of the day off to take us on a tour of Sainte-Chapelle," she lied.

"He said he asked a favor from one of his professor friends. I told him he didn't have to, that we would be fine on our own, but he insisted."

"Why is he being so nice to us?" Angela asked suspiciously. "I mean, are we going to wind up as a case for *CSI Paris*? Will they have to hire someone like that French detective Hercules Parrot to solve the mystery of our deaths?"

"Who?" Nicki asked.

"You know, that man who solves crimes in those Agatha Christie books."

"His name is *Hercule Poirot*, and he is a *Belgian* detective," Sissy said while staring at Angela.

"Oh, I just love him," Nicki sputtered. "The guy who plays him is David Suchet, and he looks nothing like the character but—"

"Whoa, Nelly." Sissy interrupted Nicki and directed her question to Angela. "What does this have to do with us going to Sainte-Chapelle?"

"I'm just saying, this stranger—"

"He's not a stranger. He's a kind—"

"Nicki, you're dazed by his charm, so you don't have a clear vision of his motives."

"His motive is to take us on a tour and possibly have lunch. He just wants to spend time with the three of us. We are not going to wind up like chalk drawings on the streets of Paris, for goodness sake!" Nicki huffed.

"I'm just looking out for our safety and

womanhood."

"L' addition śil vous plait," Sissy called out, having just about enough of the mystery movie theme that was getting way out of control.

***

"I see three stunning women in the lobby. I wonder if I could persuade you to join me on a sightseeing tour this morning?"

"I'm not sure," Nicki said as she turned to face Ermenegilde. "I'm waiting on a handsome gentleman who looks somewhat like you. I'm not the type of girl who walks off with just any extremely sexy man who comes her way."

"*Mademoiselle*, I assure you that you will have such a delightful time with me, you will not think of this other guy you long for."

The women sat, shocked at the flirtatious exchange of words. "Is that our Nicki acting like a courtesan?" Angela whispered.

"She looks and sounds like her."

Ermenegilde placed his hand in Nicki's and assisted her to a standing position. For a brief moment, he looked directly into her eyes, smiled, then turned to her friends.

"*Bonjour*, ladies. Are you ready for a wonderful history lesson that will leave you astounded?"

"I don't know about her," Angela said, pointing toward Sissy, "but I am."

"You are a delight," he chuckled.

They passed through the doors of the hotel, then turned left in the direction of the Metro station. "It is best that we ride the trains," he explained. "I do not wish that you be too tired to enjoy the site that will leave you 'breathless,' as you Americans say."

43 | THE JEWEL BOX

"We are in the area called 'Île de la Cité,' considered by the locals to be the center of Paris," Ermenegilde announced once they paused outside of the Metro station. "You will find many policemen in this area because the chapel is within the complex of Palais de Justice."

As the group approached the church, the women could not believe the line that twisted and curled like a snake in waiting.

"Oh my goodness," Nicki said after she stopped and noticed the crowd.

"All these people are here to see that little church?"

"*Oui, Mademoiselle Angela.* It has more significance than you can imagine. Just wait until you step inside. You will be amazed."

They moved forward, joining the line that appeared to be a mile in length. People of various ages and races made up the rich population of tourists who assembled to claim a look at the famous chapel. The building appeared to Angela like any ordinary one until she looked closer at its design. The darkened, gray stones and structure reminded her of a client's home she visited a few times during a consultation. What was it?

She pushed through her memory and finally recalled it—Gothic, just as this style, but it didn't stop there.

"What was that word, that particular style?" Angela whispered to herself. She looked up and noticed the radiating stone spokes in the rose window of the cathedral.

"*Rayonnant*," she said proudly with a snap of her fingers. Wouldn't Paul be surprised and even a little pleased that she remembered. Angela suspected that he would envy her slightly for visiting such a great building full of history. Now those same gray stones that she snubbed just minutes before took on a whole new meaning. She brightened at the thought of the knowledge she would gain and planned to report her discovery to Robert.

After thirty minutes, they finally reached the first stage of entry when Sissy noticed two guards inside a small inner office. The slighter of the two was attractive enough for her taste. Dressed in dark-blue slacks, shirt, and sweater, the rifle strap crossed his chest as the weapon itself lay across his back.

I wish I could take the place of that item of destruction and show him some real French kissing in the chocolate version, she thought.

"How many tickets, *madame*," the clerk at the doorway repeated.

"Oh, I'm sorry," she said. "Four, please."

Ermenegilde stepped in front of her as he reached for his wallet from the inside pocket of his topcoat. Sissy could only make out part of the conversation he held with the thin gentleman who reminded her of Ichabod Crane with his long, oval face, beak-like nose, and thin neck. The words "professor" and "Sorbonne" were mentioned. Soon, the gentleman broke into a long tooth smile and patted Ermenegilde on the back after an exchange of money and tickets that allowed the group to enter at a discounted rate.

They crossed the courtyard and stepped into the lower chapel, a rather somber, but no less important, area.

"Saint-Chapelle translates to mean 'Holy Chapel.' The area we stand in is dedicated to the Virgin Mary," Ermenegilde began. "It was used by servants and court officials of lower standing."

"The colors remind me of royalty," Sissy said, touching one of the columns.

"See the trifold arcades?" he pointed out. "The patterns on the columns are French *fleur-de-lys*." The chapel was erected by King Louis IX of France, while this magnificent building was seen as a sort of jewelry box. It held the most important relics of history: the Crown of Thorns, a fragment of the True Cross, and relics of the Passion."

Sissy noticed a stone figure atop a pedestal. "It says this statue is of Louis, or Saint Louis, I guess you would say," Sissy said.

"This chapel was built for the royal palace that no longer stands. King Louis IX purchased the sacred relics for a hefty sum and used this place," he swept his hands outward, "as a reliquary. During a crusade, the king died of a plague and was later canonized by the Pope and became known as—"

"Saint Louis," Sissy said, then smiled at the tie-in of the name with the town in Missouri.

"*Mademoiselles*, I have a treat for you. Follow me."

He led them through a narrow doorway and up a flight of winding stairs. Ermenegilde took Nicki's hand and assisted her up the last two steps. She moved to the side as he helped her friends.

"My Lord!" Nicki said, grasping her chest as she looked around the room. "Oh my goodness!"

Angela's mouth opened, then quickly closed. "I must be dreaming. I've never seen such, such—"

"Absolute beauty," Sissy interrupted her. "I can't believe this. I want to cry."

So overcome by the exquisite site, Nicki tried to discreetly wipe away the tears that trickled down her cheeks. Ermenegilde wrapped an arm around her shoulders while placing his handkerchief in the palm of her hand.

"This is the famous Upper Chapel, a wonderful example of Gothic architecture. Only the king, close friends, and family were allowed in this area. It's said that the religious relics were displayed over there." He guided them farther inside the chapel to view the immense size of the room.

"The stained-glass windows are 6,458 square feet, designed in rich blues and deep reds to best illustrate the," he looked at the information card he picked up earlier, "the Bible's 1,130 figures depicted." He pointed to the other end of the chapel. "In the 15th century, they added the rose windows."

Sissy placed the 150-300mm lens to her Canon TSi 3 and sighed when she viewed the portrayals of Exodus, Daniel, and Genesis from what she could see. The panes held the story of humankind and creation. She flashed away, capturing the resplendent depictions and understanding the tears that fell from her friend's eyes.

"I'm sorry I lost it over there," Nicki apologized.

"For what reason do you say these things?" Ermenegilde asked. "Because the beauty of the room touched your heart?" He picked up her hand and placed it in his. "Look at the light that comes through the panes, making each story come alive. The windows are divided into arches and read like a book—left to right, top to bottom. When the sun is very bright and shines through, the walls and floors are a mosaic of colors, like one would find in a kaleidoscope."

Absentmindedly, she nodded her head as her eyes traveled across the room. It was the most fantastic thing she had ever seen. The craftsmanship was impeccable. The faces displayed emotion: fear, pain, love. Even the clothing depicted pleats, folds, and other fine details. She would never be able to repay Sissy for suggesting this trip—one that exposed her to history she never knew existed.

Angela sat in a seat that became available, cradling in her arms the camera she had been using. "It always comes back to the church," she whispered.

Her eyes swept over the expanse of the Upper Chapel, appearing like an oversized storybook. Ermenegilde mentioned that fifteen of the windows were the oldest in Paris, with two-thirds of them dating back to the 13th century.

Which ones, she thought. *Here is the depiction of the Old Testament crafted by hand.* Briefly, she thought of her church back home and exhaled deeply. "Always watching over me," she said before picking up the camera, changing the shutter speed, and firing away.

***

Ermenegilde looked up at the partly cloudy skies as the group stepped outside. "Ah, winter in Paris," he sighed, then turned to the women. "I hope you enjoyed your visit."

"More than I would have imagined," Angela said.

"Thanks to you, we learned so many things. This was a chance to see something we may have bypassed in our search for things to do," Sissy added.

"I had plans to take you to lunch, but unfortunately, I have a class to teach this afternoon that I cannot get out of. What will you do with yourselves now?"

"Since our time is almost at an end," Nicki began, "we thought maybe a train ride would be nice."

"Brussels in Belgium is not that far. It will be a nice ride if you sit in first class. The ticket price will be somewhat higher, but it is worth it for the space, peace, and quiet. They serve a nice meal as you travel there and back. The only high-speed train from Paris is operated by Thalys. You will arrive near a very nice part of the town called the Grand Place," he suggested. "Maybe a little shopping will be available, also."

"Why not?" Sissy said while looking at her friends. "An unplanned trip will be nice for a change, and we can call it our last hurrah."

"I'm game if you guys are." Angela held up her hand as if voting on the passage of a bill. They all agreed, then turned to Ermenegilde to say goodbye. He gave them directions to the train station. After kissing each woman on the cheek, he whispered something to Nicki and then said "Be careful" to the trio before he turned to leave.

Angela led them to the subway. As Sissy followed, she looked back at Nicki. "Well, there's no doubt that he likes you."

"It won't last."

"With that attitude, you're right, it won't," Sissy shot back.

"Come along, Scarecrow and Cowardly Lion," Angela called over her shoulder. "We're off to see the Wizard."

44 | AN UNPLANNED TRIP

It should have been the first clue that neither of the girls took heed to that more trouble would follow. First, they had to figure out how to use the bright-yellow ticket machines at the train station. After a few "*Pardon, madames*" and "*Excusez-moi, monsieurs*" to find someone to assist them—and not in French—they found the customer service area.

After a fifteen-minute wait, the cheery, thirty-something woman called ticket number thirty-five to her window.

"*Parlez-vous anglais?*" Sissy asked.

"*Oui.* How may I help you ladies?" she asked in a muted voice.

Sissy went into detail about their travel plans while asking the best route and possible travel in first class.

"If you have the extra money, I would suggest first class. It is much quieter and not crowded. We provide a lunch, and upon your return, a dinner is served. It is much better than second class."

After they spoke amongst themselves, they agreed to pay the $141.00 fare for peace of mind, if nothing else.

"You will travel Paris-Nord to Brussels-Midi for an hour and fifteen minutes," the ticket agent explained while typing some information into the computer. "Train 9361 at track 9 will depart in 45 minutes." She gave them further directions to the departure gate. With tickets in hand, they made their way to the customs line.

**

"I didn't think we had to go through this just to ride the train," Angela said while looking around the room at the other passengers.

"Since we are going to another country, we have to go through the same process," Nicki answered.

Once they were cleared to continue, they located their train just as boarding was underway. Several train personnel were standing outside to direct passengers to the correct cars. As they approached the clerk, he took one of the tickets and, after scanning it, pointed to his right and said, "Car one."

"Of course ours would be the last in order

to be the first car out," Sissy huffed as they jogged their way toward the back.

Once the conductor of that area confirmed that they were his passengers, they located their seats at the double seating area. The bright lighting enhanced the alternating burgundy-and-red seats that caused the eyes to delight in its color. After a series of whistles were blown, the train shimmied at first, slowly down the tracks, then gradually picked up speed.

The car was quiet as predicted, with the exception of two children. The grandparents went about their duties to temper down the noise with gentle discipline. Drowsiness placed its soothing hand over Sissy's eyes, lulling her to sleep as the car rocked and creaked along the rails.

Nicki pulled out her journal, once she knew her friends were distracted, and made a quick entry before lunch was served.

Our European trip is nearing its end. Currently, we are aboard a train heading to Brussels, an unplanned trip. We don't know what to expect, but we've decided to take a chance to find out what lies beyond the yellow brick road.

As the countryside rolls by, it is as I have

seen in several travel television shows— variegated green grass along rolling hills and trees with heads full of thick, olive-colored leaves.

I had a lovely time at Sainte-Chapelle. It was unbelievable beyond words. Ermenegilde proved to be a wonderful host. I find that I think of him often, but just as quickly, I stop and allow reality to take its place. My secret has been revealed to Sissy and Angela with better acceptance than I expected. The next hurdle? To tell Ermenegilde, but not until it's necessary. If I were to look into his eyes and see any sign of disgust, it would break my heart. This is why NOT dating has been the best route for me; no emotional hang-ups.

Lunch is being served, so until next time.

Angela placed a hand over her mouth as a deep yawn left her feeling woozy. *How long has it been since I rode the rails?* Through the window, haystacks, pastures, and an occasional house captured her attention. Another yawn caught her off guard as her mouth widened and her face scrunched up, forcing her eyes to close. When she opened them again, one of the children—a little boy—was staring at her. She feigned a smile, but he continued to stare. Finally, she stuck out her tongue, causing him to blink then mirror her action.

She pulled out her thin leather journal just as the grandfather reprimanded the child regarding his behavior. "That's what you get for staring at me," Angela chuckled as she opened her journal.

For whatever reason, we are headed to another country. I can't believe that our trip is coming to an end. I'll really miss Paris and London while envying the fact that Nicki will remain a week or two longer. Maybe one day I will have the chance to return, even if I have to join one of those tour groups. I can't wait to show Paul the photos I've taken and tell him about what I've seen and learned.

It would be kind of cool if he could join me, you know, show me the places he enjoys and teach me things regarding Paris architecture. Hold up! I must be trippin'! It isn't as if he and I are dating. Besides, I like my dark-chocolate men too much. Maybe we could do a sort of business trip. Yeah, search shops for fixtures, light switch plates, and stuff like that! Now that's what I'm talking about. I'll mention it to him when I return to work. Well, it's lunchtime; got to go.

45 | DISAPPOINTMENT

As the train shifted, slowing its approach into the station, the women, groggy from their shortened naps, tried to come to life.

Angela's thumb and first two fingers balanced an ink pen that hung precariously in the open journal she started again after lunch. The page revealed some unintelligible scribble and a line that trailed down the page.

Sissy's bracelet had branded its embossed imprint across her forehead where it had lain, while Nicki's hair was pushed to one side, giving her a lopsided, cockeyed look.

Before the train came to a complete stop, people had begun to fill the aisles and doorways. Announcements in French blared overhead as the crew made their final walk-through, pulling tickets from the slots overhead.

The women gingerly stepped from their car onto the platform as they tried to figure out which direction to take. They watched the other passengers head to the left where an overelaborate clock with striking hands, hanging above the station's opening, pointed out the time—five fifteen. To the right of it, a metal statue of a couple in a loving embrace, nine feet or more in height, caught Nicki's attention. She pulled on Sissy's jacket sleeve and pointed in its direction.

"Yeah, it looks okay," she said.

"That's what you and Robert will be doing in a few days, all locked up on each other."

"Maybe, maybe not."

"What's that supposed to mean?" Nicki walked faster to catch up.

"Just what I said. I'm not trying to think of Robert at this moment. I'll deal with that when I get home—not on a train platform in Brussels."

"Why you little snob," she called out as she stopped and waited for Angela to catch up.

"What are you waiting for?" Her friend was standing beside her.

"Something is up with Sissy. She has become so, so—"

"Glamorous?"

"A snob when it comes to Robert. She's about to lose a good thing with her stuck-up behind," Nicki complained as they walked to catch up with Sissy.

"Don't fret. Once she lands in Kansas and sees that fine man, she'll try to suck his lips off from kissing him so much."

"I hope you're right."

They stepped through the station doors and were taken aback by its starkness. They joined Sissy and made their way to the back of the building and through the doors where red exit signs were posted. Twilight had settled over the town as neon signs announcing restaurants and bars for the choosing dotted the background.

"It looks a little dark around here," Angela said while pulling her purse closer to her body.

"Yeah," Nicki agreed as she looked up and down the street. "I think we wound up on the wrong side of the tracks."

Perturbed about their situation, Sissy pointed to her right and said, "Let's go that way. Maybe the heart of the city is farther down."

"The way this place looks, I'm afraid someone will mistake us for some chunky call girls," Nicki said while looking over her shoulder.

"If he's good looking, I'll say, hey baby, won't you give me your digits so I can check you out later." Angela chuckled, then broke out in a full laugh while trying to keep pace in her three-quarter-inch heels that she insisted on wearing.

"See, there you go, being nasty again," Sissy said while crossing the street to the other side of the road.

As they walked farther, all they found was more darkness and less safety. They remained on the side of the sidewalk with the most streetlights as they turned and headed back to the train station. When they approached the area, Nicki screeched, "What is that foul smell, and where is it coming from? Are we near a port-a-pot?"

Before another word was spoken, their pace slowed as they noticed several men with their butt cheeks to the wind.

"What in the hell. . .," Angela stammered as her hand flew up to cover her nose.

Sissy finally gathered her voice after staring at a fine set of buns and pointed. "That's where the smell is coming from. It looks like upright urinal ports for men."

"That's so unfair," Nicki said through the tissue that acted as a veil. "The men have toilets at the ready for them, but we have to stand in endless lines to pee behind closed doors."

"No you don't," Angela said. "I'll bet you'll get a boyfriend in no time if you step up and squat at one of those things."

"Nasty heifers," Sissy said as she finally dragged her eyes away from the variety of butt cheeks at the stalls and entered the doorway of the train station.

"I know you're not calling someone nasty the way you were eyeballing those men," Angela said while following her inside the door.

Nicki led the girls in the direction of a ticket counter. "Let's ask someone where the shops and stuff are located."

The answer was not what they were expecting.

***

"We did what?" Angela said.

"The woman said we got on the wrong train and departed at the wrong station."

46 | CRAZY!

"The wrong what and what?" Nicki practically shouted while drawing attention to herself.

"Could you take that down a notch," Angela said. "You sound like a banshee."

"You have nerve to talk, heifer!"

"You better lock it up, girl," Angela shouted while reaching for Nicki's shirt. Sissy stepped between them just in time.

"Have you two lost your cotton-picking minds? Do you want to try spending time in jail, in another country?" Sissy looked at one and then the other woman before continuing. "People are looking, and soon security or the police will arrive if you *both* continue. And if you do, I will be more than happy to leave your butts right here. Now act like the grown women you're supposed to be and sit down while I figure this thing out."

When the two women walked off in different directions, Sissy returned to the ticket counter and spoke to the clerk. She explained that although they were in Brussels, they were in the wrong section of town, and there were no other scheduled stops going out that evening.

Great, Sissy thought as she walked away. Now she had to return to the fighting tigers and explain that not only had they wasted their money, but they had to wait to take the return train home.

For two hours, they hovered around the station shops and boutiques before returning to the main hall. Angela, still upset with Nicki, drifted over to the staircase. Just as she was about to sit down, she noticed a sign forbidding such action. Her frustration mounted since there were very few seats to be had. As soon as one was vacated, people converged on it like vultures on a ripe kill.

Nicki kept her distance from Ms. Thang, strolled over to a nearby reading stand, and leaned against the wall. *What a way to spend a Friday night,* she thought. She noticed the high police presence in and around the station. Not only was it payday for some, but she concluded the party people would be out in full force and could wreak havoc.

She continued to scan the station for an available seat when her gaze stopped at a homeless man digging through the trash can. He pulled out slightly empty bottles and cups, pressed their rims to his cracked, dry lips, and sucked down the remaining contents before tossing them back into the receptacle. He rummaged through food sacks as his pants hung off his hips, exposing his butt— not because of a silly fashion craze, but more to the fact that he lacked food and proper clothing. Her heart went out to him as he made his way to the next trash can. All of a sudden, the fight between her and Angela seemed so petty compared to this man's situation.

Sissy was the only one in the trio who was able to secure a seat. It took some fast moves and a stare down with a few people competing with her, but she won the prize as she sat on the hard plastic. The cold, drafty station caused her to tug on the lightweight jacket a little more while wrapping the shawl-like scarf over her head and shoulders. She noticed her friends, each on opposite sides of the station's interior like enemies of war. What was she going to do with them? The least little thing seemed to set them off, and that bothered her.

Could it be that Angela is jealous of Nicki because of Ermenegilde or the fact that she'll remain in Paris?

And what's going on with Nicki? Nervousness or the fear of being left behind without her buddies to support her? A breeze—brisk and assaulting—coursed through the station, startling Sissy from her thoughts. Just as she was about to return to her conclusions, an overhead announcement stating that their train to Paris was starting to board all passengers was a welcome relief.

***

The click-clack of the train wheels on the rails was the lullaby needed to place the trio into a deep sleep. Prior to that, dinner was served and they ate in silence, refusing to acknowledge the tension between them. Each fighter had returned to their respective corner in the ring.

They finally arrived in the city and disembarked the train. Just as Nicki stepped onto the platform, Angela walked away.

"Hey," Sissy yelled out.

Several people turned in response, including Ms. Thang. "*Désolé*," she said to no one in particular, then looked directly at Angela and waved. "Get over here."

She stormed back. "Look, I'm not a child whom you can order around. I'm about fed up with you and Ms. Sugar Breeches over there talking down to me."

"Girl, don't start," Nicki hissed.

"I'm not doing this here on a train platform where both of you can fight and fall on the rails and die. How would I explain that to your families? Let's take it outside, right now," and she led the way.

***

Sissy stormed up the concrete staircase, occasionally taking two stairs at a time. Enough was enough, and she planned to have it out with both of them. She paused just outside the entrance of the subway and waited. The two women deliberately lagged behind like puppies that *knew* they had done something wrong and feared the consequences ahead. As soon as they stepped in front of their friend, she let them have it.

"What in the world is wrong with you two? You have been going at each other like two alley cats over a bowl of hot milk."

"Wouldn't that burn their tongues?" Angela kidded.

"Don't play with me; I'm not in the mood. We're not going back to that hotel until we get a few things cleared up."

Once they moved away from the crowd, Angela began. "I just don't appreciate you guys constantly getting on my case about the least little thing."

"Like what?" Nicki insisted.

"I can't come up with an answer off the top of my head with the two of you staring me down as if I were a wanted criminal."

"Try," they said in unison.

"Okay, fine. But remember, you asked for it. First, Nicki," she pointed. "You walk around here all highfalutin and stuff because you're dating a foreigner."

"What did you just say?"

"I didn't stutter. Who cares that you get to stay in Paris and hang out with that white guy and go 'Ooh la la' all the time. You better watch your back and hope he doesn't use you up for the fun of it all."

Nicki unfurled her arms and leaned forward. "Why you selfish little—"

"Keep it clean," Sissy yelled out while stepping between the women once again. "Remember, we don't want to eat our words later."

"Girl," Nicki said, pointing in Angela's direction. "You better be glad that somebody is praying over you because you were about to get a new kind of christening."

Once their friend walked away, Sissy

looked back at Angela. "I take it you have some words of wisdom for me," she said sarcastically.

"Well, since you mentioned it, I do. You need to get your fast behind in check and tell Robert how much you want and miss him. I've told you before that you're about to lose a good man because you think you are too fine and sexy now."

"Boy, you sure have gotten bold in the last few days. Who do you think you are?"

"I'm still Angela, the beautiful one," she laughed at her own joke, "but at least I know I have a few loose screws rolling around that need to be fixed. I still love my black men— although it's been hard to find a good one— but I roll with my own."

"And that is why you are going *to grow old alone*. Try thinking outside the box for a change. And a little word to the wise. You better stop riding Nicki about her interracial dating. Let her have some fun. If he breaks her heart, we need to be there to help her. In the meantime, if this man makes her feel like she's the best thing since peanut butter, then leave them be."

"Alrighty then," she huffed. "You do you, girl, but remember I was the first to tell you so."

"Angela, do me a favor."

"What's that?"

"Shut up!" Sissy marched off to find Nicki.

47 | OFF THE DEEP END

I don't know what the heck is going on with us, but we have lost our minds in Paris. Sissy paused after the journal entry and looked toward the lobby. It was four in the morning and she couldn't sleep. She found refuge in the small sitting room. She shook her head and continued.

We had to take a break from one another yesterday, so we dispersed around town. I walked the few blocks back to Notre Dame Cathedral to admire its Gothic styling. The flying buttresses in the rear of the building were used to stabilize the fractured walls during that period. I have to admit that I went inside and took a little time to pray for my sisters and I. Okay, so we are lifelong friends. We feel closer and treat each other more like family than our actual ones. Either way, we needed prayer, so I sent up a few. Later, I meandered the streets, not caring if I got lost, and did a little window shopping while taking in the sights and sounds around me.

The desk clerk paused in the doorway.

"Would *mademoiselle* like a cup of tea while she writes?" the dark-haired, pudgy clerk asked with a dimpled smile.

"Oui, merci," she said.

***

Angela tossed back and forth in the bed for what seemed like the eighteenth time. "Enough is enough," she mumbled while throwing the sheets back. As the rain pounded against the windows, her skin tingled with fear. As a child, she never dreaded rain until the night an intense hailstorm sent a tree branch soaring through the window of the bedroom that she and her baby sister shared. From that day on, she slept with her back to the wall and her face forward, as if watching the window would prevent any other such mishaps.

She turned on the bedside table lamp, then walked over to the opened carry-on bag, pulling out her pen and journal. "I still can't get the hang of writing in this thing," she said while climbing back into bed, "but I guess it's cheaper than a psychologist."

Angela turned to the bookmarked paged and began to write.

I don't know why everyone is wound so tight. I tried to be honest with my point of view, and they flake out on me. And why does Sissy always have to be the lion tamer in the group? I mean, every time I look up, it's "Angela this and Angela that." She might as well say, "Down girl, get back in your cage." At this, she chuckled then continued.

When will I get my turn at love? Sissy has Robert, but from my point of view, she isn't being very nice to him. Then there's Nicki. She's all gushy and strung out over that Parisian. So what if he looks like that man from Gigi . . . oh . . . what's his name? Not the old man but . . . Louis Jourdan with his fine self. As I was saying, he's only going to break her heart once he gets her into bed. Poor child. I guess when it's been a while since you've been loved, you go with whomever and whatever looks your way.

She continued to write for another thirty minutes before she felt the pen fall from her hands. She fought to stay awake, but lost out to her eyelids as they began to close in slow motion.

***

Nicki bolted upright in bed and felt as though someone had thrown a pitcher of water on her chest. She was drenched in sweat as she ran her hand through her hair. "Yuck," she called out, then fumbled around in the dark to turn on the overhead light. She crashed into the desk chair, tripped on her own shoes, and stubbed her toe on the leg of the desk.

"Freak, freak, freak" was all she could say as she hobbled to the wall panel, finally flipping on the light switch. After a quick wash-up at the bathroom sink, she sat on the opposite side of the bed—the dry side—and tried to make sense of what happened.

"Oh, what's the use," she mumbled, and made her way back to the desk to sit and write, hoping it would relax her enough to go back to sleep.

The trio is falling apart, **she scribbled.** *Maybe this trip wasn't such a good idea. We seem to be getting on each other's nerves, and it's not pretty. This is our last day together, and soon the girls will be gone while I remain here, in Paris, alone. Well, maybe not totally alone since my boss will be in town, but still.* . . . She touched her damp hair, looked around the messed-up room, then continued.

Somehow, someway, The Fat Girls Club

will have to pull it together or we'll be The Fat and Lonely Girls Club. She gave a wide smile, closed the book, and after turning off the lights, fumbled her way back to bed.

48 | BACK TO THE GRIND

Angela practically tore the door off its hinges as she yanked, pulled, and twisted her body and suitcase into the hallway. "It makes no sense that this thing should be this heavy," she huffed after patting her face with a handkerchief.

Sissy watched in amazement as her friend fought with the overstuffed suitcase. "You know that's too full, girl. You might as well divide some of that stuff into your carry-on tote."

"Sis, I'm full to the gills," she whined.

"Well, no one told you to shop like there's no tomorrow," Nicki chimed in after she sashayed down the hall and paused beside Sissy. "Look, just take out what you don't need right away, and I'll go to the post office and mail it home to you," she offered.

"You'd do that for me?"

"Yes, I'd do that for your raggedy behind."

"Now see, was it necessary to say all that?" she huffed as her hands flew to her hips.

"Ladies," Sissy called out. "Not today, please. Let's put the fighting on hold and have breakfast. I'm starving."

"That's the best idea yet," Angela agreed and closed the hotel door behind her. "I'll meet you guys downstairs. I'm going to check out."

"Bet. See you in a few," Sissy agreed and returned to her room to finish packing.

***

Sissy stepped away from the airport check-in counter, allowing Angela to move her suitcase onto the scale. The clerk frowned. "I'm sorry, miss, but you are twenty pounds over."

"What? But I pulled a lot of stuff out of that thing."

"Do you have another suitcase or tote bag that some of your things could go into?" she suggested.

Angela turned to Sissy.

"Hey, don't look at me. I barely made it under the wire, and my tote bag is full."

Nicki put both hands up and shook her head. "Don't even ask me."

"Fine. That's just great." She looked at the airline clerk. "Well, I have no other option but to pay. How much will it be?"

"$100.00."

"You've got to be kidding!"

"*Mademoiselle*, you must pay the amount or step out of line and do something else," the clerk's stern voice replied.

"Okay, okay," Angela huffed as she snatched the credit card from her wallet.

"What a great bunch of friends' you guys are," she said as they walked toward the departure terminal.

"No one told you to shop like you're a rock star," Nicki replied.

"I've got your rock star," Angela quipped.

Sissy butted into the conversation before it turned nasty. "Hey, you two cool it. Let's not leave on a sour note, okay? Besides, here's where we need to go to get to our flight," she said while pointing toward the hallway on the right.

"Wow," Nicki sighed. "This is going to be rough. It feels strange not to be boarding the plane with you."

"But look on the bright side. You will have more time to hang out in Paris and get to know that handsome hunk of a man. What time is your boss arriving?"

"Around noon." Nicki took a deep breath,

then walked over and hugged her friends. "Have a safe flight home. Despite everything, I really had a great time."

"Yeah, it was a blast in more ways than one," Angela said. "Okay, sister girl, stay safe and watch out for men with wandering hands."

"Let's pray," Nicki said. They stepped out of the path of the foot traffic near an unoccupied seating area. With heads bowed, they held hands. "Lord, keep my friends safe as they make their way back home. Protect not only the aircraft, but keep the crew alert and attentive. Thank you for the time we've shared. And Father, I ask for one more favor." She paused before continuing. "Please assist Sissy in her relationship with Robert and help Angela find someone who can get her under control. Amen!"

Angela opened her eyes and looked up. "You think you're so funny, don't you? Ha ha," she said sarcastically.

"Yes ma'am," Nicki said and gave each woman a kiss on the cheek and a quick hug. "Love ya. Later."

Angela and Sissy started down the hallway, turned, and waved once more while yelling out their goodbyes. When they could no longer be seen, Nicki turned and walked away. Tears streamed down her face as she dug deep into her jacket pockets and retrieved the napkins she had taken from the restaurant during their breakfast. Reality had begun to set in.

"I'm all alone and have to prove not only to my boss but to myself that I can do this job. And what about Ermenegilde and the secret I may have to share with him? Well, here's to looking forward." Nicki straightened her back, let out a deep sigh, and began to sing "Ain't No Stoppin' Us Now" by McFadden & Whitehead as her hips sashayed out the airport doors.

THE FAT GIRLS CLUB

QUEEN OF HEARTS

When your mind and body have been on vacation, the last thing you want to do is deal with the realities of life. But deal we must.

Sissy rested the rollerball pen in the crease of her journal and looked up. Angela's soft snores filled the space around them. She chuckled, and when her eyes scanned the seats of the other passengers, she noticed a rather handsome man staring in her direction. He gave a wink that startled her.

No, he's not trying to flirt with me, she thought while giving him her sexiest smile. She watched as he unfastened his seat belt and made his way in the semi-dark cabin to her row.

He leaned on the seat beside him and whispered, "Hello. My name is Jonas. You caught my eye earlier, and I was wondering if you'd join me. The seat next to me is empty, as well as the next."

"And how did you get lucky enough to

have two empty seats?"

"I paid to have the whole row," he said before straightening.

The smile that followed was the sexiest thing she'd seen in a while. She drank in his 6' 2" athletic frame. No fat or flab on that sexy body. His round, well-scrubbed face held a pair of luminous eyes that peered out from thick lashes, causing her breath to stop briefly. His upper lip protruded slightly initiating sinful thoughts in her head. This total package was drenched in a russet skin tone that made her toes curl in her shoes.

He stepped aside to allow her to get comfortable and then sat and refastened his seat belt.

"Tell me about yourself," he said.

From then on, the night didn't seem so long as they talked and laughed the hours away..

Made in the USA
Columbia, SC
18 August 2019